MOS LABS

MOS LABS

MOS LABS

I0593532

First Published in Melbourne, Australia
by Mos Labs

First Edition
978 0 6457526 1 8

brandon young

REFLECTIONS
of FONTAINE

a MOS LABS novel

contents

part one
reflections

ONE
The Fat Man, Pt. 1

My breaths are echoed by something outside of my own body, but at a quarter to four a.m. there's nothing, just the snow. I'm watching it sizzle against the tip of my cigarette like hot whispers on a cold winter's night. Beyond this, the words **Paris, 1959** shine in the storm clouds, a classic titles sequence. The score is Bernard Herrmann.

The reviews will be *stellar*.

I watch the darkness gush through Paris as floodwater does when poured through a miniature town. It splashes thick and nebulous across the brick buildings and lamp posts, strangling their meagre yellow lights. I've grown to enjoy this. The all-engulfing darkness. The quiet. I continue to chew on the end of my cigarette, bitter and wet.

There's something about this city at night and you can't quite capture it in a cartoon strip in the *Canard*. The monochrome palette, the repetitive blizzard winds, over and over and over, the drunkards moaning on sidewalks and the leftover music tiptoeing out dead-hour establishments. How to spin a feeling into something tangible. It's the snow, it's the fumes, it's the booze stuck against the sidewalk—well, it's booze or vomit.

I take a drag of my cigarette and feel the city suck in a breath too.

Yellow headlights catch me as I exhale smoke into the air, dropping the cigarette to the tips of my fingers and letting it dangle by my side. Staring through the yellow haze, I can vaguely make out the face of the car's sole occupant, a middle-aged man with a clean shave and large red ears. If you asked me, I'd imagine his ears are red because of the weather and not because of some disease of the skin, but who can be sure. This is the fifties, isn't it, and there's a lot to be shared around in times like these.

The man isn't looking at me because he's peering around at the parking signs, all bent like they're puking out the snow. You can't make out a single thing they say, but who's checking where cars are parked at four a.m. amidst a storm like this.

The car engine goes silent, the headlights vanish in a gasp, and the door clicks open. I shiver as the city gives out a tremble that sounds like brass.

The city freezes frame and the words **Nicolas Fontaine** flash against the skyline, like the beginning of a Hitchcockian thriller. There's smoke in the air, gone morbidly rigid; and a woman's silhouette through her frosted window, fingers gripping the curtain, watching the car, watching me. I look up and she disappears behind a curtsy of fabric.

The large man exits his vehicle, one stocky leg kicking out

with theatrics, and then the other. He wears black business pants and glossy shoes, and his suit jacket is congruously black and professional. From the darkness he withdraws a satin hat and slaps it on his horribly-balding head. Then the car door swings shut, scraping the snow-covered footpath with the sound smokers make when they snore.

The Fat Man.

This is all I can glean from him as he locks his car door with a jangle of keys, then walks underneath the streetlamp beside mine, throwing his swollen hands into his pockets. The only thing that marks him as anything besides ordinary is the simple fact he's out so early and he's here in front of me. I continue to watch him as I let the cigarette sail from my fingertips and land in the snow, the burning end face-up like an industrial tower pissing smoke.

"Good night," says the fat man.

His voice alarms me. Baritone and sleepy, it's as if you crossed the singer Distel, and Constantine from the *Lemmy Caution* films, rolling out of bed. I gaze at the frost vapour oozing out of the fat man's fat lips, and suddenly I'm struck with the urge to draw him. He is not a particularly short man but his voluminous suit jacket gives the illusion of stout legs. His top hat speckled with frost provides comical height. My above-average olfactory glands can't smell anything besides Paris, but I'd imagine his hat carries the stench of dirty backseats.

The fat man's eyes lift, peering at me ponderously.

"What," I ask in an unpunctuated tone.

The winds howl in response and the fat man clutches the brim of his hat.

"I said *good night*," the fat man repeats. He walks closer with his hands outlined through his pockets, disappearing in the dimness between the two streetlamps, then reappearing in the ambit of mine. He has good skin for a fat man, clean and unblemished.

Finally, he stops. "What did ya think of the show, then?"

The lamp we're standing under burns out, and then flickers back on again, suddenly accentuating the frost that's gathering on the fat man's bushy brows.

Now that he mentions it, I don't remember much about the show, but my fingers scour my coat pocket instinctively and brush up against a cold ticket stub, which is flimsy and small.

"You got a problem hearing me, boy? Eh? The show's what I'm talking about, the one down at the theatre just two blocks out. You were there, weren't ya? Now no use lyin' about things yet."

It's hard to notice a city during the day, when the streets run hot with car fumes and choking exhausts and thrumming engines, but on nights such as this one, an ordinary night in February 1959, even despite the blizzard, you notice it.

For example, the city snickers.

"Have you been following me," I say.

The fat man glides closer still, his head moving through his most recent gasp of frost. Our close proximity exposes his lack of any substantial height and I find myself almost face-to-face with his top hat. He steps up onto the tips of his toes and says, "Not following you. Just paying attention."

He looks at me as if that is any reasonable response.

"How do you know who I am," I say to him.

"I asked at the laundromat," says the fat man.

"I don't work down there anymore."

"Takes more than a resignation to make a person disappear."

There's a sudden cramp in my chest, the kind that conjures the thought, *I couldn't be having a heart attack, I'm only twenty-five,* and yet the thought passes my head nonetheless. Did I lose consciousness sometime during the night. It would explain why I can't remember the show, for one.

My hands are riffling my coat for another cigarette. It finally appears in my right hand, lighter in my left. *Snap. Hiss. Sizzle.* There's a brief spark of amber. Smoke belly-dances in front of my face as I light the cigarette.

I focus on the fat man, who makes a sound between a cough and a chortle, like a man choking on a really good burger. He's staring back at me through a sheet of falling snow. If you listened now, you'd hear the scuff of tires on frost-slick roads, of a dog barking across the street, then abruptly stop, as if sensing something in the air had changed.

"Where are my manners, then?" says the fat man in his dulcet voice. "I'm a representative from a corporation currently testing a new kind of **drug**. We're looking for participants in a brief trial and your name came up as a potential candidate. Have you ever signed up for anything like this? Been asked, ya lookin' for a way to earn quick money? That's probably how we found you in the first place." A slip of paper crinkles against my fingertips. I clutch it involuntarily. I'm staring over the fat man's shoulder down the deserted sidewalk, where one of the streetlamps is turning on and off like morse code. I can feel the fat man's warm breaths reach my neck.

He keeps his voice low and baritone. "I've slipped a piece of paper into your hand. On this piece of paper is a number, and if you dial that number you will speak to a man who sounds like a woman but I assure you, he is not a woman, that's just his voice. This man will put you into contact with another man, and this man will ask you a question, and if you answer this question correctly, you'll wake up the next morning to find one hundred fifty francs in your bank account." He shrinks down to his usual, below-average height and looks at me.

"What do you want with a failed cartoonist," I ask him.

"As the lottery chooses its winner," the fat man says, "Moscati Research has chosen you." Despite this, I sense things aren't so straightforward, and this is no simple lottery.

"Moscati Research. What the hell is that."

"Moscati Research Laboratories is one of the pioneering forces in scientific development in the twentieth century," says the fat man. "I have slipped you a piece of paper with a number on it. Once you speak to the man on the other end, you will learn more."

I remain silent. I don't recall ever putting my name down for something like this, but all things considered, I don't trust my memory so much tonight. All I can think of is that I used to pop one every now and then, but then again, how would the fat man know this; and besides, it's not been for some time. There's no other reason why I'm being approached except that it's a con, and it certainly sounds like one. But the look the fat man gives me suggests he's not playing around, and why did he come looking for me at the laundromat.

The snowing winds suddenly change direction, like a man walking through a grocery store he has never been in before. I become aware of the warmth that a human body gives when its standing nearby another, but at the same time goose bumps spring up on my arms. I think about the fat man's words, and about the piece of paper enclosed within my cold fingers. There's not enough space between us for any snow to fall.

"What was the show," I find myself asking.

The fat man smiles without teeth. I search his eyes for some sign of anything, but it's like staring into a puddle of trodden-over mud. "Marcel Aymé's *A View from the Bridge*," he says matter-of-factly, frost flying from his mouth. "You ever thought about going to America, Nicolas?"

"Wait a minute, how do you know my name."

"I told you, I asked at the laundromat where you no longer work, but like I also said, it's not so easy to disappear completely."

"Oh."

The fat man makes a hmph noise, but it could just be a bit of food stuck in his throat, rather than much consideration for anything in particular. "I've heard it's nice over there. America. They have all the good movies, don't they."

I have no answer to this. So, without another word, the fat man turns and leaves. All that's left is the spitting of snow through the space where he had been.

I shiver, clutching the piece of paper and thinking about

A View from the Bridge, not that I can remember much from it, pieces of the night censored and forgotten.

The fat man inserts a key into his car door, then climbs in and turns on the ignition. Headlights drench me in hot mustard and I squint, lifting a hand to shield my eyes. Slowly, the car rolls forward until it's side-by-side with me.

The window rolls down clumsily.

"It's just a bit *old-fashioned* isn't it, the theatre," the fat man says, directly quoting something I wrote for the *Canard* maybe three months or so ago. His eyes look askance but his smile stays where it is. He's lit a cigarette and he perches it on the edge of his mouth. "I liked your cartoons, Nicolas. Very progressive." He looks back at me—

"Now how the hell'd you end up gettin' like this?"

I stare at the fat man until the tinted window chomps him up. Wheels screech in the snow and the car disappears up the road, and I'm thinking about the show that I can't remember, and I'm thinking about what the fat man has told me.

For the first time tonight, I lift the piece of paper in my hand. The left edge is crone's teeth jagged, like torn from a lined notebook. The phone number has been written in blue pen, obtrusively smudged from the snow. As my phone line was recently disconnected, I don't currently have access to one directly, but there's a booth about twenty metres down the road. I glance at it now, covered in frost.

I look back down at the phone number scribbled in blue. By all accounts, ordinary. According to the fat man, if I dial this number there will be a man who sounds like a woman, and then there will be another man who asks me a question. I wonder what sort of question he will ask me.

But if I answer correctly, they'll pay me one hundred fifty francs, which, times as they are, is decent money. Far more than a few days' work at the laundromat.

A strange sense of unjudgmental calm comes over me, and I throw the piece of paper onto the ground. Like rats that are hungry, the snow opens up its maws and engulfs it. I kick it with my boot to be sure, and sure enough it's gone. The cigarette I left there, still sizzling with faint amber, also vanishes under the ravenous snowbank.

At last, with hands in my trouser pockets, I walk away.

In a band room deep down in the catacombs of Paris, one February night in 1959, or a morning, if you have some place to be, a trumpet vomits notes into the city air, and the rest of the band splashes around in it, turning it into music.

I look up as white text dissolves into the air.

It's the title of a film, superimposed over the darkened sky, untouched by the frost and the streetlamps. Synthetic white text, the font simplistic, *Clarendon* or *Aldine*.

Reflections of Fontaine is what it says.

TWO
Paris, 1959

There's a blue pen between my fingertips and I'm sketching on a napkin out the front of a breakfast café. Two coffees send massive plumes of steam into the air.

I slide the napkin across the table.

My older sister Colette examines it with introspection as I watch people pass us along the sidewalk, clutching umbrellas and drowning in gigantic fur coats. Often brand name. Their breath is vapour, their boots high, the snow shifting underfoot. I lift my cup of coffee just to warm my hand.

"You ought to be employed by *Vogue*, or *Elle*," says Colette as she holds up the illustration to the light, her voice much like the timbre of a bird. "Mister Lazareff is in television. Perhaps mother knows him. Though, I have to say, he seems quite a spineless man at times—not that I've worked with him, that is just what I've heard."

Taking a sip of coffee, I study Colette across the table.

With care, she lays the napkin back down, letting it catch underneath her plate of crumbs that used to be a croissant. "Have you been working, then?" she asks me.

I shake my head. "I wouldn't be employed by a fashion magazine. The industry doesn't so much appeal to me."

Colette gives a simple "hm" and hurriedly sips her coffee. I notice how her deep brown hair grips her shoulders with above-normal flair. Her eyes are large and round, like when you look at something under a magnifying glass. I collect the napkin and hold it up in front of her, letting my eyes go back and forth.

I take up the pen again.

"Mother seems happy," Colette tells me.

"She doesn't write to me," I say, shading my sister's firm yet soft jawline. It's the sort you find in fashion magazines, carefully-carved and highly-marketable.

"They're filming in a place called Ushant tomorrow. I've never even heard of it."

"It's an island, I think." I slip my pen back inside my coat pocket and hand Colette the finished sketch.

"Oh I love it," she says to the napkin.

I finish what's left of my coffee and spit out a bean.

We walk abreast down Saint-Lazare, buried in the early morning rush of cars. An old man gives Colette a genteel nod as he slips through a gap between us, his black dog plodding along behind him, jowls hanging.

The score is slow and introspective, a piano and wandering violins. You spend enough time in Paris, things like the traffic, the people, and the corner stores become background noise, and you start to pick up on other things.

The E-flats and major sevenths in the wind. The weight of the shadows cast from tenements. The growl underneath your feet, as though gears lie on the underside of the footpath.

You see a woman in her thirties pull aside the shutters from her bookstore on Rome Street. You've seen her other times you come down to Saint-Lazare with Colette. She wears her hair a little differently each morning; and today, curls of grey streak her usual red. Your gaze drifts from her, to her blue dress—typical for her Monday mornings—and then to the faded parking signs out the front of the bookstore, then eventually closer still, like a camera pushing in, to the road.

We speed-walk to the other side of the road. Two men in black suits and ties blow past us without breaking stride, and I look over my shoulder as they hurry in the opposite direction.

I remember the fat man.

"Mother met a gentleman on their vessel, a violinist," says Colette. Thoughts of the fat man are thrown from my mind in the same way a strong breeze can dispose of a hot fart, and I sense I'm better for it. "He's Spanish," Colette says, tossing her dark hair back across the ashen furs of her coat. *"Camarón que se duerme se lo lleva la corriente.* The shrimp that falls asleep is carried by the current. I just like that one."

"You just like shrimp," I conclude.

"Solo me gustan los camarónes," she says.

I look at her from the side.

"I just like shrimp," she says.

"Well, when is our mother *not* having affairs on film sets."

"True," Colette says with a sigh.

When we're outside the metro entrance, Colette slides a gloved hand into her leather handbag and fetches around in there for a moment. "For the illustration," she tells me, withdrawing a bundle of money notes and pressing them into me.

I grab her hand and force it back against her. "I don't—" My retort is cut off suddenly by a tickle in my nose. I throw my face into my sleeve and let loose a sneeze. "I don't need any money, Colette," I tell her. "It's really okay."

"You aren't getting sick, are you?"

I don't respond to this.

"Well," she says, "you make sure you go see Doctor Morel if you are. And please, Nicolas, don't be honourable now." She folds my fingers around the notes and offers one of her kind, well-rehearsed smiles. "It isn't much since I'm on a bit of a break, but take it anyway."

With a sigh, I pocket the money and let Colette throw her arms around me, desperately rising to the tips of her toes. Her warmth is that of good family, her smell of strong perfume. But I know the money isn't really for the drawing.

"Take care of yourself, Nicolas," she tells me in a voice that's more of a plea than anything customary. She kisses me lightly on the cheek and bids me farewell.

When I return to my apartment at 66 Lepic Street, there's a letter from the landlord containing my utility bill. The first thing I do is kick it across the floorboards and watch it skitter to the edge of the white couch. I close the door and throw off my coat, hanging it.

The muted morning light presses against my curtains like ghosts. A French horn erupts from my plasterboard walls. I imagine a flash of light coursing through a slit in the curtains, accenting my eyes.

The floorboards creak contemplatively beneath me. It's the television static that makes me stop. It's throwing silver wisps of light around the threadbare apartment dressings. Plucking the remote from the couch, I switch it off. Suddenly I can hear the wind against the window glass, like an old crone scraping it with overgrown fingernails. I can hear the occasional honk of detuned cars, and the couple arguing in the room next door.

A blue flame flashes upon the stovetop and I boil water.

My right hand collects a wet teacup from the rack by the sink and my left selects a teabag, slipping it deftly inside. Suspended over the sink is a calendar flipped to February 1959. There's little to be found on this besides grocery reminders, overdue payments, and missed deadlines from the *Canard*.

By random, the television turns back on, blasting the room in light. Julie Adams shrieks, the subpar speakers crackling. The screen fizzles with static. Sinister trombones shape the scene with suspense. It's a Hans Salter score, in collaboration with Herman Stein and Henry Mancini. I used to own the vinyl of it.

I ignore the remote control and unplug the power from the mains. Then, with this resolved, I dig into my pocket and withdraw Colette's offering. Thirty francs; one of the notes has a half-moon of coffee on it. I can't say she's never done anything for me. If it weren't for Colette, who's to say I'd still have this apartment, just down the street from where Van Gogh built his first studio. I briefly glance at a newspaper clipping on the kitchen bench: a promotional stub for *The Sinking of the Elisa Maree,* our mother's new film. She's one of those golden age film stars whose career intertwined with the likes of Myrna Loy and Loretta Young, so it's not so much a surprise she's gone mostly unnoticed—though, she did win an Academy Award in 1933. But they say this could be her comeback.

The Sinking of the Elisa Maree, it's her second feature with Alfred Hitchcock. She had starred in one of his early films, about the time I was born.

The kettle screams. I turn off the gas dial and the flame vanishes with a puff, leaving only boiled water in its wake. I pour it into my cup. Condensation bubbles against the engraved YOUNG CARTOONIST OF THE YEAR in red, celebratory lettering.

It's an award designed for headlines, but I was sitting at the top of the world. Twenty years old and I thought I was going to be writing *Tintin.* Fair to say, that did not eventuate, and I'm drinking the cheapest tea they sell in a bitingly-cold apartment I won't for much longer be able to afford. I hiss as the tea scorches my tongue, cursing it.

I've never published a cartoon under my real name so if you ask most people who Nicolas Fontaine is, they wouldn't have a clue. That was something our professor told me back when I was a fledgling artist fresh out of the School of Fine

Arts. It's because of what I drew, of course, they said it was contentious, but the guys at the *Canard* liked it, that's what they publish.

But the fat man knows Nicolas Fontaine.

I shiver.

The silvery light of sun off dew burns against the edge of my cup. The steam is thick and intense. I never won another thing after this. A cup. They couldn't even make it in a good font.

Fog clouds the windows of the grocery store on Martyrdoms Street, and occasionally a mote of frost breaks, sending a single drop of water down the glass.

I stop by the pickle jar and pluck one from its murky depths when the vendor's looking away. This is at least the fifth one I've taken this month. I feel only moderately sorry for the man who's forced to stand here selling pickles to reluctant customers, so I throw him two coins instead of one, before walking away with half of the pickle in my mouth.

Canned food clatters in my wire shopping basket when I toss in a loaf of bread, which immediately tumbles from one end to the other. I'm navigating the aisles like a man who knows what he's doing, expertly turning corners and picking items off the shelves. An old man I've seen plenty times before is mopping in the baked goods aisle. I might bake a cake one of these days, but then again, eating a whole cake to yourself is a sad visual.

I grab two cartons of frozen fish and chuck them in with

the rest. There's not a lot of space left in my freezer but the fish is discounted, and it saves on time.

I set the basket on the cashier's bench. There are mechanical clicking noises. The sound of pen on paper. The greeting. "Good morning, sir. How are you? And how are you? And how are you?" And I respond like, "Good. Not bad."

"Fourteen francs," says the cashier.

I complete the exchange and then slip out into the blizzard. It's enough to knock back my grocery bags, and a woman's umbrella down the street lurches inside-out, and a college student with fogged-up glasses loses his entirely as it sails up and catches a tree branch.

"Oh you're kidding!" cries the student.

My life is tiny, disconnected moments. I can't even begin to piece them together. There's a jammed line of cars on Abbesses Street, which stretches further than I can even see. There's a red *Facel Vega* that reminds me of the car my mother drives, its exhaust shitting out the carbon dioxide equivalent of diarrhoea. The man inside it adjusts his side mirrors with an arm that's more hair than skin, and for a brief moment I get the impression he looks at me. But he doesn't, he surely can't see me from where I'm standing, hardly within view.

Or maybe it's that he stares into one of the city's eyes.

In one motion, I turn and leap up the road onto the sidewalk. This is one of those disconnected moments. My ankle twisting, my shoe making a full revolution on the ice, the rest of me plummeting to the icy ground—

There's something about February in Paris, and the

worst of it's not the cold, or the snow, or that lull in good films. There's a harbinger of bad news. An ill fate's set to befall me one February. Maybe this year, maybe the next. The city knows it, too—well, it knows everything. Whispering it to me when I'm asleep. I feel it when I'm standing at the edge of the road, a warmth on my back when the only thing around is the cold. Something off in the pickle I just ate.

The city releases its held breath.

Grocery bags go flying, cans and fish and spices spraying everywhere. The paper receipt flutters through the air and catches a gust of wind, never to be seen again. My teeth crunch down on my tongue and I grimace in pain, watching after a can of beans, which rolls along the ice for some time, before sharply turning and tumbling onto the road. A car honks and tires screech, but all he's doing is avoiding the beans.

"You all right there, pal?"

I heft myself from the snow to hands and knees as a middle-aged man in a large fur coat peers down at me, two cans already in his hands. "You left quite the mark," he says.

Standing up, I notice an imprint of myself left in the snow. Thanking the man under my breath, I steal the two cans from him and chuck them into one of my plastic bags. "I'm fine," I tell him hastily without looking him in the eye.

And then I'm standing there.

And the winds have grown more fierce.

Sometimes, when you open your eyes and see—*truly* see—the things behind the monochrome façade of Paris, when you pull back the curtain of blizzard winds, the bustling hive of cars and people, when you do all of this, you might spot a ghost. But you have to look closely, and really pay attention. It's in the subtle tremor of snow that was previously settled in banks. The forming of shadows on brick walls, detached from anything in particular. A shiver through shaking bones, and it's not from the wind. Like a breath, somebody moaning into your bare skin.

It's watching me as keenly as a camera on the leading man. I don't look up, but I pause for a second, and feel a heaviness grip the air, and my ear lobes have become hot.

I pick up the second box of frozen fish but it's been ripped open—they're lying scattered in the snow, no less frozen than before, but still. Sighing, I resignedly toss the leftovers back onto the ground and watch the snow leap up to consume it, hungry. An engine roars and a snowbank gets kicked up with the exhaust, and then its wheels screech as they circle around me.

I catch an old woman watching me from the bus stop. She's wearing a grey cloak, and a layer of snow shines on her hunched shoulders. Not everything that's in Paris belongs here. It's like finding a gigantic sex toy in a children's store. This is the old woman. Her walking stick, like something from the eighteenth century. Her undulating cloak.

The woman seemingly exists here in Paris, but does not fit. And I figure, hell, then I'm the same. I walk the rest of the way home without looking anybody in the eye.

Back at 66 Lepic Street, I take the stairs. It's only two flights and I prefer this way; the elevator is broken most days of the week, and even though I can see the little light on, it's hard to trust something like that.

A black man stands outside room number seven. He turns around when I approach him, hanging up a phone call and offering a kind smile. He's a tall man, this fella, taller than myself, with thin wire-frame glasses and good hair, greying at the sides. The lines that crisscross his forehead give the impression of wisdom, rather than age.

"Is something wrong," I say to him.

The man is still smiling as he adjusts his black tie against his white collar. "Either you've been swimming fully-dressed, or it's still raining like all hell's flipped out there."

I don't respond to this.

"Detective Francis," he says. *"Agence Duluc.* I'd hate to take a moment out of your day, but you wouldn't happen to've noticed anything odd about these parts lately?"

My first thought is the fat man.

I glance further down the hall to see another detective a few doors down with a notepad out, and something's happened in there. "What's going on," I ask.

"A girl lived down this hall, a, *erm,* Louise Duchamp?"

I think for a second. "And. Am I meant to know who that is." The truth is, around these parts—and I've lived here for some time—I wouldn't even be able to describe the person who lives next door, nor the couple who's always arguing in the room on the other side. The other occupants of this building are as much spectres or mythical beings as they are real.

"Okay," says Detective Francis. "Go about your day then."

His partner comes down the hall towards us, eyeing

me briefly, then murmuring something to Francis. Francis smiles at me and the two detectives from *Agence Duluc* walk back down the hall, their boots thudding. I sense he's smiling all the way to the elevator, which *dings*. People who smile all the time are dishonest, is what I've always thought. Nobody is that happy, certainly not a detective.

I open the door to my apartment and walk inside. The television is playing a foreign language film, and the curtains are pulled open, letting in the cold noon light. I drop the groceries by the entrance and kick the door shut with my heel. This time, I go for the power cord immediately and tear it from the wall, killing the television with a hot sizzle.

At last, the room goes quiet.

The couple next door are fighting again. I hear her shout and footsteps ring out against the floorboards, from one side of the room to the other. A door slams and she's gone.

The quiet deepens, to a silence.

I can see myself in the dead television screen. Little old me, surrounded by mess, illuminated by the minimal light. I think back to the ghost on Abbesses Street and realise there's a room in my brain that I've blacked out, where *she* still lives, though I've done my best to lock the door using every key. The spot where she is hurts, like an aneurism that hasn't yet burst. I was in love for a time, or I thought I was.

She-she-*she*-**she!**

What was her name.

I realise I'm ravenous. I'm tired. Hell, I can't draw a comic worth anything these days. The apartment smells like cigarettes and all I want is to sleep and to be sober and I want this blizzard to stop. Did I ever really see that show like how the fat man said. If I don't remember it, who cares.

Montmartre, Paris. I've lived here all my life.

So why does it feel like an alien planet.

I take off my coat and start unpacking the groceries.

THREE
Meeting Miss Blanchot

You become a hot prospect for high school talks when you can put "young cartoonist of the year" after your name. It's *Lycée Victor Hugo*, just off Sevigne Street, a place I spent my four years, a proud school, but it says something that they're fetching back for me.

It's an early Tuesday. There's a girl in the second row hanging on my every word, but most of them appear indifferent, and I haven't come to expect anything else. The students ask the same questions. What's it like turning your hobby into a real job. How much money do you have. What's it like working for the newspapers. Where did you study.

The lecture ends with some form of general advice, and a well-rehearsed joke that hits with success. I toss up my coat from the wooden chair next to the lectern and let their half-hearted applause usher me out of the classroom.

Their art teacher, an older gentleman with a bold

moustache and a mottled-red nose, shakes my hand on the way out and gives me an appreciative look. "Great presentation," he tells me, and I nod and smile as I walk into the warm hallway.

It's only thirty francs for the half-hour talk, but you take what you can get. The period bell rings as I walk into the teacher's lounge. They often serve snacks, it's one of the things that helps them justify the meagre pay.

Nobody looks up when I walk in, but the group is small; most of the teachers are in class. I stack some macarons in one hand and put a tea in the other, skirting the room, looking at the various class photos on the walls. The door to the lounge opens with a loud creak and somebody leaves; I don't look over there. Instead, taking a bite from my pink macaron, I find a photo of the 1952 rugby union team, nineteen young men posing on benches. At the very front, with a cheeky grin on his narrow face, is a man with the name of Nicolas Fontaine.

I don't recognise him.

"Are you here for the training?"

A bespectacled face slides into my peripheral vision, about my age, maybe a little older. I finish my mouthful of macaron and lean back against the photograph of Nicolas Fontaine and the rugby team of '52. She glances at the macarons piled in my hand. I offer the handful to her. She takes one and continues to study me, her black sequin dress—bold for a teacher—shimmering.

"I'm sorry," comes out of my mouth as a question.

"You were just standing near the photos."

"Oh. I'm not here for the sports. I'm just doing a talk,"

I respond brusquely. "They like bringing you back to talk to the students because you're a connection they've got. I'm a cartoonist, that's why they asked me to come. Class of '52. I don't remember much of the school. They've done work on it." I look back at the rugby team photo. "Gilles Jordan. Vandooren. Now those are names I haven't thought about in years."

"Class of '53 myself." She slides the macaron into her mouth and I begin to feel slightly nauseous, like the room is spinning. She smiles, her sallow cheeks puffing out like a blowfish, and I take a long drink of room temperature tea.

"Maybe I saw you around." She props up her glasses.

"Maybe," I respond.

"You ever do anything worth remembering?"

"I did lots of things back then but you wouldn't guess it."

She smiles softly, licking a crumb from the corner of her lips. They're red, for a teacher. Her blonde hair's a tangle, her ear protrudes from the left. I notice how her breasts are forcibly propped up against the stack of books in her arms.

"█████████," she tells me.

There is static when she says this. "What."

"My name. The students call me Miss Blanchot."

"Oh." That's weird. I want to ask her for her name again, afraid that I've missed it. I search for a nametag but she's not wearing anything—that is to say, she *is* wearing that black dress, just no nametag. I search the books in her arms. I can see essay pages poking out the top.

"I teach English," Miss Blanchot says, probably noticing my eye. The novel at the very top is *Bonjour Tristesse*, by

Francoise Sagan. We look at each other in the eyes again. "I know, it's a contentious move. But her writing is splendid."

"'Ain't it funny how fate loves to choose unworthy and mediocre faces,'" I recite, thinking about how the fat man had approached me two nights ago.

Her eyes narrow the same way ████████'s eyes do, blonde hair falling in front of her murky green eyes, like a rainforest being thrashed by a storm. Again, I'm alarmed at how the name is censored in my head. ████████, now why is she so strong on my mind. "You're a word or two off," she says. "But still, very impressive. Who are you, cartoonist?"

"Nicolas."

She shakes my hand. Her skin is soft, as if moisturised, and mine is crumby. I apologise and she says it's okay, before brushing the crumbs off on her dress.

"It's weird that you have her name," I say.

She tilts her head. "Whose name?"

Ghosts on Abbesses Street, they stalk me, watching from the shadows. I realise I'm standing there, not saying anything, and in the very back of my mind, the place where it hurts, I can hear soft piano, a leitmotif from long ago. My lips begin to sing it but no sound is coming out; it's in my head.

I was in love, and I lost her.

Suddenly, I refocus on Miss Blanchot's face.

"I don't know," I respond to her question.

She furrows her brow, makes to leave, but stays. "I live around here. Number 13 Charlot Street, it's a little place I'm renting above the ceramics store."

"Okay," I respond.

"If it ever gets lonely."

She's staring into my soul so much it hurts, and my mouth has gone dry and I've forgotten the tea in my hands. Miss Blanchot looks like somebody who's lost, and I understand what she means.

"I should be going," she tells me, and leaves.

I spend the rest of the day riding the metro around the city. My right ear is pressed against the frosted window as I sketch people in my small notebook, and every now and then I have to stifle a sneeze or else the other passengers will think I've got something.

I keep thinking about Miss Blanchot, which I suppose, I think I'd rather have her on my mind than the fat man, but nonetheless. I sketch her black dress and the books stacked in her arms, a pile of four mismatched and disorderly. Textbooks and *Bonjour Tristesse*. Her yellow-blonde hair is accentuated by my shading strokes, coloured that way only in my imagination. Her ears, small and round like the way these train tracks curve as you go down the Aubervilliers line.

When I'm finished, I hold back the page and stare at it. Immense horror comes over me and I tear it from the book, scrunching it up with both hands. A young boy, on all fours, stares at me from a bench seat, his mother lost in a fashion magazine with Colette on the front page. The look on the boy's face is one of contemplation, if a child this young can contemplate anything more than the fact he's shit his pants again. Slowly, his small lips smile at me and he giggles uncontrollably.

I can only think he's mocking me.

I gather up my materials and shove them deep into my backpack, slipping my pen into my pocket, as the train reaches Rambuteau station, and then I hurry out the doors before they're completely open.

We fuck with the curtains drawn shut, which makes the three thirty-seven light look like a more respectable hour. Miss Blanchot's room above the ceramics store is shoddy and the mattress is hard but she has a gas heater installed in the bedroom, which makes up for anything else.

It smells of dust but I only notice it when I walk in, and then we're on the bed and the grey blanket's been torn off with the turquoise sheets exposed. Her lips taste like tobacco and when they smack together, it's with a wet sloshing sound. Her tongue flies, and not because she's talking. She tears off my shirt and a shiver goes through me.

She throws me onto my back. Flings her glasses onto the bedside table. I cup her bare breast and stare into her green eyes. Her nose is dusted ever-so-slightly with freckles.

And I imagine she's ███████.

She's ███████.

She's—

With the heater against my back, I get my hands underneath and fuck her in the dull grey light. You become a hot prospect for women when you can say I'm the young cartoonist of the year, but it's been some time since I've been with anybody.

Not since—

You hold a breath, eyes sewn shut like a horror movie monster. It's her claws in your shoulder blades. Her teeth in your neck. Sweat drips from your forehead onto her back, which is scored with what appears to be cigarette burns. You can count the ridges of her spine protruding through her pale skin, pulsating up and down, up and down.

Fuck.

I retreat out of her with a heavy gasp, landing on my back on the edge of the bed. For the first time I notice the ceiling, which is slanted and unpainted, broken by cracks and occasionally patterned with shadows of trees. Miss Blanchot rolls over too, and I grab the sheets, yanking them well-and-truly over my nakedness.

I'm trying to catch my breath.

What's your name.

What's your name.

What's your name.

My cock is aching, like a muscle ache, more from the fact it's been so long. I can feel a dribbling of semen and can smell the stench of afternoon sex permeating the room. When I look at Miss Blanchot, she's staring at me in a familiar way.

"I'm sorry," I tell her.

She slides across to me and finds my half-flaccid cock underneath the sheets, gripping it hard. Her wet lips attack me unexpectedly and I melt into her kiss. Slowly, but with an above-average level of expertise, she climbs on top of me, the covers arching then falling off us, to the cold wooden floorboards. Her arse lights up with goose bumps.

"Don't move," she murmurs to me.

I don't, but I'm thinking about my talk. She's stroking

my chest and pumping up and down, her juices dribbling across my cock and onto my pubic hair. I'm thinking about ███████.

Miss Blanchot screams.

"Christ," I mutter as she collapses on top of me, her elbows on either side of my face. She sinks down towards the mattress and her lips blow shuddering breaths against my ear. Her heartbeat thumps against my chest. She's got her eyes shut, occasionally giving a spasm and a moan.

She rolls off me and my cock flops out of her and into the cold air. The bedsheets sail to the floor and stay there. The only sign that I ever reached climax is the fact there's goo-like semen on the bedsheets, and her thigh.

I study her on my side.

"You know what I do when I'm not teaching?" she says, opening her eyes and crawling on top of me, breathing heavily against my face, a tang of macaron and tea in it.

"What," I say without a question mark.

"I look around for sad people to fuck."

"Great," I say in monotone.

She shoves my ribcage to prop herself up. A bead of sweat falls from her face to my bottom lip, and I lick it. Her white breasts swing softly like a hypnotist waving a pocket watch, except they're not making clicking sounds.

Her gaze is dreamy, her cheeks are red.

"That's why I teach at a school," she says.

"That can't be true," I tell her.

She looks at me with her head resting on her knuckle. "Well, it's not like I'm offering sex in exchange for passing grades or anything like that. What kind of teacher would that make me? It's just that they're all sad. It's consensual, anyway."

I roll onto my back and blow out a breath of air.

"If you say so," I tell her. "You know, you could go to jail for that. I don't think it matters if it's consensual."

"Yeah. Well. It's just a bit hard at the moment."

I find it difficult to disagree with her, resting my hand in the tangled hairs of my chest, damp with sweat. We lay there, our thighs touching together, for some time.

"Who's ███████████?" she asks.

"I never said that name."

"That's why I'm asking."

I pause to think about it. Her name has been a black mark for as long as the past few days—though, it could be much longer. "It's funny, you know," I say. "It's like there's this static every time I hear that name, so much so I seem to have forgotten it completely. Say it, I'm not lying."

"███████████."

"See."

"It doesn't sound like static to me. ███████████."

"Okay. That's enough."

I sigh again, closing my eyes. I imagine I'm falling through a sea of darkness, but the darkness is warm, and my descent slow, deliberate. Sometimes I see flashes of things in this darkness, and once I was afraid of the things I see here, the faces of so many people, voices manifesting as literal words spelt out across my vision, white on black, but now I let them come, and then go, and so they pass like tides on the shoreline.

"I want to know about her," Miss Blanchot says.

I can't access this part of my brain. She's a smudge in the back of my memory, and when I knock on the door she's standing behind, I'm struck with the most painful of headaches.

"There's something wrong with you," I tell her instead.

Miss Blanchot does not object and so in her silence I slide out of her bed and pull on my trousers, my shirt, and then collect my coat, throwing my arms through the holes. My feet hit the cold floor and I jump onto one foot to mitigate it.

I peer through a parting in her curtains. The early-week sun turns the snow the colour of urine when you haven't drunk enough water, but it's no different to any other day in Paris. The timid sunlight touches pores in my skin and I feel mildly rejuvenated by it, as much as you can be.

When I look back at Miss Blanchot, she's up and clutching the bedsheets across her chest. Her cheeks are a soft red. Her bottom lip is puffed up. She's chewing on it like a lolly.

"You're right," she says. "There *is* something wrong with me, something really wrong." She stops and I notice the muscles in her shoulders tighten. "Come visit me at the school tomorrow."

"Aren't you afraid I'm going to tell someone," I ask her.

She shrugs, the blanket slips from her swollen nipple. "It was a joke. I don't sleep with my students, *or* the teachers."

"But the first part was real. About the sad people."

"I fucked you, didn't I?"

"You don't know me," I respond, throwing my hands into my pockets and touching the pen that's in there.

"And you don't know me," she says.

"You're right, not even your name."

"You'll come then," she says decisively.

"We'll see." I walk out of the room, using my shoulder to nudge open the door. I descend the narrow white steps through to the ceramics store, wet smell of pottery in the air. Then I'm walking onto the Parisian streets and the snow has stopped, but I know it won't be for long. Never is.

I pull back my sleeve and glance at my watch. The clock hands have stopped at one minute past four, which I know is wrong. The sun sits directly overhead, its white light illuminating the frost that's gripped the city. There's a room in the corner of my brain with the door locked, and I'm starting to think I've thrown away the key for a good reason. Or I just lost it.

██████████. Why don't I remember.

My breath glides out between my lips and vanishes as soon as it touches the Paris air. I'm standing on the edge of Charlot Street as the lights go green and cars fly past, plumes of ice in their wake. I walk along the side of the road, not looking up at anyone who passes.

The winds die late-afternoon just as the shadows are growing long. Snow's settled against awnings and trees, tucked against the glass of tenements and storefronts. Paris has grown eerily quiet save for the minimal traffic and occasional voices peddling wares, and work friends departing for home.

And the ringing of a telephone.

It's a teenage boy in a grey school uniform and a cigarette poking out of his mouth who notices the ringing phone. He removes his gloved hand from his pocket, tugs on his red woollen scarf, and picks the cigarette from his mouth, dribbling smoke into the air. In the absence of any meaningful wind, the smoke simply lingers there and he walks through it.

The phone booth is empty and the telephone is ringing.

The boy looks around for a moment, then furtively sidesteps inside the booth. He is surrounded by plastic-glass walls that are scratched with names, digits, quotes and sketches. There's the back of a piece of paper stuck to the other side of the glass, and he can vaguely make out the advertisement for an old show at *Le Bal Blomet*, November 1954. The telephone itself is red. There's gum on the wall beside it, and a single coin worth one franc on the narrow benchtop.

He sneakily pockets the coin and with his other hand plucks the telephone off the rack, guides it to his ear. There's empty space on the other end, as though the phone has been left on the table in a room where nothing is happening. There's just the faint hum of . . . jazz music, so faint that the teenager thinks, briefly, he's imagining it.

"Hello?" he says.

He catches a breath on the other end, the kind of long and forced breath you only hear when somebody wants you to.

"Who's there?" he says.

There is no response.

The teenager hangs the phone back on the hook and looks around. The Paris streets are empty and quiet. Yet, he gets the sense he can still hear that music. He eyes the phone for a moment longer, debating whether or not to pick it up and see for himself, but he thinks then, there's no way.

So with this, the teenager, though perplexed, walks out of the phone booth and slings the glass door shut, throwing his hands back into his pockets.

The telephone starts to ring again.

He stops and glances at it. *What the . . . ?* is his only thought, and he feels a tingle on the tip of his tongue. The phone appears to quake as it rings. He feels the urge to pick it up, to discover who's calling on the other end.

Another person is coming up the sidewalk and so the teenager decides to leave the phone be. Without thinking about it again, he kicks his feet and walks off.

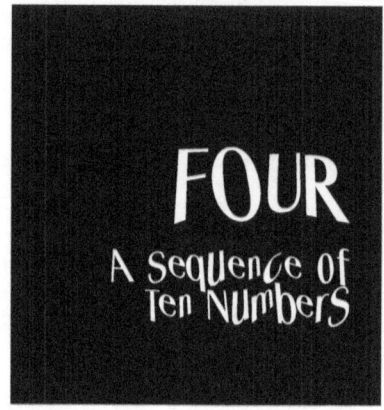

FOUR
A Sequence of Ten Numbers

I walk out of the *Studio 28* cinema into the cold night, standing in the pool of soft red light that's being cast from the building's signage. Rubbing my hands together for warmth, I peek at my watch, clearing frost from the cheap glass.

Stuck on a minute past four, as usual. Feeling no desire to keep staring at it, I pull off my watch and throw it onto the ground, where the snow quickly devours it.

All I know is it's dark and late enough that more lights glow on the street than in all the frosted apartment windows combined. Wednesday nights are the quietest round these parts, though you can't say that any night is truly quiet at *Studio 28*. A young couple walk up the steps as I feel for my cigarettes, but my coat pockets come up empty except for a small mass market paperback. I must have thrown them out.

Buttoning up my coat, I walk up Tholozé Street from the cinema. It's probably for the better that I try to kick the smoking habit anyway; I can't say it's done me much good over the years. Soon I'm back amidst the narrow streets of Montmartre, wiping my nose with the back of my coat sleeve and continuing on. Street artists flit about, and I catch glimpses of myself in the reflective windows of barbershops, jewellery stores, cuisine spots, and hardware stores. All the windows are dark, no movements in or around them. It all rises up and over me in complete dominance, the lampposts and buildings, the grey fog that crawls unrelenting over the city.

Suddenly an oncoming car screeches past, flicking snow across the sidewalk. I backpedal just quick enough to avoid the splash of ice, and watch after it.

Fucking Paris traffic. No matter whereabouts you are, and it doesn't matter the night, or the arrondissement, believe me, the streets aren't wide enough.

I'm taking the long way home, up Burq Street and through a playground. I vault the rusty green fence and feel my shoes against the dirt path. The playground is empty except for the play equipment and malformed trees. Wind sends the swings and I catch one by the chain, letting it squeal to a stop. It's a pathetic-looking plank of metal but I sit on it.

There's just enough light for me to see the pages of my paperback, which I tear from my pocket and open up in my left hand. *Of Mice and Men* by Steinbeck on the front cover. I picked it up from a second-hand store and you can see moderate wear on the edges, creases in the spine. The sound of crinkling paper fills the air as I turn the page with my thumb.

Owls hoot. Bats chirp.

A sequence of ten numbers pops into my head.

And I'm not thinking about the book. Not its characters, Milton and Small, nor the feel of the pages in my hands. All I can think of is that sequence. Ten numbers, scrawled on a little tear of paper that the fat man gave me.

I shudder, looking up from my book and over my shoulder. A bush shakes as though something has moved. But there's nothing here, only trees and a metal slide covered in ice. I stare straight ahead, to the road, and, on the other side, dark tenements. Windows slammed shut against the winter's bite, lightbulbs out, the day's papers rolling in the wind.

Suddenly a breath tingles the hairs on the back of my neck, sending me to my feet, boots sinking into a bed of snow. The paperback shuts with no bookmark left in it.

Yet, there is nobody else in the playground.

Then footsteps sink into the snow with the sound of sizzling sausages. I can smell them now, can see their flaming firepit in my mind's eye, and the warmth, it takes my body. But it's as if those metaphorical sausages have begun to emit an off stench. They crackle now, not only oozing fats and oil and grease, but pus, maggots writhing from the pores in the meat. I imagine them whining like babies over a gigantic fire.

And then it vanishes, and only the stench remains. It's a vaguely familiar stench, still only as faint as a single type of perfume in a crowded auditorium, the smell of a funeral home. Are there ghosts out tonight. What do they want with me.

A stick breaks and I turn around just in time to see

something disappear, only the ghostly fabrics of her dress catching the wind. Just for a second, and then she's gone.

You live in one place long enough, you start to see ghosts.

"Get out of here!" I shout.

An animal darts through the shrubbery and a bat takes flight from a street post.

My forehead opens up and a bead of sweat crawls out. I'm gripping the paperback in one hand, its pages soaked. A car door slams shut somewhere and another car honks its monotone horn. Somebody giggles. The leaves quiver. Snow, it falls.

She's gone, only the smell remains.

"Nicolas . . ."

Her voice clangs against the back of my mind with a sharp gust of wind, my right ear pops and begins to ache. Her tone is taunting, like bullies in the schoolyard.

There's the image of a room, murky and half-dressed like a sketch in someone's visual diary. There in the light filtering through wooden blinds is a woman's figure, slender and golden, wearing the sunrays like a dress that she's sewn. Her blonde hair turns with her, shimmering golden in the light. A cat purrs on the half-made bed. The clock on the wall ticks, but only between two seconds, back and forth, back and forth.

I'm in this room as well, in the space where the light doesn't touch, the back of my hand scored with burns which have started to blister, the damage from boiling water.

The woman is speaking.

What is your name.

What is your name.

You know what I do when I'm not teaching?

I shudder over to the swings and throw up, losing my knees in the process. They dig deep into the snowbank. My paperback tears, soaking in the dirty snow.

The sky breaks with thunder.

"Happy birthday, Nicolas."

Colette's face is illuminated by the candles of my birthday cake. It sits there in the middle of the dining table, a simple dacquoise, but I know if it's coming from Colette it's not as simple as it looks. She's smiling broadly, still wearing her work clothes: a white coat and black skirt with matching leggings. The card she gave me is on the edge of the table. It's one hundred francs and a handwritten letter.

Rain spits against the windows of my apartment. The television, which is tuned to muted grey ants, only picks up the slightest tangle of the ten p.m. screening. The monochrome lights flash across the room sporadically.

"Make a wish," Colette tells me.

I circle the table so that I'm standing beside her. She puts her hand on my back and hisses into my ear:

"Quick!"

I lean over the cake and blow out the candles in one go. A darkness splashes in their absence. There's a rolling of thunder, which sends the television into a hard fit of more static. Somewhere behind all that distorted motion and noise, a monster roars and an orchestra of strings keen.

"Twenty-five." The number leaves my body like the last bit of air leaving a balloon. I look up at Colette and she rests her head against my arm. "I thought I was going to be writing for *Tintin* by twenty-one," I say with a half-contained laugh.

I boil some water and fill two cups, steam filling the air. Hanging above the sink is the calendar which reads Thursday, February 12. I'm sceptical; the days all blur into one. It's only the films they play on the television, and the showtimes at the theatre, which give me any indication of what day it is.

I return to Colette at the kitchen table, passing her tea. We sit down together and start cutting up the cake.

"Mother sent another postcard," Colette says.

"Is she still shooting in . . . where was it."

"Ushant," Colette says with grandiose. "She tells me she saw the most beautiful red bird. 'The most stunning thing I've ever laid my eyes on,' is what she wrote me. She really is enjoying herself. I must say, I'm almost envious of her. But then, how could I live with missing this blizzard!" She throws back a spoonful of cake and then washes it down with some tea. Meanwhile, lightning opens the sky outside my apartment.

"Good lord!" she exclaims. "It really is bad out there."

Bubbles rise to the surface of my tea as I lift it to my lips. I take a sip and smack it back on the tabletop, then sneeze violently into the nook of my arm, all snot and mucus.

"You should see someone about that."

I wipe my face with a handkerchief, feeling like I really might be coming down with something. I finish blowing my nose and stuff it back inside my pocket. She's still looking at me and I smile softly in her direction, without making eye contact. "Have you ever seen it snow so relentlessly in Paris," I say to her, now catching her eyes. "And for so damn long."

"Once when we were children," she responds.

"I don't remember much about those days."

"Well, it wasn't much to speak of." She smiles and digs into her cake. "Mother kept us well off, I will give her that. It's a shame the two of you no longer get along."

I take some cake. It's not that I hate our mother. I really don't, in fact her resistance to my work only ever made me double down on the messages I wanted to convey. Our mother is stuck in her ways, always has been, but what can you expect of someone who came of age in the world she did. The space between us, these days it's not so much filled with anything in the way of malice or scorn, but there is space. Just empty space.

"I feel like it's more than just my work with the *Canard*, though, sometimes," I admit, watching the vague images coming through the television static.

"Certainly."

"I remind her of things."

Colette gives no verbal response, but says enough. She sips her tea, then swirls it with a spoon.

After a while, she says, "I'm sure it's complicated," and looks at me through the dim lights. "Mother is critically inhibited in regards to conversation."

"Tell me about it."

We continue watching the movie screening together. A man's voice suddenly cuts through, stern yet passionate. "Oh, it's *Suspicion*," I say, noticing Cary Grant.

"Have you gotten it working then?"

"No, it's still turning itself on and off," I assure her. I draw a spoonful of cake to my mouth. "Well, that is to say, it's predominately when I'm not home, and preferably gone for the night. My bills are growing by the quarter." I eat the cake.

"You really ought to bring it up with the landlord."

"I wouldn't want him to see this," I say through cake.

"I always thought he was a nice, grumpy old man that Michel."

"He's corrupt. You know he makes all his money bootlegging films. It's no wonder he doesn't run the entire industry out of business, certainly the *Gaumont-Palace*."

"I'm not saying what he's doing is right, but he does what he can to make ends meet, we all do in this city."

Her mention of the city makes me feel as though something is watching us, but the curtains are drawn tight.

"You're always seeing the best in them," I say.

"Well, there was that one occasion in which Eric—that tool—gave my beloved Bengal a haircut and I forced him to sleep in the rain for a night, so be careful before coming to that conclusion, Mister Fontaine." She wags her cake-crumb fork at me. "You know, I can be vicious when I choose to. But Michel, by god, the man is in his seventies!"

"That's very cruel," I suggest.

"Eric? He had it coming for him."

We take mouthfuls of cake each.

"The other day, there was a detective down the hall," I say. "I'm not sure what he was after, a couple of them, from *Agence Duluc*. Looking for a Louise Duchamp, or something."

Colette hums. "*Agence Duluc*? You think a murder?"

"Could be. Probably not."

"More like someone gone missing."

"Probably." The sound from the television has gotten lower so that all you can hear is the rain hitting the windows and the boiled water still fizzling on the stove. I slide my empty plate aside and take the envelope she had given me.

Colette tidies up the last bit of cake on her plate while watching me. "That's for you before you try to give it back. You're my little brother. Well. You're my little brother who's roughly a foot taller than me. But nonetheless." She takes my hand across the table. Hers is warm, unbelievably so, and I'm just so damn cold. "Why *are* you so tall?"

I'm struck with the urge to tell her about the fat man. But what difference would that make. I hardly remember the night and it might have been a fever dream as far as I'm concerned. I certainly don't remember the show I saw.

"Are you okay?" Colette asks.

"I don't know why I'm so tall," I say, before standing up. "While I do appreciate the thought, I don't want to be living off these anymore." Suddenly the room goes black and it's the television going off. "I know it looks bad, it does." I'm gesturing at the screen when it comes back on with the rest of Hitchcock's *Suspicion*. "And I know you can afford it, everybody knows you have the means, but you know . . ."

I grab the *Zenith* remote and hit mute.

"I'm in a position to help you," Colette says.

"It's just," I say, "it's just a little hard right now."

She doesn't respond to this. Anyway, she isn't wrong, no matter how much I want to resist it. I have no means of affording any of this anymore, we both know that. My savings are wasting and I'll lose the apartment soon. I'd have lost it already if not for their help, I'm just living off their residuals, but it isn't sustainable. You're a failure, Nicolas Fontaine. Your mother's making movies with Hitchcock. Your sister's a fashion icon in the fashion capital of the world. And you can't even draw pictures anymore.

But it's just a little hard right now.

But how the hell'd you end up gettin' like this. **The fat man.**

Colette takes my hand in her own and pulls me back into the real world. The images across the screen burst against my retinas; I've seen them a hundred times before.

"Have you been on something again, tell me the truth."

I see the fat man in the headlights of his expensive car, his shadow slammed across the road. His dress suit and pants and top hat. *Moscati Research,* that's what he said they were called. I don't remember putting down my name for any sort of jobs, not since leaving the laundromat.

Then how did they find me.

I'm looking at Colette.

She reaches into my coat and snatches out a box of cigarettes. "What is this? Nicolas?"

"Give it back—"

"You're still on these damned things!" she snaps, her spittle flying. "What's it going to take?"

The apartment shrinks, or maybe it's just the temporary high that comes from birthday desserts with your sister wearing off. He slipped a piece of paper into my hand. On the piece of paper is a number, a number composed of ten digits.

A man who sounds like a woman.

A man who will ask a question.

One hundred fifty francs. That's more than Colette even gave me tonight, and just for answering a phone call.

But then what.

"I'm sorry," Colette says, throwing the pack of cigarettes onto the table by the cake and sitting down, drinking her tea hard and fast. She grabs her face and wipes tears from her eyes. I suddenly sneeze awfully-loud, so loud she jumps.

"Sorry," I mumble into my sleeve.

"You know how you get," is the only thing she tells me, and I know what she means, but I'm not like that anymore. I wish I could convince her of it. That I'm doing the best I can, given the circumstances. And besides, it could be worse, couldn't it. After all, it's only a cigarette. It could be . . .

You know how you get.

She jumps up and throws her arms around me and there's nothing I can do but hug her back, staring through the television's silvery lights. "Promise me you'll stop," she says. "I hate to see you like this. Promise me you'll let me help. I love you, Nicolas. I know it hasn't always been the best but you're my little brother. I love you. I love you!"

"I'm trying," I tell her. "I'm trying."

The four thirty-five a.m. film is *Dinner at Eight*.

I sink into a plastic chair on the small balcony out the side of the apartment, which leaves little room to move around. A matchstick strikes a box and comes alight. I lift it to the cigarette that's jutting out of my mouth.

Then stop.

Sighing, I extinguish the matchbox and throw the cigarette off the side of the building, then lean back into the balcony chair, watching a drizzle of rain fall in front of me. It's as quiet as it's ever been out here. The thunderclouds have withdrawn into the stars, snow falls as only a gentle patter against the rusted railing and the trees, which whistle.

A sequence of ten numbers dances in my mind like a chorus line. I imagine my cold thumb, glazed with frost from the undying winter, slotting into the loop of a telephone dial and turning it clockwise. Click. Return. Twist it to the second number. Click. Return. Again and again and again until . . .

A voice on the other end. A man who sounds like a woman.

I exhale deeply into the falling snow, and close my eyes.

The **city** does too.

Miss Blanchot is not teaching the next day. Morning light, illuminating the frost that sticks to windowpanes, flows like vapor across the teacher's lounge where she had been the previous day. As if sensing the reason for my visit, a man in gym shorts and a whistle around his neck tells me, as he walks to his desk, she's not in today.

My eyes are heavy, and sore from my constant rubbing. I'm sure they're red. I grip my hands to stop them from trembling. In the corner of the teacher's lounge is a formidable shadow, and that shadow appears to grow each time I blink. Soon it will consume me, I think. Will grow hands and grab me by the shoulders and say you've disappeared, Nicolas. Those who know you in this city are dwindling, one after the other, forgetting.

Blowing my nose in a tissue, I begin to walk around the teacher's lounge. Two students sort through a pile of papers, and one of them comments on my yellow jumper. The way I tower over them makes me feel old and out of place. Eventually I find Miss Blanchot's desk and pick up a folded letter there underneath a copy of *Bonjour Tristesse*.

I take the letter and open it, reading what's inside.

I knock on the door of Miss Blanchot's room above the ceramics store, and listen. The owner in the shop below softly whistles an incoherent tune; she doesn't concern herself much with what happens above her head, she says she's used to people coming and going all the time. The only other sound besides her whistling is the soft blues emanating from under Miss Blanchot's door. Receiving no response from the knocking, I gently lean into the cold door and am surprised to find it open.

Soft light breaks through the curtained windows, giving the room a hazy feel. The pungent smell of pot is tangible, the odd scent filling the room. A gramophone splutters the blues, a genre of music I never quite fashioned. Sitting by the gramophone is an ashtray collecting burnt cigarettes. I close the door behind myself and focus now on a shadow being cast from her partitioned bedroom, smattered across the rear wall.

"Is anybody in here," I say, throat dry.

The floorboards creak as I cross the room, past the unwashed clothes and the umbrella leaning against the solitary couch, chequered blue and white with a blanket hanging off it. Carefully, I peer into the bedroom.

The curtain is drawn but not all the way, letting in light which paints the scene. The white bedsheets mangled. The naked body on the bed, tangled in its own assemblage of sinuous, feminine limbs. Needle jutting out of her forearm. She hasn't begun to smell yet, so I suppose she hasn't been dead long.

I sit down on the edge of her bed, gently nudging her bare foot to the side. Her toes curl unnaturally, in the grips of early rigor mortis. I suppose Miss Blanchot is someplace else now, far from the room where she breathed her last breath, had her last orgasm, tasted her last cigarette. Actually, I'm disappointed, in a way. I'll never know her name.

There's a crumpled note tucked near her thigh.

Apologies for the mess, is all it says.

I turn over the note but there's nothing on the other side except a faint dampness, not sure from what. I fold it back up and tuck it underneath her stiff, milky thigh.

Down in the ceramics store, I tell the owner to call the police, I tell her what's happened. Then, once I know that the police are on their way, I flee back out into the snow and don't look back. A black car kicks a snow bank rushing past. I thrust my hands into my pockets, wipe my leaking nose on my sleeve, and walk the other way.

She's swaying about the room with no clothes on. Slides a dusty record from its sleeve and slips it onto the record player.

Mainstream blues dribbles from the gramophone, crackling with all its imperfections. She sucks on a cigarette and lays down on her bed, legs spread, a knee to the ceiling. The curtains are drawn except for the very edge, which gets caught on a thread and lets in a butter knife of sunlight.

She's sliding her smooth fingers in and around her vagina and humming to the hot blues. There's a needle sticking out of her arm, quivering with each excited movement.

A bird sits on the balcony outside her window, looking in. Then the windows fog up and she exhales sharply, the cigarette dropping from her lips to the side of her face, sizzling. If she had remaining any ability to feel, she'd have noticed.

Her vision clouds and she closes her eyes.

Death and orgasm occur simultaneously.

I hurry on past the bus stop with a handful of rowdy youths inside it. A police car rattles past on shaky tires, its siren tearing through the air like sterilised needles through pulsating veins.

I lean against the brick wall opposite the phone booth on the corner of Pastourelle Street and Archives. A man in business attire enters the booth and calls someone.

After some time, the phone returns to the hook and the door clicks open. The man lights a cigarette and glances in my direction, doesn't say anything or even acknowledge me. Hands slipping into pockets, he steps inside his awaiting vehicle and I briefly glimpse a woman inside with him. Her black sunglasses glint at me, then the door's shut. Without making a fuss, the vehicle drives off into the mid-morning city light.

My breath gushes white in front of my face as I step

forward onto the sidewalk. A red car honks as it rolls past me.

I approach the phone booth, its plastic walls covered in frost and drawings. My stiff hand finds the door and I pull it open, sliding inside. The red telephone hangs from the hook. I pull the door shut and am surprised by the quietness.

There's a sequence of ten numbers.

I dial this number now. Twist right. Stop. Click. The rotary dial snaps back to zero. Twist right. Stop. Click. Frost spits from the telephone. My fingers reflect against the phone booth walls as I turn the rotary again. Stop. Click. Screaming as it returns to zero. Twist right. Twist right. Twist right. Twist right. Number. Number. My finger burns with frost as I slide it into the little circle dial and turn right. Past one. Past two. Past three. Four. Five. Slow. Slow—

There it is.

I hold my breath as I release it.

Snap to zero. Frost chips from the telephone to the floor. A soggy newspaper curls against my shoe, where it stops. I raise the telephone to my ear.

If you dial that number you will speak to a man who sounds like a woman.

A sharp *click* rings through the telephone wires and cracks against my ear with such force I nearly drop the phone. Lips smack together. Somebody takes a breath.

"You will be redirected to the offices of Doctor Moscati. Please hold momentarily."

A beep. Just my breath into the silence, the words spoken by the man who sounds like a woman ringing through my head. He really does sound like a woman, come to think of it. The doctor's name is Doctor Moscati, but what he's a doctor of, it's hard to say. I change my grip on the cold telephone, swinging it from my right ear to my left and glancing through the walls of the phone booth. Across the street, I catch a flash of movement, somebody disappearing behind a black van.

This man will put you into contact with another man.

A male voice answers the call in the offices of Doctor Moscati. *"Good evening."*

This man will ask you a question.

"Can you state your name and date of birth for the record?"

The telephone creaks within my grip. Frost burning my palm, I switch it to the other hand, other ear. My heart is drumming the way it does when you're in some place you shouldn't be. I want to throw up and hang up simultaneously.

From the blacked-out part of my brain:

Sir, are you there?

"Nicolas Fontaine," I respond.

Fingers tap-dance across a mechanical keyboard.

"Date of birth, February 12, 1934."

"Ah. Happy birthday."

I am inclined to resist the late-birthday greeting, and instead hold on the phone without saying anything.

"Nicolas Fontaine, then. As expected. Please be assured that your details will remain strictly confidential with the company and its associates. Prior to your visit to Doctor Moscati's labs, please be advised that we will require proof of identity. Once there, you will be given everything you need for the impending trial. Mister Fontaine, in the meantime, we require nothing further from you but will be in contact within the next twenty-four hours with

instructions on how to proceed. Please keep an eye on your mail. And allow me to stress, the information packet you receive is for your eyes only. Please acknowledge that you understand the nature of the trial and the nature of your responsibilities going into it."

"Okay," I respond.

"Wonderful. Can I assist you with anything else?"

I notice a faint buzzing in the phone wires.

The man is sitting behind a desk in a nondescript room, with an open book in front of him. The walls are white and unmarked. A single fluorescent light spans the midsection of the ceiling, giving off that low buzz. Warm air drips in through a grate by the ceiling, just above the single, shuttered door.

The man's large, slightly-hairy hand engulfs a cold coffee cup. It's red and on it is the symbol of Moscati's practice, a large and statement-making "M." He wants to drink some of that cold coffee but you can't drink when you've got someone on the line, and all he knows about Mister Fontaine is that on the record he was given, this name has an asterisk beside it.

"Is there anything else, Mister Fontaine?"

I feel my eyeballs return to their usual position.

"No," I respond, the words fogging up the booth. Snow hisses against the glass. Yellow light washes over me as a black car passes. I watch it with my eyes.

My eyes.

"I'm sure the team looks forward to meeting you."

The line disconnects and all I'm left to do is stand there, staring at the rotary dial, still warm from that sequence of ten numbers. I hang the red phone back where it came from and think about what I'm going to do while I wait for the delivery.

It arrives with next morning's mail.

FIVE
Moscati Research Laboratories

The white envelope hisses as I retrieve it from my designated mailbox in the complex lobby. I slam shut the compartment and step outside into the Saturday morning frost. The streetlamp outside my apartment block is still on from last night, surrounded by a haze of lingering fog. Snow trickles in much the same way dust falls from the ceiling of an attic.

I tear open the envelope and unfold the letter contained within. The entire thing is typed in neat rows of Courier. It's directly addressed to Mister Nicolas Fontaine. And, underneath this, in parallel lines, printed on a slight angle with ink bleeding across the page:

Dear Mr. Nicolas Fontaine.

We wish to thank you for your impending participation in the clinical trials of the latest invention from the **Moscati**

Research Group. The trial will commence **this Tuesday**, the 17th of February, at Moscati Research Laboratories. The session will be preceded by a guided tour and briefing held **this Monday**, the 16th of February. This will be your chance to ask questions, and to learn more about our new product.

Find below the address of Moscati Research Laboratories, and your appointment time. We wish to remind you that this letter, along with any general information associated with the impending trials and the Moscati Research Group, is strictly confidential. Upon your arrival at the laboratory, you will be required to sign a non-disclosure agreement. Refusal to do so will result in the immediate removal of your participation.

Thank you again for your cooperation.

Kindly,
The Moscati Research Group.

I throw my back against a brick wall under the eaves of the first floor balcony and continue to study the letter. My breath turns to mist as it bounces off the paper. As it's the weekend, I currently have some time before visiting the laboratory.

I fold up the letter and slide it back into my yellow coat.

———

Cans of spam, baked beans and pickles rattle about my wireframe basket. I grab a block of cheese, crudely wrapped, and use the remainder of my grocery budget on bread and milk.

As I walk through the checkout, each movement is slow yet automatic. How are you going, sir? Good, good was the usual. My items go through in three satisfying beeps. The clerk tosses them into a plastic bag, which pulls under the weight. Next goes the cheese, then a loaf of bread, carton of milk.

"Good day," says the cashier.

I smile and walk off.

Up through the frosted streets, black tar reflecting the dun sunlight like mirrors. A nondescript car honks its horn at me and I glance at the man inside, business suit and top hat and a healthily-fat cigar jutting out the corner of his mouth. Has Paris always been so full of them, or am I being watched.

I cross D'Orsel Street as a black dog scurries out of a toppled trashcan, soggy papers and banana peels floating off its damp brown fur. It brushes the side of my leg, leaving a wet stain. White and green lights carve through the snow and reflect off the frozen sidewalk, the words they make only barely legible in the haze. *Pharmacie la Providence.* I'm looking up at the large sign, gusts of snow circling the individual letters. Some of them are flashing intermittently, but not by design.

The door squeaks as I open it, ice detaching from the plastic frame. The warmth hits me first, and then the dry smell. I walk to the counter without looking around at much.

The middle-aged woman, with her blonde hair up in a clumsy bun, smiles at me. "What can I get for you?"

I can taste codeine. My hands are shaking.

But I'm clean. It's been a while.

The woman is staring at me.

I tear my prescription slip from my coat and slide it across the counter, into her hand. She takes this, gives it a look. I've had it for some time and I'm not exactly confident she'll accept it. Nonetheless, these concerns are quelled as she writes down something in a notebook and smiles.

"One moment," she says warmly.

I watch her back as she collects the antibiotics from one of the shelves, and I continue to watch her as she returns to me, still smiling. The way she constantly smiles reminds me of that detective I ran into outside my room not long back. Francis, or something, and something about Louise Duchamp.

The small container of pills clicks against the table and she prints a receipt. I listen to the sound of zipping gears as they churn out the slip of paper, vaguely transparent under the bright fluorescent ceiling lights.

Antibiotics and receipt go inside a small bag and the bag slots neatly into my hand. I nod to the pharmacist, she says have a good day, and then I walk back the way I came in.

Sometime shortly after three o'clock in the afternoon that same day, I'm tidying up the kitchen while another run of *Suspicion* gives me something to listen to aside from the scratching of Colette's pen on paper. She's in the adjacent living room, receipts and invoices scattered in orderly piles around her.

Time moves slowly. I count each tick of the wall clock, feel the earth shudder with each one, too much time between each second.

I'm seeing Miss Blanchot on the backs of my eyelids, how she had been lying there on her mattress. I'm disappointed I'll never get the chance to learn more about her, learn what parts of her are true and what she kept secret. Anyway, there's no point in commiserating; she's dead and what's there to be done.

I hang a plate on the drying rack and tug the tea towel from where it's hanging by the oven. The wall heater hums and yet I'm still cold. I glance at Colette across the room, occasionally grappled by those crackling silver lights coming from the television. She's looking at me over her shoulder.

"Everything okay?" she asks me.

"Yes," I respond, hanging the damp towel.

Tell her about the trial.

This voice is not my own. It comes from far away, beyond the apartment. Tell her about the trial, about the fat man and what you're doing. She's going to find out eventually, isn't she, so why do you feel so timid to get it over with?

She's giving me that look, like something's wrong. She knows. She suspects. She's reaching for the smell of cigarettes, of alcohol. You can smell it on the air, vaguely, but it's not from recently. But now she smiles, and I can hear the clock again.

"It's Valentine's Day," Colette says.

I let go of the breath I've been holding.

You lose track of the days after a while. I nod, and I don't respond, remembering why I made myself forget.

I don't tell her about the trial.

I leave before the end of the two p.m. Sunday showing of *The Fly*, the threadbare crowd thoroughly disinterested.

Outside in the foyer, I sip loudly through the straw of my soda and loiter nearby a radio playing *Gone With the Wind*; I own a copy of it back at the apartment.

I comfort myself with the smell of popcorn and that artificial warmth you feel every time you walk into a movie theatre. There's a poster on the wall: *North By Northwest*. A striking piece of artwork in visceral colour. Beside it, *Ben-Hur*, the latest epic from William Wyler.

And there's something else.

I avert my eyes, soda dripping from the tip of the straw to my scarf. There's a man standing near this last poster, a man who I don't recognise, but he's looking at me through a shimmer of thick, ballerina-esque smoke trails. Catching my eye for only a second, he sticks the cigarette back into his mouth and walks off, out of the theatre complex. I watch him until nothing but the black splotch of his business suit against the white city remains, and then the city swallows that too.

They *are* watching me.

But they've been watching me for a while.

Why.

On the way back to my apartment, I light the last cigarette in the box and suck on it deeply, tasting that sweet balloon of relief as the smoke massages the back of my throat and fills my lungs. Colette would disapprove. It's almost enough to make me put it out immediately, but what's one more cigarette. As one sighs at the end of a very long day, I let it all out and hang my arm, the cigarette dangling between my fingertips.

Meanwhile, I think about many things.

First of all, while passing a florist casting warm light onto the footpath, I think about why that man with his black clothes and top hat visited me that night and why he knew so much about me, things he couldn't possibly know. My name, where I worked, hell, he ought to have known even where I lived, at least where I'd be at that specific moment. I get the impression the man must work for Moscati Research Laboratories, but he certainly wouldn't fit the stereotype of a doctor, nor a scientist. He was a businessman, there was no doubt about that.

Between the *Gaumont* and my apartment on Lepic Street is a fruit shop which closes soon, as well as an oddity shop and a cigarette store. You pass brick walls covered in soggy advertisements. A comedy show at the *Théâtre Montmartre Galabru*. A new season of *Lucy Crown* at *Théâtre de l'Atelier* near where I pick up my groceries. One poster, halfway caught in a stacked snowbank, undulates wildly and I step on this with a tear to see what it says: a new television show.

How many others have been invited to participate in the trial and how does the selection process go. I suppose I *must* have signed up for something, a consideration at least, but who was picking. A part of me is surprised by the formalities of it all, but then again, I probably shouldn't be. Not when I take into consideration their black suits and protocols.

I laugh at the obscurity of it all, like I've become the protagonist from some Hitchcockian film. I take a drag of my cigarette and send a plume of smoke into the air. It's just after two in the afternoon now but the city doesn't lighten much, the shadows cast from the tenements engulfing everything in darkness. I walk beneath a streetlamp and it turns on with bravado. I wonder if it sees me, if any of them do.

And then I begin to sing. It's the first thing that comes to my head, and I imagine myself strolling through a Hollywood soundstage surrounded by lights and cameras. I imagine that the snow falling over the Parisian streets is fake, that the sky is fake, the tenements . . . that *I'm* fake myself, just an actor wrapped up in a role. I suck hard on the cigarette and then flick it to the city, the red glow burning into oblivion.

I crescendo, dashing forward and skidding through a snowbank, feeling the ice crackle under the soles of my shoes, water soaking through to my socks.

I'm singing at the top of my lungs, and streetlamps flicker on and off like faces. An entire orchestra plays, the conductor waving his baton like it's the last thing he'll ever do. And I grab onto a lamppost and hurl myself around it.

I skirt past a quiet bus stop, a phone booth on the corner. The door is slightly ajar and knocking the doorframe to the four-four rhythm of the blizzard.

Then, looking up, I see a Caravelle plane flying over Paris. And the music ends. The city falls silent. I stop to catch my breath, watching the plane drift through the sky. I turn around in a three hundred sixty degree motion to keep my eyes on it, until eventually, the plane disappears far beyond the snowstorm, far beyond Paris.

The city bows out.

I'm alone again.

"Welcome to Moscati Research Laboratories."

He speaks with a thick German accent and with his spindly fingers interlocked as if containing something volatile. Standing before our small group in the laboratory's visiting space, the man has put on his very best introductory smile and, you can tell this for certain, his best set of clothes.

"My name is Doctor Anton von Brandt and I will be taking you through the laboratories this morning."

I would sketch Von Brandt with a kind, yet borderline artificial smile, a rather unkind combover, and with enough wrinkles and depth around the eyes to suggest a man of late forties. His lab coat is an extra-large, but he is as tall as he is wide. The pudgy hands that emerge from the ends of his white lab coat feature sausage-like fingers, a ring on his left hand, and yellow blistering of the scientific accident kind.

There isn't much else of Moscati Research. It spans only two floors of its shared building space, a building of plain white walls and dark windows, which leads me to believe the laboratories are either new or underfunded, and the teams small and contained, yet most likely not so secretive as to require their own building altogether.

Our group is made up of only seven, and yet it's enough to make the space feel claustrophobic.

Von Brandt is standing before a large wall with an impressive "M" situated within a hexagon, and under this:

MOSCATI RESEARCH LABORATORIES

"I want to start by thanking you all for coming," continues Von Brandt. "Our work on the Jazz Project is brand new and cutting-edge, but let me assure you that every single detail of it has undergone prior testing and, well this is a given in our industry, we have your safety first and foremost in our minds. In fact! there is not a safer pill on the market, in terms of the sheer exhaustive testing we have done." Von Brandt covers the length of the room well. His side profile reveals shoulders of a slight-forward shape, and between his eyes are red pressure marks which suggest he wears glasses on occasion.

The Jazz Project.

The other people in attendance to undergo the trials appear each so out of place that nobody really does, some of them in business suits, others in more casual attire, like myself. There are four men and two women, all appearing of similar age except for one older man who looks, let's say, sixty-five.

"You will be required to sign on this piece of paper before we begin," Von Brandt tells us, holding a clipboard full of papers before us, then beginning to hand them out along with pens. I already have my own pen, taking it from my pocket. I collect one of the agreement pages and scan it over. The information is similar to what was written on the letter I received a few days ago in the mail. The trial is secretive, and will run for a number of sessions beginning tomorrow, a Tuesday.

My blue pen scribbles a signature.

"If you'll follow me," says Von Brandt.

I slip my pen back into my pocket and walk with the group through the cold corridors of Moscati Research, near the back. Windows look into expansive laboratory rooms with equipment scattered on tables, and in each one you see bespectacled scientists at work, bewitched by numbers and data.

At last, Von Brandt leads us into one of these low-ceilinged research rooms. The scientists look up from their notes and at us, but only briefly, before returning to their work. There's a foul stench in the room, like bodily fluids mixed with something vaguely sour. A machine-like buzz whirrs with consistency.

I'm immediately drawn to an upright test tube, the likes of which are suspended every ten feet or so throughout the room, each one containing nebulous specimens.

Green ooze bubbles in one of the test tubes and I find my reflection in it. Inside this tube, probably three feet tall and half a foot radius, is something I am incapable of describing, but whatever it is, there are two.

"What is that?" another one of the participants says.

I take a step closer towards it, and the other man touches the glass. The fluids do not react to this, but as I approach it, I can hear the bubbling of liquid; there's a low hum emanating from it, generating heat. I make up in my mind that it's some sort of incubation device.

Suddenly a face appears on the other side of the tube

and we both jump. A thin scientist with black spectacles and blue eyes rounds the test tube and stares at the two of us with contemplation. He says nothing, but his look is enough to send us away, back to the rest of the group.

Von Brandt takes us through this room and into a second corridor, eventually stopping at another laboratory with the door shut. A horizontal window spanning the length of the room looks into a moderately-sized research lab not so unlike the previous one. Several blackboards are situated around the premises, all of them covered with writing.

He waves and a single man inside, very white and ghastly except for the horrible bags underneath his eyes, lifts his head and motions for Von Brandt to enter.

"This is Doctor Lippmann, the head of development on the Jazz Project," Von Brandt tells us as Doctor Lippmann presents with all smiles. He's got a twirled moustache and half-moon spectacles. His eyes scan the group passively. From my position towards the back, I observe the other researchers at their tables. I get the sense they're faking it, half-listening to hear what this is all about, half-stealing glances at us.

"Thank you," says Lippman in a nasal tenor, looking at me.

Something moves towards the back of the laboratory and from behind a blackboard appears half a man. I see his business suit, balding head, the top hat clutched in his hands. He's staring straight at us—at myself. I avert my eyes.

It's the fat man from that night.

Lippmann makes a motion with his hand. Another person wafts across the lab and the light dims. A projector ignites with a click, and the familiar rumble of film flickering through a roll completely consumes the room.

"Jazz is a synthetic pill created in our labs," Lippmann says as a square image flashes onto a projector screen on the far wall. JAZZ, it says in dull white lettering; and bracketed, you can make out its unmemorable scientific name.

It clicks to the next slide, a complex web of chemical and elemental links, which turns the entire room to an ugly red-blue-purple. The projector hisses as the slide changes, this time to a burlesque dancer mid-performance under hot red lighting. A soft jazz arrangement rings from the speakers, one I swear I've heard somewhere before.

"This brand new pill from Moscati Research calms the user, placing them in a spot of uninterrupted bliss," says Lippman. "Besides this, it certainly has its quirks. My favourite, for example, is the sudden and inexplicable taking towards *jazz music*. However, as all good jazz ought to be, at least in my opinion, its melodies and arrangements are that which have not been written or heard before in our time or a time before ours."

The slide changes to a brain activity map.

"The effects of jazz last approximately thirty minutes to an hour, during which time the user is expected to remain in a calm state of consciousness, nearly fully-taken by the euphoric effects of the jazz. This is the brain of a rat. As you can see, despite its pleasant and therapeutic trance, its brain is very much alive with activity. You know, on top of its common effects, one can only imagine the possibilities such a thing might present for, let's assume, musicians." His eyes sparkle when he says this, but there's minimal response from the room. I am not a musician by any stretch, so I can't say I share his excitement. I just want this to be over with.

On cue, the projector goes off.

The lights turn back on.

I glance sidewards, back to the blackboard, and notice that the fat man in the suit who had slipped the piece of paper into my hand has vanished from the room.

"What we have today," Doctor Lippmann says, "is the product of nearly seven months of development and testing—but decades of *dreaming*. Tomorrow, I'm excited to begin the first round of human trials." He averts his eyes from the group, and says, "My colleague will take it from here."

Lippmann recedes into the shadows.

Doctor Von Brandt steps forward once more with a clipboard in the nook of his arm and his eyes find me amidst the group. "You will all leave here with a new appointment time. Each session will last approximately an hour, during which you will be offered precisely one pill of the jazz. The controlled environment will ensure your safety, in the unlikely scenario that you have an adverse reaction. You will then return throughout the following weeks for additional sessions." He pauses, throwing his glance across the group. "I'm here to answer any questions you might have."

The questions come slowly and with great distance between them, and Von Brandt, along with infrequent input from Doctor Lippmann, answer them with no degree of difficulty.

It's three hundred francs for every day you're in.

Pills will not be administered outside of the labs.

No, Moscati Research is not a government operation.

Yes, they have developed drugs before.

Each answer is rehearsed and proper, and I'm looking around the room at the other researchers, all of them trying not to acknowledge us, yet every now and then stealing a glance.

No, Von Brandt says, they are not legally obligated to give any more information regarding anything.

Yes, jazz is intended for the market.

No, they are not going to discuss the legality of it.

I can see the fat man in my peripheral vision, but when I look there he's gone. I see those things in the test tubes again, the things that are of no possible description, their nebulous forms immemorable and defiant of all known illustrative rules.

Yes, Von Brandt says, the trial is perfectly legal.

I leave the research laboratories with my appointment for eight thirty a.m. the next morning folded away inside my coat pocket. The sun is still rising and a heavy mist enshrouds much of the city. I stop on Raspail Boulevard, gazing ahead at a black car that's parked suspiciously off the road.

I walk over to it slowly.

Suddenly, the lights flash on and the car drives off, leaving tire wheels in the snow behind it, as well as a plume of black smoke. I watch it until it's out of sight. It's the same type of car that the fat man had driven. Why was he here. Sensing something, I turn the other way and glance up to the heights of the Moscati Research Laboratories.

There is a face peering out one of the third floor windows.

Somehow, I know that this is Doctor Moscati. The man, who appears to be in his early fifties, a gross figure of a man, stands there for only the briefest moment, before disappearing from sight. I shiver as the city lets out a breath, snow rising from the ground, then settling again. And with this breath, I take one too, only mine is sharper and less relaxed.

I do not look up again until I'm home.

Monday, February 16. 7:06 p.m.
Property of D. Francis.
Subject: Louise Duchamp.

We found the Duchamp girl yesterday morning, earlier than the melting of dew from the grass. Though it's always dark in Paris nowadays, it was as dark as it gets out, with light bulbs insufficient. Claude and I took the *Peugeot* up to the sixteenth arrondissement. The girl had been spotted around one of the parks there.

We made first contact with the Duchamp girl at approximately 5:14 a.m. on Sunday, in the most unsettling of circumstances. The girl was stark naked, her skin bluish, and clearly visible beneath her skin were enlarged veins and frost burns, both severe. Her skin also appeared bruised in places, but her injuries contained, all things considered. Aside from her bruises, there was no distinct sign of trauma, just hypothermia.

When I approached her for the first time, she did not appear frightened, nor particularly bothered by the cold. Judging by her apathy, the girl was most certainly suffering from shock. I offered her my jacket and she wore it, though begrudgingly, for even though she showed no signs of discomfort, her body was riddled with shivers.

Louise Duchamp is approximately five feet, one inch. Petite, probably on the flatter side of forty kilograms. Her hair is roasted coffee brown. Her eyes are small and blue. She has no distinguishing features that I could make out. By all accounts, and notwithstanding her current circumstances, she is a healthy fourteen-year-old girl.

It was Claude's opinion that the girl had been kidnapped, and had later escaped, perhaps as recently as twelve hours ago. It's difficult to survive a night in the snow without shelter or clothes, and I happened to agree mostly with his analysis. The Duchamp girl was not carrying any possessions and did not appear fully-conscious; more like in a daze, incoherent. It's likely she wouldn't have survived another four hours. However, her bruises did not match up with those of a victim under any sort of bindings. Her wrists were clean, the bruises rather covering other parts of her body, including her arms, stomach, and shoulders. Her fingernails displayed signs of trauma, but could have simply been eaten away at over a period of years.

We debated the facts of our investigation while we waited for the Duchamp girl to recover at *Chardon Lagache* hospital. Once during this time, I looked in on her as she slept, the curtains in the room pulled shut and tied, the room a stark grey colour.

Certainly, the likeliest outcomes are that she either ran

away from home, or escaped a potential kidnapping; missing persons cases are our specialty and I've dealt with them before. But I couldn't help but wonder if there was something else, as I watched her sleep there. She didn't stir, in fact you could hardly see the rise of the bedsheets as she breathed.

It was only when a nurse came by and suggested I go home that I left the scene, but even as I returned to the *Peugeot* and drove back to the offices with Claude, I couldn't shake the sight of her from my head. The drive back was quiet and neither of us offered much in the way of conversation, just the low music from the radio. Claude dropped into the office to work on the court letters for the Gilles case, and I drove back home.

We got the call again this morning that Duchamp was awake, so Claude and I returned to the hospital without so much as having more than a bun and some coffee for breakfast on the drive. As I peered in through the door shutters, ducking my head to do so, I saw that her mother and father were in the room with her. Beside me, Claude gave the scent of coffee and cigarettes. He said, "She seems to have recovered well."

I chewed on this for some time. The Duchamp girl's recovery was certainly of note. Through the window, her skin appeared warmer and a rosy tinge had returned to her cheeks. Colour touched her small lips, though her expression hadn't changed; her eyes remained wide and unblinking. I made all these notes in my book while standing there, as Claude peered over at me doing it. Eventually, when Mr. and Mrs. Duchamp made eye contact with us, and stood, I opened the door and we walked inside her room.

The first thing that struck me was the distinct way in which she moved, as if animated in fourteen frames per second. Every movement was clipped and jagged, particularly unnatural, and I wondered if anybody else could see the same thing. The next thing that struck me was how her knuckle was white from gripping the bedsheets. I looked from this, back to her face— she averted her eyes—and I wondered what compelled her to grip there so hard.

Mrs. Duchamp said that Louise had not spoken a single word since she had woken up. I asked them to leave for a moment so we could question the girl, and they obliged, though not without a period of hesitation. Claude and I were in there for approximately thirty minutes, which was enough to confirm their statement. Duchamp was certainly aware of us being there, and occasionally she made eye contact, shifted about, scratched an itch, gave off a quiet (yet audible) yawn. But she wouldn't speak.

Every so often, she looked to the corner of the room where the window met the wall, sometimes for a few or more seconds, to the point Claude became paranoid that something must have been there. Though, having checked the corner where she kept looking, it was clear that the only thing there was plasterboard faintly discoloured from the sunlight.

We took Mr. and Mrs. Duchamp down to the agency to interview them independently. With coffee and biscuits, they seemed open enough to talking. Mr. Duchamp is a healthy-looking man who runs every morning, and works at a small accounting firm. He is soft-spoken and fidgety, and his nerves during our interview were apparent. He appeared more reluctant to divulge information, and more anxious, in the absence of Mrs. Duchamp.

What we learn about Louise through the course of our

initial sessions is that she was an ordinary girl who studied at *Saint Jean Gabriel* and played the bass in a student jazz band. She was organised with her studies and social life and showed no indication of wanting to run off. In fact, by all accounts, the family relationship was a good one. Her grandparents lived with them, but this was only a temporary arrangement. She has no siblings.

During my time with Mr. Duchamp, I asked about Louise's movements in the days before her disappearance. She had attended school the week prior and had jazz band on the night before she disappeared. Arriving home late, she ate dinner alone and they listened to the radio together. Louise often reads before going to bed, or catches up on study.

A perfect-enough girl, was the impression I got, but perfection is often constructed out of something far less so, and even though I gave Mr. Duchamp no indication that I suspected him of anything (and really, I kept any suspicions as nothing more than protocol), I made a note of his anxiety and his stumbled words, and the way he kept shifting in his seat.

We let them return to the hospital after our interviews, and Claude and I conferred over our notes. He shared many of the same sentiments as myself, but we weren't going to be quick to pin anything on the parents. Though, we could agree they were withholding *something* from us.

We currently suspect that Louise did not run away from home. Perhaps it had been a kidnapping, but with no evidence of a break-in, this is also unlikely. I believe the Duchamp girl may have gone out for a late-night stroll and the incident had occurred then; or, she had left for someplace early the next morning, before notifying anybody, but had never made it there. Could she have lived a secret life?

Now of course, this is all based on the assumption that Mr. and Mrs. Duchamp are giving us all the information—an outcome I doubt. If there's more to this story, facts they're covering up, then it really might be a possibility that the Duchamp girl ran away. The question is why?

Deciding we were both tired, Claude and I grabbed dinner together and discussed the football, and then we both went home for the night.

SEVEN
Daydreams in Jazz

Light hits the back of my eyelids and I'm awake. I clamber up in bed until I'm in a sitting position, and check my bedroom for the source of the disturbance. I spot a parting in the blinds, through which, every now and then, headlights flash past. It must be early morning, then, but well before sunrise.

I fight my way through the tangle of sheets to my bedside table, where I yank a tissue from its box and blow as hard as I can. Then, certain no amount of sleep's on the agenda going forward, I steady myself by sliding onto the very edge of my bed with feet flat on the carpet.

I focus on the patter of snow against my window to distract from the dull throbbing in my head. I must have slept six hours by now, and yet I feel as if I hadn't slept at all. Faint bursts of colour continually light up my curtains, occasional white light spreading across the room like a shopping scanner. After stepping out of bed and into my slippers, I cross the room and pull aside the curtain fully, peering out at empty Lepic Street.

I walk into the kitchen and take my antibiotics in the darkness. Squeezing my eyes shut, I swallow the two pills with cold water and then put the box back on the bench. I draw a cross on Monday 16, yesterday's date. This means that rent is due by the end of the day, and I'm going to have to dig into either Collette's gifts or Moscati's first payment to make it.

Looking around, I realise Colette has gone.

I check to see if she's asleep on the couch, and then the bathroom, but there's nobody else home. From the kitchen table I find a letter and switch on the lamp there to read it.

She's been called to work. Smiley-face.

Sighing, I walk over to the couch and sit down. On the coffee table is a small brochure from the *Gaumont-Palace* and I look at it, open to a double spread featuring the actress Julie Adams. I can still taste the antibiotics in my mouth, plastic and bitter, and wish I had something else to wash it down.

I give a small cough and then reach into my pants.

I grab my cock in the darkness of my apartment and, while looking at the monochrome still of Julie Adams in *Creature from the Black Lagoon*, I slowly begin to stroke it. It doesn't grow much, but it's enough to get the job done. I eventually relax against the couch backrest and close my eyes, my hand gripped firmly around my phallus—which, on most days, hardly feels like it's a part of me.

As outside, snow falls over Paris and the clocks strike somewhere around seven. You can hear the wind as whispering breaths, strangely erotic. For a second, as I bend my knee and yank on my cock harder, I feel something exhale into my ear.

A piano sounds, there are violinists playing pizzicato.

It's breathing in my ear, against my neck. My hand goes mechanically, my knuckles occasionally rapping against my balls, and there's something else here with me.

My cock stiffens and swells and my wrist starts to ache. The piano music quickens, as does my pace. I open my eyes and see Julie Adams in that brochure from the cinemas, her breasts and her white bathing suit, and then I imagine her small hands grasping my cock and going to work.

The strings crescendo and a breeze comes through the room.

It's just past eight thirty a.m., Moscati Research Laboratories off Raspail Boulevard. I'm let into a small room by a short man with a softly-freckled face and an appearance otherwise not worth much description. There is a single window spanning the wall, shuttered with vertical cream-coloured blinds, and a large brown leather chair to sit on. A single video camera, like from the movies, watches keenly atop a tripod.

There is the sound of a door creaking shut and then a clap as it slams against the latch. I look back at the freckle-faced man as he settles inside the room.

His name is Doctor Fred Bobin, far younger than the kinds I've seen around here—it's quite possible he's only been here for a modest time. He tugs on his white lab coat as he makes himself comfortable, puts on a gentle smile and, thus far, he has always looked at me when he speaks.

"This session will be recorded," Fred Bobin says in a kind voice, directly to my face, before switching on the camera. "I hope that's okay. Please, take a seat."

I sit in the brown couch, immediately becoming engulfed in its leathery abyss. I grab the armrests and feel the room rapidly enlarge around me. A wash of heat flies through it with the sound of a machine roaring to life, and the faint smell of smoke. Fred Bobin offers me a pill.

I accept this pill and, thus, am introduced to jazz.

Jazz has no distinctive features, but an unremarkable purple strip following the circumference. It smells vaguely metallic, weighs very little, and feels as though you ought to be able to crush it quite easily between thumb and forefinger. The pill slips into the palm of my hand and I stare at it.

Fred Bobin sits in the couch by the camera and I'm looking at him. A clipboard leans against his forearms and a black pen clicks. "I will ask you a series of questions so we can use them to compare any changes in your body, before and after the ingestion of the jazz. I should also let you know that anything that happens in this room, and the recording currently taking place, will remain strict property of Moscati Research. You are not to discuss this outside. We will do likewise, in keeping your details confidential."

He gives a friendly smile. "Any questions?"

I shake my head.

"Excellent," Fred Bobin chirps. "Let me reconfirm your name and date of birth for the record."

"Nicolas Fontaine," I respond. "February 12, 1934."

He nods and occasionally writes something down.

"Any medical history?" he asks.

I shake my head. "No."

"Past reactions to drugs?"

I'm popping a codeine pill and swallowing it down dry. The feel of it in my throat is sore. The image is gone just as quick as it came, and I'm still shaking my head. "No."

His pen scratches the page.

"Are you currently on any medication?"

I pause for a second. There has been no suggestion thus far that being on any medication such as antibiotics would cause any problems. But then, I can't know for sure.

He's still staring at me in that way he does, cocks the head. "It's no problem, really," he tells me.

"No," I respond, one-wordedly.

"No there *is* a problem or . . ."

"I'm not on anything."

"Okay." Fred Bobin's pen scribbles across the page like a stick over rough stones. My eye twitches. I squeeze it shut and then reopen it. The room blurs, then comes back into alignment, and Fred Bobin is staring at me.

Why are you staring at me.

"Upon taking the jazz, you may feel displaced, like a leaf in the winter. I will be closely monitoring you, should anything go wrong. Once the effects wear off and you have returned to a normal state of consciousness, I will ask you further questions and you should be clear to go home."

I nod and unclench my hand.

The jazz is staring back at me as if it has eyes.

"When you're ready," Fred Bobin says.

I take it.

A cabaret bar, almost anywhere in Paris. The walls

are red velvet. Lamps throw warm light across round tables. There's a woman on the stage and her voice is sultry. Her red dress sparkles in time with the mellow piano chords.

This is what it sounds like.

You're lying in bed next to ██████████—her name is censored in your brain, why is it censored. Her blonde hair flares out across the white pillows like a nuclear explosion frozen in motion. And she's looking at you with the bedsheets pulled to her unpainted lips. Her hazel eyes glimmer in the pale morning light. The bedroom smells like perfume washed with sex. Her breast pokes through the parting in the sheets like a child peering out of a closet. You want to cry, and you don't realise it but you're holding your breath.

Let go, or you'll suffocate.

There is a hotel room with a bed, a writing table, a clock ticking and the sound of jazz music. Floral green wallpaper stretches everywhere you look. The floorboards are wooden and chipped in places. There's a window, and on the other side, the white that people must see when they're about to die.

And this is where I am, the transition silent. It's almost like waking up from anaesthetic.

I orient myself in the middle of the room. Look from the bed, to the writing table. Window. Clock. Jazz. *Door.* I move towards it and grasp the bronze handle. I turn it to the left—nothing. Turn it to the right—the door snaps open.

I step out into a hotel corridor with green wallpaper and wooden floorboards, lacquered with an inky coating.

There's the smell of dust and mildew, which makes me want to sneeze. I lift my arm to my face, hold it. It passes.

Where am I.

What I do know is this is out of the ordinary, but it's hard to tell whether or not it's real. I have certainly not been here before, nothing sparks any sort of memory, so then I must be someplace tangible and outside of myself. I'm aware that I took the white pill, the jazz, from Fred Bobin.

I can hear a television movie behind one of the doors down the corridor. From the score and the dialogue, it's no film that I've ever heard of, but definitely American.

My hand finds the handle to this apartment door, but I do not take it. Instead, I stand there and slowly press my ear to the wood, hearing a woman softly moan on the other side.

"Is someone watching us?"

I continue listening, hoping to hear something that might explain where I am and who these people are. Can they be trusted. Are they even real, or no different to the movie.

But nothing else comes, and I have no choice but to continue further down the corridor. The lift at the end is in disuse due to maintenance so I take the stairs.

Snow falls over Paris.

I shiver, my arms instinctively reaching for my coat—but there's nothing there. Rather, I'm stuck wearing the clothes I had brought into Moscati Research Labs, plain chino pants and a white long-shirt, a scarf around my neck. I do my best with what I have, starting by fixing the scarf so it's secured around my neck. Then I put my hands in my pockets and walk to the edge of the street. Yellow light washes the road as automobiles rush by, unaware of me standing there, or of anything really. The first thing I do is look up at the street sign, which, though obscured in frost, says Biot Street, and it's where I thought I might be.

The street is packed, stores and restaurants on both sides. It's at least eight o'clock but it can't be any later than nine, judging by the stores that are still open.

Why have I awoken here of all places. It's on the other side of the Seine, close to where I live, yet so far from Moscati Research that the idea that somehow I walked here is out of the question. So I continue down, towards Clichy Place.

Eventually I'm out of the narrow street and staring up and around the frozen city. Somebody on a bicycle uses the pedestrian crossing, and the street lamp over me keeps flickering on and off. Buildings are stark black against the ever-darkening sky, haze of snow surrounding all. I walk to a nearby bus stop where a businessman reads the paper.

"What year is it," I ask him.

He looks up with some degree of uncertainty, pauses. "What are you, some kind of time traveller?"

"Just tell me, man."

He stands up. "It's 1959."

I watch him walk away. Same year, then, at least. I continue walking up the plaza in the direction opposite from the man, my shoes occasionally slipping in the mounds of snow. It's harder to walk than usual, almost like there's something about this place which is lined up differently.

Eventually I enter a street corner café. The glass doors fall shut with a clap of snow.

It's warmer inside. The red radio on the countertop plays jazz music. Disinterested eyes glance up over the folded edge of a newspaper and watch me. The woman behind the counter looks at me like somebody looks at a fly that has landed on their food. A middle-aged man in a blue sweater and matching beanie walks out of the bathroom and does not look at anybody, including me, until he's out of the restaurant. I move away from the door and find a booth with a view of the street.

I took the drug and now I'm here.

This is my first realisation, but it doesn't make sense.

I took the drug and now I'm here.

I repeat this to myself, but figure something's missing. Something must have happened in the space between swallowing the pill and then coming to stand in the middle of that odd hotel room on the other side of the Seine, a room I've never seen before, with that green wallpaper. And I know it must not belong to me, because I would never live in a place with green wallpaper, and I would certainly remember it if I had.

You took the drug and now you're here.

Something is wrong with the window.

I'm on my feet and staring at the place where my reflection should be. Only, it isn't me, though he wears my clothes and my face. The man is not me. I grab my own face and the man in the glass does the same. I turn around and the woman behind the counter fleetingly looks at me again. I imagine her snickering at me, a stranger from another dimension, a man who should not be. Why are they all leering at me.

I run from the restaurant.

Something must have happened in the space between the jazz and here. How am I so far from Moscati Research. Is it possible that I'm just dreaming about this. But it doesn't feel like a dream. I think back to my first meeting with the fat man. It seems like years ago. What did ya think of the show, Nicolas Fontaine, the show you've forgotten.

I run until I hit the intersection, and then the bright and looming *Gaumont-Palace* engulfs my view. I soon enough reach its lit-up façade, and this is where I stop, bending over to catch my breath. I stare up at the showtimes. *House on Haunted Hill* at eight twenty-five. *Room at the Top* at nine thirty on screen two. *No Name on the Bullet* at nine thirty-five, screen five.

Shivering, I purchase a ticket from the box office and stroll through the glass doors into the foyer.

A breath like hair from an old man's head leaves my mouth and rolls in the air like tumbleweed, suspended under the yellow lights. The double doors close with a squeal. There is music playing on a radio, a song that I don't know the name of, something slow and distinctly jazz.

Always jazz.

It reminds me I've taken the drug. I wonder, are the effects of the pill that everything you see turns into jazz music. Is it that you forget where you are, reconstruct a city of your imagination. I touch my cheek beneath two fingers.

And then I see her.

What's she doing here.

She's a blur, standing in the lobby with a black coat buttoned up to the chin, a bucket of popcorn cradled like a child in the nook of her arm. Her skin, despite the distortions, is unusually pale, her cheeks reddened, lips tight. Her blonde hair has been flung out as if by the wind, but it looks more like intent than any sort of disruption from nature.

She's an A-lister from Hollywood, torn from the pages of a Hitchcockian screenplay, and the world is frozen around her. She stands there, the heroine on the centre of a poster framed by the warmly-lit theatre lobby. For a split second, her face becomes bitingly clear.

██████████.

What was her name.

██████████'s hazel eyes meet my own and I feel a spike of something old and forgotten rush through me.

She looks at me.

Does she see anything.

The corner of her mouth twitches. And it seems as if we're standing within whispering distance of each other. I can smell the butter on her popcorn, warm and familiar. She's looking at me but I can't read her face anymore. She's just looking.

Just a look from a stranger.

But we're not strangers.

I hear a ringing phone.

Riiiiiiiiing—

I turn to my right and see a person with a gigantic rotary phone for a head in front of me, the telephone ringing.

"What the . . ."

My muscles begin to clench, pins and needles in my hand. Like I'm holding onto something really sharp.

Riiiiiiiing! Riiiiiiiiiiiiiiing!

And I'm back in that room.

"Fuck!" I gasp as finally I come to.

Light pours through the frosted windows. Heat fills the room from the vibrating heater ducts, and Fred Bobin is staring at me from the other seat, clipboard in hand, and his thumb on the top of his black pen going *click, click, click.*

"You were really out for some time."

The only thing I can comprehend is my heart racing. He's looking at my eyes as though there's something wrong with them, and then he's writing words down on the sheet.

"How do you feel, Nicolas?" Fred Bobin says.

I think about this for a moment. My first question is how am I back here, and where did I go. I can still feel the sensation of my feet on the snow, and the wind surging at me from all angles. I had to have been physically there, *had to.* I'm not looking at Fred Bobin when I say, "Same as before."

His pen makes a brief movement.

"Are you experiencing any pain or discomfort?"

There's nothing that immediately comes to mind, nothing I hadn't felt before taking the pill.

I shake my head. "No."

I answer each of his questions truthfully. Do you have any notion of the time that has passed. If you had to guess, then. Did taking the jazz evoke any overwhelming feelings, such as fear or anxiety. My answers are short and each response is followed by a nod from Fred Bobin and his black pen scratching the page. I have no reason to lie. He asks me, can you tell me what day it is, how about the time, and I answer with confidence, though I'm thinking about the green hotel room, the man at the bus stop who told me it's 1959, which means I haven't travelled through time or anything crazy like that. As I formulate my responses, every now and then I glance into the camera lens, the little red light telling me it's recording.

And something is not right. I feel chewed up and spat back out. I can still hear jazz music in my ears. I can smell the perfume that ███████ had worn, the same she'd always worn.

She's in Paris.

No. **That wasn't Paris.**

"There's one more question," says Fred Bobin.

He does not look me in the eye when he asks this.

"Was there . . . anything else in there with you?"

In there. In the drug, is that what he means by that. He's got his black pen over the page and it's not moving. My first thought is of ██████, but Fred Bobin's not talking about her. He couldn't possibly know her. I think about the strange person with the telephone for a head, the piercing ring that eventually awoke me. Yet, I'm inclined to think that even this is not the "anything else" which Fred Bobin is referring to.

"Like another participant," I ask, to clarify.

"Not another participant," says Fred Bobin.

And so I respond with a shake of the head. "No."

And Fred Bobin's pen moves across the page.

I close the bathroom door and toss my white towel onto the

rack by the wall. There is a crack there, right through the tiles, one that seems to be getting worse every time I look at it. We used to look through it, see if we ever saw anything on the other side—we never did.

It's a reminder. Everything is a reminder. The apartment. The music. The films. *Get out of my head.*

White and black chequered tiles cover every inch of this bathroom, except for the mirror. I toss my clothes onto the sink and look at myself. The person staring back is wearing a week's old stubble and his eyes are sunken and dull.

I shave my face, all the while thinking about what happened in Fred Bobin's office, about what I'd seen. Or experienced. I still don't quite know what really happened, only that this little drug was unlike anything I've ever done before. It was first thing in the morning I visited Fred Bobin, and yet the moment I took the drug, I remember stepping out onto those icy Parisian streets, and it being the middle of the night. As it cannot be both night and day at the same time, how . . .

I splash my face with warm water and then run the shower. The handles squeal when I turn them. Hot water hisses from the faucet, always too hot or too cold. My finger flicks against the fan switch and it rumbles to life, much like those heaters in Fred Bobin's office. Steam from the burning shower water withdraws into the fan, the remainder of it bubbling against the shower window. The mirror bubbles too.

I unbutton my shirt and toss it into the clothes basket by the door. I finally turn on the light, and my shadow spits out across the floor tiles. The shape of a flaccid cock emerges on the wall as I remove my pants, tossing them on top of the rest of my clothes against the basket.

I step into the shower and immerge myself under the hot stream. Each droplet of water smashes into my face and skin like tiny bullets. My dark hair, past due for a cut, flattens and streaks down the back of my neck.

I close my eyes and stand still. You can faintly hear the television from the living room. I imagine the scene, that monochrome room, a 1930s horror film, probably directed by James Whale, apartment lights shining against the curtains.

I received a telegram from Colette when I returned home.

Six months sober. Proud of you.
Let's find a time to do something special.
I've deposited some money into your account.
Love you lots. Colette.

I grab the cold water handle and turn it. I'm standing under the downpour, imagining being in the middle of the street. Car tires chew up snow on the side of the road. A dog is barking. The ceiling creaks with pacing footsteps.

Was there . . . anything else in there with you?

Somewhere in Paris 1959, in the middle of winter, a black car is parked. This car belongs to a fat man who wears fancy top hats and knows something he isn't telling someone.

You tell me, Fred Bobin.

You made me take it. You should know what's there.

Nobody responds, except the faucet starts spitting out

cold water. I immediately let out a gasp and sidestep out of it, reaching round the stream to turn back the handles. They screech horrifically, like pigs being slaughtered, and the water stops. As it's sucked down the drain, the ground beneath me gurgles, the sound somebody makes when they're vomiting.

I walk into the living room to find *The Invisible Man* on. I grab the remote and switch it off. Then, I cross the room to the curtain and draw this fully-closed. I button up my black coat and tuck my scarf into it.

I walk to the kitchen and fill a mug with hot tea and take it with me. The apartment does not make a sound as it watches me open the door and walk out.

I'm standing outside the *Gaumont-Palace* again with my tea in hand, its tendrils of steam wafting up against the gentle downpour of snow and rain.

It's just past seven thirty now and the streets are quiet. Cars roll past, spraying me with ice and yellow light.

Across the road, a streetlamp goes out.

The air becomes stale. I saw her there, *her*, when I took the jazz, and I feel my heart racing, as though at any moment she'll be back, smelling of perfume, clutching the bucket of popcorn. I'm a ghost on an amusement park ride and I can't get off, can't think, I'm just here and I don't know what I'm doing.

You don't belong here.

She doesn't belong here.

A man lights a cigarette and I watch him. He does not notice me, blowing the smoke and staring towards the heights of the buildings across the road. His blue cotton beret is on the wrong way, but he doesn't seem to mind.

I circle to the front of the theatre and peer through the glass doors. Very few people are inside. Nothing is out of place from the way it was when I went there before—if I did; or was it just a product of the jazz, like a daydream.

I raise the mug to my lips and take a sip. Hot tea runs through my body as I swallow, it burns the roof of my mouth.

You're standing in the snow and it's seven thirty-seven p.m. and a man is smoking a cigarette next to you. You can smell the smoke, and you wish you had some tobacco. It's the *Gaumont-Palace*, always the *Gaumont-Palace*, and it's on Caulaincourt, number one, and some nights it's the brightest thing in the city. The *Gaumont-Palace* never changes. Only the posters and the prices and the names that shine in bright letters over the box office. These are the only three things that change about that movie theatre on the corner. It's just the same machine all the time, rented out by different faces each and every night.

You know what I do to make myself feel less sad?

I don't care.

I step away from the theatre into the cold Parisian streets.

A shiver slams through my body so hard I gasp and turn around. I'm standing on the edge of the sidewalk. A streetlamp flickers, teasing light. "Get out," I speak into the wind.

The man in the backwards beret looks at me.

"Go!" I scream.

It wasn't real. None of it was real.

My hand touches my face.

I'm still here. She never was.

Just a dream, or something of the sort.

Letting out a deep sigh, I walk away from the theatre with my head down and I don't look back up. Somewhere in Paris 1959, in the carpark behind a grocery store, there is a black vehicle. A man is sitting in the front seat eating Chinese food with the window open. A dog barks in the distance.

There is a gun on the seat beside him.

This is not a dream.

EIGHT
Fred Bobin Again

Fred Bobin is smiling as I walk back into his office. It isn't snowing at this time but the room remains chilly. Without the whir of the heater, it is near-silent.

"They haven't been working all morning," Fred Bobin says regarding this, with quiet despair in his tone. He closes the door and walks to the camera. He begins filming the session before I've even sat down, that little red light blinking on. I look into the lens, seeing myself distorted in it.

Quiet on set. Rolling.

"It's Friday, February 20," says Fred Bobin into a tape recorder as I sit down in the large couch. I look at the wall clock at the same time he says, "It's ten forty-five a.m. Participant is Nicolas Fontaine, session two."

Keeping the tape recorder going, Fred Bobin sits in the seat opposite mine, and asks, "Have you been well?"

I nod without much thought.

"Enjoying the snow," he suggests.

"Yeah." I rub my nose with the back of my hand. It's sore, but I'm weening off the antibiotics and I'm the best I've felt all week. "I'm not sick, by the way," I assure him, running my hand through my greasy hair. "Just coming off it."

"Excellent." Fred Bobin smiles softly, shy creases appearing in his otherwise youthful face. "Let me open the session by asking, have you experienced any of the following symptoms over the past few days? Reduced hearing in either ear, or both? Continued, daytime hallucinations? Sudden increase in sex drive or unusual feelings of arousal. At any time since our last session, have you felt as though you were not yourself? Have you experienced a loss of interest in activities that you once found enjoyable? Has the passage of time felt different than normal? For example, if once you were frequently on time, have you found that you've been running late to appointments, or forgotten to eat a meal when the time came round?"

To all of these, I offer a simple shake of the head or a muttered no. Nothing out of the ordinary. Nothing that I can think of. And so, Fred Bobin gives a smile.

"Are you currently on any medication?"

"No," I respond, one-wordedly again.

"Lovely." Fred Bobin holds out his hand, palm facing towards the ceiling. Cradled within his palm is a single white pill. The couch quivers as I pull myself up out of it, taking the pill from Fred Bobin. It stares at me, trembling in my hand the way pills tend to tremble in anticipation. I knock it back, swallowing the jazz without thinking.

And it's four-thirty a.m. on an empty street. You're sitting passenger side in a car with the engine running, and beside you sits ███████████. Rows of houses stretch to your left, more to the right. It's the middle of summer but the night is cool, stars and moon above. "It's all felt so surreal, hasn't it," says ███████████, leaning forward over the steering wheel in such a way a dagger of light from a streetlamp hits her face.

"I keep wondering if we're not in some movie," you say. She turns to you with a wry smile.

"Would be something, trapped in a movie without even knowing it," she says. "Imagine, invisible writers pulling strings, and all this is just some backlot across the sea in Hollywood."

You've never been happier.

This is what it **feels like.**

I feel my body shudder and I stand up from the couch in the office of Fred Bobin. There's a pain in my chest that feels like suffocating but this didn't happen last time. A ghost of my other self is still sitting down on the couch and Fred Bobin is watching it, but he's moving slowly, evident when he turns his head and the space around him blurs. Everything feels large and voluminous. I get the sense that I'm floating, although this is not true at all, my boots firmly on the floor.

"Participant is stable," into his tape recorder.

I open my mouth but find that I cannot speak. Yet, in the moment, I think nothing of this, simply accept it as the fact. There is the distant sound of jazz music, the sort that gives off hot pink wallpaper and black lights and women in scanty clothing. I look to the window and notice snow has paused mid-drift, little bits of ice suspended in animation. I see my distant, pinprick reflection in the glass.

Is that really me.

Fred Bobin walks until he's standing over my apparition-like, semi-conscious state. I side-step so that he doesn't go straight into me, not that I know if he can, or if I'm even really here. Once standing over my . . . *Other*, Fred Bobin kneels so that he's eye level with it, and he simply studies it, like it's a scientific subject. Which I suppose, it is.

He raises his tape recorder. "He's out."

This isn't normal.

And then I'm—

It's Vendôme Place, a wide expanse of open nothing. The bricks underneath me are jagged and mismatching. My elbows, the skin there is grazed right through. I look up and see black sky and dotted yellow lights, and the falling of snow. The Vendôme column's there, so tall it sooner disappears in the icy haze than my eyes can make any sense of wherever it ends.

I climb off the ground and catch my breath, grasping at my chest, where that breathless feeling has begun to subside. I give off a shiver and the city does this too.

Lifting my scarf up over my mouth and nose, I survey the area, and decide that, all things considered, this does not feel like a dream-state. The snow, the chatter, the people, all of it's too real to be faked.

Would be something, trapped in a movie without even knowing it . . .

As I take off, a black car comes out of nowhere along the bouncy cobbles, sending up a tuft of papers with its back tire. I stop suddenly, stumbling out of its path. Somebody punches down on their horn and I see another car skid to a stop, its driver visibly up-in-arms over the whole ordeal. I hear a rattle, and to my right a boy unchains his bicycle from a frosted metal pole and departs.

What is this place. What use.

What use is a drug that just sends you to some place.

Why is it sending me here.

I stroll through Vendôme Place with my hands in the pockets of my woollen grey coat, and my scarf against my mouth and nose creating a warm trap of air.

Eventually I reach the corner outside the fully-lit *Louis Vuitton* building and look in. Snow sails past in the wind. You can hear a train go by underneath the city. Somebody's running down the steps into the metro.

I pull away from the building as my ears pop, letting in a high-pitched ring that's almost shellshock.

Was there . . . anything else in there with you?

What are they looking for.

I peer in closer through the windows of *Louis Vuitton* and see multiple faces reflected back at me, each one slightly different. I cannot recognise them. The tousled hair both frayed and unwashed, hasn't been cut for some time. Oiled skin, creases between the brows, chapped lips, all of it dreadful.

People pass and avoid my eyes.

I look to the side and see a man in a black coat further down the street. I glide onto the crosswalk and try to catch his eye. The man wears black shades so that his eyes cannot be seen, though his austere black clothing makes it difficult for him to blend in. Like agents in a Hitchcockian thriller, is what I think of it. The man turns and walks off.

I follow him through the yellow glow of this wide street down from Vendôme Place. Snow crunches beneath my feet. There are nights—even here inside the jazz—nights where you can hear the city breathe. It purrs, like a cat asleep on a quilt in a cold apartment. In fact, it only seems more intense here, like the jazz has of a mind awakened it. With each breath the city takes, ice tears from overhanging eaves and traffic lights, and drizzles to the people on the sidewalks. They don't lift their eyes for anyone, moving like spectres.

I follow the agent onto Saint-Honoré, where everywhere you look is another clothing store. Colette lives somewhere along here, all glittery clothes and jewels. I look at the shuttered windows and newspapers, soaked through from the melting ice. The footprints of the black-clad agent draw a path forward, which I decide to follow. The gap between us remains considerable, but I'm not exactly ready to confront him.

On nights like this, in whichever upside-down world I've ended up in, the city runs like a great industrial machine, the road like a carapace over gears.

Nicolas Fontaine . . .

The hairs on the back of my neck twitch and I stop in the middle of the open road, where a car is parked by a payphone.

There.

No, it's gone.

My breaths reverberate with low frequencies in my ears

and there's ice burning my cheeks. I face forward again and see the agent disappear inside one of the shops to the left.

I hurry my steps and reach the store. A single mannequin poses out the front, its face expressionless, naked. A plastic head rolls through the snow, leaving a trail behind it. Purple curtains cover the windows but with my nose against the frosted glass, I can peer through them and make out a light on the other side, which illuminates clothes, scarves and other fashion accessories. I grab the handle of the door—it's still warm from the other man's grip—and creak it open.

Inside the shop it's no warmer than on the street. Minimal light finds its way into the lobby, cast out from a room down the back, and the voices of two males, low rumbles.

I hold my breath and try to listen.

"What did you see, Moret?" one of them says.

The floorboards groan and I retreat slightly, closing the door a fraction. I peek through it with just one eyeball and all I can see is the glow of light emanating from that back room.

There are at least two men, and Moret.

"I don't know . . . it was all very quick." This is a woman's voice, it must be Moret. "I'm not lying, I just—"

"Where'd you get this then, eh?"

The city shows me what he's talking about: a small tear of paper with the appearance of a ticket, flapping in the hand of the second man. A ticket, sure enough, but the writing on it is blurred and I can't make it out. I hold a breath, once again trying to press myself as close to the door as I can to hear.

I miss something, the voice is mumbled. Shit.

Then, Moret: "There's something called the jazz town, isn't there. The jazz town, is that what this is about?"

One of them groans. "Do you hear what she's saying?"

The other one: "Yeah, I heard it dammit. I heard it. Well tell me, Moret, where did you hear of that?"

Meanwhile, Moret is still talking but her voice becomes background noise as I close my eyes and try to hone in on what exactly the two men are speaking about.

"Goddammit, Moret, start making sense!"

"I told you, I don't know what I saw," she says in a hurried, ever-more-agitated voice, "but I don't want to do it anymore, I just don't, okay, I've had enough of all of it."

"Now come on, Moret, you need to cooperate."

"Cooperate? Cooperate! I don't have a clue what's going on!"

"Moret, did you go there? To the jazz town? Moret!"

She lets out a full-throated scream and one of the men swears. Moret cuts off with a gasp and a body slumps to the floorboards like a muted sack of potatoes.

I jump, reeling back.

The hell was that, I wonder.

"You've broken her fucking cheek," one of the men says in a slightly-hushed voice. "Her fucking cheek!"

"Grab her up. The boss is gonna want to hear about this and where the hell she got this . . . this . . ." He's waving the ticket, and every now and then it hits a ray of light, yet in my mind's eye the text is still too blurred to read.

"Just clean it up," says the other guy.

"What do you think she saw there?"

"I don't give a damn, it ain't our problem now."

They haul the body and I shut the door before they have a chance to find me, backtracking onto the street. Then, without a second thought, I hurry from the dress store.

Riiiiiiiing!

I stop, eyeing a homeless man on the sidewalk. He's looking at me from inside a sheathe of wet furs, his head a black telephone. *Riiing. Riiing. Riiiiiiing!* Cautiously, I begin to approach him, the sound of ringing from his face growing louder.

"What does it mean," I mutter against the homeless man.

I feel the air begin to loosen around me and I reach for something to grab onto. Nothing is there. The phone keeps ringing and my legs buckle. Snow burns my hands as they sink into it. My wrist grows numb, and then my forearm.

"What is this place!" I demand.

And then it's Fred Bobin on the other side of the room by the window. His reflection's in the glass between the parted curtains, which sway in the breeze. I'm still in the deep couch, my tongue feeling heavy and bitter. That's what the pill does to me, leaves a bitter taste on my tongue, a dry mouth, the feeling that something isn't quite right. Ringing in my ears.

Fred Bobin smiles at me. "Oh, wonderful."

Unsure of how to respond to this, I simply nod. I can hear jazz music, but it's just my imagination. The only real sound in the room is the traffic. I don't meet Fred Bobin's eyes.

He walks over to me, sitting down in his chair and retrieving that clipboard and pen.

"Are you in any pain or discomfort?" he asks.

"No," I immediately respond, not thinking about his question so much as I'm thinking about what Moret had seen, or what she'd known, or what was . . . the jazz town.

Fred Bobin studies me for a longer time than usual, as if reading my thoughts, and then begins writing things down on the back of his clipboard.

His questions I answer as truthfully as before, though I leave out the detail about the dress store. I don't mention the ticket, or about the jazz town, nor whoever they were referring to by "boss," though I suspect it's the fat man, who else. Each time I give a response, Fred Bobin follows it with the scribble of his pen against the paper, but says nothing else.

I glance at the window and watch the green curtain flapping. I look at the white teacup there, unmoving as teacups should be.

"You saw nothing out of the ordinary, then?" he says.

I feel a shiver run through my body, and I do remember hearing something call out my name in the middle of the street, and then the hairs on the back of my neck prick up again.

I shake my head.

"Not that I saw," and Fred Bobin writes it down.

I visit the dress store again while there's still daylight. That car I saw in the jazz remains parked by the payphone, except there's a man sitting in it with the window down, smoking a cigarette. There is a white dog on a leash, shackled to a metal pole, watching me as I walk past.

There is that mannequin outside the store, only it's wearing a red coat. I peer through the windows and see that it's business as usual. No Moret and no agents wearing black. I start walking back the other way as a woman leaves the store with full shopping bags, not looking at me. There is no homeless man on the side of the road with a telephone head.

Which means that, whenever Fred Bobin gives me the jazz, I'm ending up somewhere that *is* different to here. It's not Paris in 1959, at least not the Paris where I live.

"Hey, chump!"

It's the man inside the car, his cigarette trailing a thin line of smoke. The way he's looking at me suggests he's after something.

"What," I respond.

"Sorry, I didn't mean to shout." He clicks open the door and walks over to me. The man is skinny, about the same age, maybe a little older, with a lopsided jawline and acne scars on his face. For some time, it appears that he's looking at the dress store, then finally turns his attention to me.

"Pierre," he says, offering his hand.

I take it. "Nicolas."

"Nice to meet you, Nicolas."

I have some recollection of meeting this man before.

"We're both part of that trial at Moscati Research," Pierre tells me with an obvious shrug. "I saw you in there. Well I saw you first in the laboratory when we all met. Of course." He takes my shoulder lightly and turns me towards the dress store, gesticulating with his still-smoking cigarette.

"They weren't too happy," he says.

"We all go to the same place then," is what I respond with.

Pierre appears confused by my non-sequitur, but he catches on. I know this because he nods suddenly, taking a relaxed drag of his cigarette. "Lots of agents watching last time. I assume because of what happened. Her name was Annie Moret, they ended up taking her back to their boss, most likely to encourage some answers out of her. Messy business, it is."

"For a research group," I say.

"You're right about that."

"What's the jazz town."

"I dunno." He sucks again on the end of his cigarette, this time while staring at me. Then, he throws it into the snow.

"What do we do about that," I say.

He's kicking the snow over his exposed cigarette and having quite a degree of trouble with it. I wonder if I should ask him about the place we've been going to. If Fred Bobin, or whoever's been testing him, if this person keeps asking about:

Was there anything else in there with you.

"We shouldn't discuss more," Pierre says in a quiet voice, looking at the ground. "They might be listening, and we don't know what they want us to know." As he says this, I look around. The street amplifies our voices with its deep quiet. There are windows open, and it feels as though the buildings are engulfing us. "My advice, take whatever money they give you and get out. You need the money, right? I mean, why else would you put down your name for something like this, right?"

"Is that how they found you," I ask.

"I guess so. I've always responded to those listings in the paper, an odd job here and there. Figured somehow they came upon my details. Most likely, somebody out there's sold my personal information. You'd make a pretty penny out of that."

I nod, and Pierre says nothing else, just taps me on the shoulder and begins walking towards the dress store with as casual demeanour as you can have, as if to buy something.

His words ring through my head.

Take whatever money they give you and get out.

Colette and I take the metro down to Trocadéro station on Saturday, and as we come up to street level, with the red "metro" sign at our backs, I notice that the snow has stopped. All that remains is a slight pattering of rain. Colette throws open her umbrella and it unfurls above us, blocking out the meagre light from the early morning sun.

We take the short walk to Passy Cemetery without talking much, crossing Georges Mandel Avenue in a bubble of pedestrians trying to avoid the traffic. The air smells of gasoline and rain, there's children talking and rubber boots splashing through puddles. From Georges Mandel, we walk to the quiet cemetery grounds, where you can hear little but the grass against our shoes, our heels tearing shards from the dirt.

We're huddled underneath our single umbrella as the rain comes bearing down, raindrops smattering on black nylon. Flowers on graves bend over. Leaves flutter. Butterflies become tangled in the wind and flop against gravestones and plinths.

Picture frames of the dead.

I pass them without looking at much, my head inclined groundward to such an extent of ignorance that my leg brushes somebody kneeling to the side and I'm forced to mutter a quiet apology. After this brief disturbance, Colette loops her arm around mine and pulls me close, our body heat mingling.

"It's down here," Colette murmurs.

We divert from the main path to a section of graves out the back. A green fence pokes out from behind them, shrubbery growing through the metal spokes, and the hill beyond rising into the grey sky. As I glance in that direction, I'm forced to squint my eyes against the haze of water being tossed every which way by the wind, until my vision is clouded.

Eventually we come to a tomb of rough stone. In copper lettering reads the name MARCEL FONTAINE, born 1901, died 1941. I was seven, and when today I look back at all the great tragedies of this family, I wonder whether the death of our father started it, or if some sort of curse had been placed upon us long before even then. I stand back as Colette ventures out into the rain and lays a bouquet of yellow flowers by the tomb.

I join her, but I don't kneel, holding the umbrella to shield us both from the rain. A gust of wind comes through, tearing flowers from a plant to my right, and I have to tighten my grip around the umbrella end, angling it against the wind so as not to lose the whole thing entirely.

Colette stands, taking my hand.

"I'm happy that you're here," she says.

"Our father never caused us any despair," I say.

"Yeah," she responds.

She glances to the grave beside our father's, though I pointedly avoid it. I see her avert her eyes, pretending it isn't there. Neither of us acknowledge the fact that there's another Fontaine and he's buried by our father, two Fontaines in Passy, mouldering underneath the wet, worm-filled dirt.

She pulls me closer to her as wind comes through and somebody breaks into weeps at one of the graves nearby.

Colette starts to recite a poem in moderate sing-song, the same as always. Its words are meaningless to me now, but I mutter them with her, monotone and quiet. When at last it's done, she kneels again and kisses the tips of her fingers, touching them to the wet, cold stone. She stands, and I'm moving off, avoiding with my eyes the next grave over.

Except Colette isn't following me.

She's stopped beside the other grave, her hands clutched to her chest and her brown hair glistening in the sparse sunlight, which tears in strips through deep grey cloud.

"Colette," I call out to her. I offer the umbrella but she shakes her head. I walk over to her while keeping my eyes away from the grave. "Let's go now," I tell her.

Without looking at me, she says, "He was just like you. Two of you would have gotten along, I can tell you that."

"I guess I sometimes wonder about him."

I look up and see the inscriptions on his tomb. It's smaller than our father's one, the brick slightly darkened, and there's a pot of grass on the top, like someone's accidentally left it there. 1924-1933, a year before I was born. He was hit by a car and that was that. In their grief, I came along.

Colette lowers her head onto my arm and I stop looking at the two graves. "He was so funny, too . . ." she says.

"Okay, that's enough."

"Oh Nicolas."

I take the umbrella and walk away. Her footsteps in the mud come squelching after me, and she loops her arm through mine.

"Back home?" she says.

I nod, and we walk back the way we came.

Another pill and that distant sound of jazz. Fred Bobin's eyes across the room. It's a Tuesday morning with the heaters running and a light drizzle of snow outside, and I'm becoming more and more convinced that this stop-start winter will never end.

A house in the Parisian neighbourhoods with tall walls and a clothesline in the front yard, spinning in the winds. It's spring for a moment, but then there's snow.

██████████ tells you she's going away for a bit.

And you're sitting there with something hot running through your system in a dark apartment kitchen in

Montmartre and it's the "pull yourself together, Nicolas" and it's the moment she closes the door and then you're alone, and suddenly it's silent. The TV throws shades of grey at you and the window is open, tossing about the curtains with nonchalance.

This is what it feels like.

I can still sense Fred Bobin's eyes on me as I awake in a laundromat after midnight. It's the same one I used to work at, the dull decorations, the plain tiled flooring. A man sleeps soundly on one of the central chairs and two machines are on, clothes sloshing, engines whirring. One of the overhead lamps flickers with a loose connection. A woman's on the other side of the room reading a fashion magazine. Colette's on it, again.

There's something in here with me, but where.

I throw the glass door open onto Burq Street. Through the haze I can see stars in the sky. As I walk, snow shakes from the footpath like thousands of tiny marbles. A bicycle flies by with blinding lights. I'm speed-walking the streets of Montmartre in this off-kilter world and I'm thinking about the agents, watching me from the shadows, thinking about Pierre, and Moret in the dress store. And this city ain't right.

And then there's something.

Coming onto Abbesses Street, I spot another one of those agents on the other side of the road. I slow to a stop and watch him, the snow kicking up against my heels. The man is the same as all the others, black-clad and with perfect circle glasses that hide his eyes completely.

"Who are you," I shout.

There's another man a few feet next to me, on the crosswalk; he looks at me with concern, but I keep staring across the road and ignore him. A car flies past. I step onto the road and the man doesn't react, he simply watches me.

"Why are you following me!"

The city hums and the agent turns to leave, eventually disappearing from sight. Nobody else reacts to this. Not the man on the crosswalk behind me, not the people walking by, not that cat slinking about the gutters. The agent was never here.

What do they want from us. What's here in this world that's not Paris 1959, the world that's some other place where a woman called Moret talks of a jazz town.

I keep walking until I'm at the corner, peering up to the heights of the *La Villa*, five windows stacked vertically as far as the grey haze allows.

Nicolas Fontaine.

I hear that voice again, speaking my name.

Suddenly I realise there's somebody else standing there in the falling snow, a lanky figure in bright colours and a hat. It begins walking over to me, one long leg after the other, and when it crosses by a streetlamp, I see its shadow get flung onto *La Villa*'s façade, a huge and grotesque shadow, spider-like and abnormal. But the man himself is nothing of the sorts. He's in loud clothes and makeup, everything of such distressing colour he appears wrongly juxtaposed against the monochrome world we both inhabit. His fingers are longer than most, grasping a closed umbrella by the handle.

"Thought I smelt something off," says the man.

Snow sizzles against his pale skin and melts. His pupils readjust to the light; they blink with animal-like intensity.

He makes a clicking sound as he approaches, slow and methodical, like weaving through a minefield. His black leather boots glisten from the melted snow. He is only slightly taller than me, which is to say, taller than most men who walk these streets of Paris. "What are you?" he says.

I steel myself, but don't move.

What am I.

"And what are you doing in this place?"

I took a drug and now I'm here. I watch the strange man as he begins to circle me predatorily, but still I don't move. I'm not afraid, though. I feel a deep turmoil emanating from within the man, and this turmoil begins to entrench itself in me too. I respond, "They gave me a pill to take. I took the pill and now I'm here." I stop for a second. "And who are you."

The man's vague, pleasant-enough face gives off the impression of contemplation. I sense something flicker in his eyes, and then burn solid, as if a decision has been made.

"You're not like the others, now," he says.

I don't respond to this.

"It's been a long time since I've felt anything down here," the man says, removing his top hat to reveal no hair and a chipped-at scalp. "Here in the reflected universe."

The reflected universe.

He—It—appears to read my thoughts. Is this the thing they've been looking for. Not a creature but a man, a man in agonising colours, full set of makeup like he's come from a show, which drips down his cheeks like a sad clown in the rain. Fractured scalp, chipped away like paint in a down-and-trodden apartment.

"Did you take it too," I ask.

A car rushes past, spraying us both with its headlights. For a split second, the man is entirely illuminated, the green stripes of his suit appearing to light up. Its shadow is longer, more absurd. "It was no pill that sent me here, friend."

"Then what did."

"It's a little more complicated than that."

I frown. "And this world is the reflected universe."

"An in-between," it says, simply.

Riiiiiiiing!

It comes from somewhere I can't see, and the city goes silent except for this ringing.

"What's your name," I ask.

The man opens his mouth slightly, pauses, and then a half-smirk crosses his lips. He looks askance, then back at me. "Don't tell them about me," he—*It*—warns, opening up its red umbrella with the theatrics of somebody performing on stage.

And suddenly I'm certain.

This is what they're looking for.

The **Reflected Man**.

Riiiiiing! Riiiiiiiiiiiing!

Behind the reflected man, a person with a telephone for a head, staring at me and *ringing, ringing, ringing!*

"Wait—" is all I manage before—

I'm awake in Fred Bobin's office. He's watching me from the opposite chair. My mouth is bitter and there's the continued sound of jazz music in my ears, disturbing and unpleasant.

I get up and Fred Bobin positions his clipboard without standing. I walk to the window, the glass glazed over in condensation, which drips down the pane maladroitly. The street below me is empty entirely and only when you look in the distance can you see anything move. It's just the grey roads, falling snow and the leaves, scattered to the wind.

And.

Don't tell them about me.

"Nicolas?" says Fred Bobin.

I turn around, feeling ill. Everything is heavier in the real world. It moves faster, like the framerate is off and we've dropped one. I wonder how long it's been since I've last gotten a decent sleep. Probably too long. Weeks, maybe. Or maybe it began long before that. My hands are trembling so I grab them, then let them go, tighten them into fists.

Fred Bobin asks me the same questions as always. I answer them the normal way but I don't sit. I feel as though I won't be here much longer. How much money have I already made from these repeated excursions into the world inside the pill. Nine hundred francs. How much is the fat man offering to end it. I'll be able to end all of this and get away, and Colette won't know.

What really happened to Miss Blanchot.

Why am I suddenly thinking about her.

I realise I still don't know her name.

Don't tell them about me.

Fred Bobin remains seated throughout all of this, his pen poised over the page. I'm waiting for that question he always asks last, the only question, I'm assuming, that really matters. The one they're going to relay back to the fat man and all his agents. The reason for all of this.

I hear Pierre first.

Take whatever money they give you and get out.

Fred Bobin's pen falls, he lowers his clipboard to his lap.

He asks me if there was anything, anything at all.

This is the only time my answer changes.

NINE
The Fat Man, Pt. II

Sunlight sneaking through the partially-closed curtains touches the spine of a hardcover book. It's a single volume containing collected poems of T. S. Eliot, a man who I've never thought much of, except that the existence of these poems reminds me of ▮▮▮▮▮▮▮▮. The dark spot in my memory.

This book belonged to her and cannot be thrown away. I've tried, believe me. Left them by the side of the road, tossed them in the garbage, set them on fire, buried them underground. But this one book keeps returning to the very spot on my shelf, and I'm wondering what it will take.

Standing in front of the bookshelf in my bedroom, I open up the book, the hardcover creaking. It still smells of her, a scent you can't quite describe, like old movie theatres. In blue ink on the backside of the front cover, there is a name.

Bernard Merton.

It's always been there, so the book must have belonged to him once, but I don't remember who that is. There's no more trace of him besides the name in the front, the rest of it printed text, poems that hold no significant meaning to me.

I close my eyes, and I feel the city do the same.

And so it's quiet.

But then there are cars, and people's shoes on the gravel, plunging through the snow and leaving their prints behind. There's gasoline in my lungs and it burns. I'm smoking their fumes. Car doors clap. Men in black suits, they watch the streets. Always watching. And the city, it watches them too. *I'm* watching them. How am I watching them.

I open my eyes and see the book again. Its weight puts tension in my fingertips. Bernard Merton. For some reason, his name sits somewhere close to that black spot in my brain. Suddenly I recall how he would come by the apartment, a man I sketched once—I'm sure I could find it—with voluminous brown hair and a grand moustache of somebody upper class, an aristocrat-looking man. And here he is giving books of poetry to 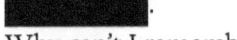.

Why can't I remember her fucking name.

I slump back onto the bed, defeated. Anyway, the books mean nothing to me. I haven't read them and, at this point, I'm not planning to. I've never been one for poetry, even if *she* had. And, whoever Bernard Merton was.

The wind picks up, causing snow and tree branches to hit hard against my window.

There's something wrong with all of this. The city reeks

of her. The poetry. The bed, it feels like her body pressed against mine in the autumn, with the muted light up against the curtains as though searching for a glance. The films they show at the cinema, they look like her; the people, they sound the way she did. I told her, once, my mother despises my cartoons, and she laughs and she says I never liked your mother's movies anyway. I said, well, she won an Oscar for them.

I don't remember her, I just remember all these little pieces, scattered around the city.

There's a distant sound of jazz music, which I can hear now, coming from somewhere outside the apartment.

██████████ hated jazz music.

"Reading T. S. Eliot?" Colette says.

Suddenly she's in the doorway, peering in. I'm almost envious of the way she's dressed, elegant and proper in a fashionable white coat that hugs her body. I tell Colette that the book means nothing to me and I put it back where it was.

Tell her about what you're doing.

I ignore this voice. Colette doesn't need to know about this, only that I'm working again. "I sold something."

This is how I'm going to explain to her the money I've been making, and hopefully get her off my back in the meantime.

"Oh," she says. "Congratulations."

Her reaction to the lie stings so I avert my eyes and pretend to have not told her anything. "It's nothing big," I say.

But my recent discovery of the reflected man in the

other universe—*another universe*—means that things might soon turn into something big. Moscati Research hasn't been in touch yet, nor the fat man, but I imagine it's just a matter of time.

I get up and walk over to Colette, taking her warm hands in mine. "You don't have to stay here if you don't want to," I tell her softly. "I'm doing rather well now."

She stares up at me and smiles. "I might as well."

We hug then, and I feel myself tower over her like a big tree, even in spite of her dramatically-heeled boots, which surely give her at least a couple more inches of height.

Meanwhile, Paris lays still and lets the cold winds of nightfall wash over her. The city rests soundly and, by the time everybody is asleep, the last light gone from the houses and apartments, it has become unresponsive to the waking world.

Just after midnight, a man in a black suit slips a sealed envelope underneath the front door of Nicolas Fontaine's apartment, and disappears without anybody seeing him.

The envelope contains nine hundred francs.

I wait until Colette is definitely asleep before lighting a cigarette and leaving the apartment.

The Paris tenements are dead at two fifty-three a.m. and only the most insomniac of the late-night dwellers remain on the streets. I examine a passing thought, and that's how do I know the time when I no longer have my watch.

I hear the muffled sound of jazz music even now. Perhaps it's the silence, but for a moment I wonder if I'm here or if

I'm *there*. But if I haven't been to Fred Bobin's office then I haven't taken another pill, and haven't even had the urge.

I walk out onto the sidewalk on Caulaincourt Street and whistle cigarette smoke into the wind. The restaurant on the corner is open and I walk through its glass doors, into the cold interior. It's a sparse audience tonight and only one man's running the booths. A single radio on the front counter by the window plays pop at a low volume and somebody turns the pages of a newspaper. There's a student with her head buried in a large paperback book, her cheek resting against her fist. A backpack sits on the table dripping textbooks and workbooks. Occasionally she turns a page and drinks from her milkshake.

I grab a burger and sit in an empty booth, squashing my cigarette butt in the ashtray provided. I have a view of the street through the window. The crosswalks go green and just one woman goes on her way. A dog snores loudly.

I finish my burger before three thirty a.m. and leave the café, having made no progress on my thoughts.

This is what you do when you can't sleep. Walk the city streets like a ghost, somewhere between existing and not. You take a bus, take the steps into the metro, and you keep on going. People don't look at you at three thirty a.m. in the Parisian streets, nor beneath them. They keep their heads down and watch their feet in the snow, making a pointed effort not to, or just wanting to get somewhere. When they look up, a breath of mist erupting from pursed lips, they don't see you, just shapes, with those hollow, vacant eyes.

This is how you distract yourself. Flipping a pen from your pocket and chewing it like a cigarette, with a trapped tune in the back of your head, walking with the ghosts through Paris. But one day, you tell yourself, one day you might be able to open your eyes and it won't be Paris anymore.

Before I know it, I'm standing outside the ceramics store on Charlot Street where Miss Blanchot died, gazing up through the light of a streetlamp and the downpour of snow. I pluck my blue pen from my mouth and spit out a bit of the plastic. I remember how I found her there, the detachment I felt upon seeing her. She fucked sad people to feel less sad and she died sad, so what was the point of any of it. When I think of Miss Blanchot, whose real name I still don't know, I only think of three things. The school where she taught, and evidently my talk; fucking her in the grey afternoon light; and seeing her there with the needle jutting out of her arm.

Miss Blanchot dies and the world doesn't miss a beat. The music goes on without interruption. I figure I'll end up dying the same, though I'm not sure how I feel about this, as I stick my pen back between my teeth and walk from the desolate ceramics store further down the darkening street.

Something's jutting out of the snow.

I kneel down to pick it up. A pink calling card slides into my fingertips and I turn it, examining its contents under the low light. I spot Miss Blanchot's face there, and beside it, a number to dial. But there's a name there too.

"Ingrid," I mutter, catching the pen as it falls out of my mouth. It certainly isn't her real name, but it's something I can refer to her as for now. Perhaps she named herself after the leading lady of Cukor's 1944 remake of *Gaslight*. I stand up, observing the card, then walk to the phone booth and slide inside, shutting the door behind me.

A sudden silence swallows me whole. There is the smell of a burrito and graffiti all over the walls, the paint still giving off a scent. I bite on my pen and pick up the phone, narrowly avoiding a chewed-up piece of gum, and let my finger dial the number on the card.

There's no answer, just a long beep into oblivion.

I eventually put down the phone and stare at the card. They've probably been shut down like the rest of the brothels in Paris. I flip it over to its back and look at the address. Number 4, Paul-Valéry Street. For a moment I'm leaning against the glass wall of the phone booth, staring at it, then staring out into the falling snow. I resolve myself to the fact, there was something about that woman, an English teacher working at *Lycée Victor Hugo*, who fucks sad people.

And she's dead but I can't help but think, if I just find out her name, then maybe things will start making more sense.

I sigh, pocketing the card and heading into the night.

It's four a.m. when the taxi pulls up outside Number 4, a modest-looking hotel with no distinguishing features. I pull my jacket up over my shoulders as I cross the sidewalk through the front doors. The interior is stark and with minimal set dressing, like a studio backlot, all wood and lamps. I go to the woman behind the desk and say, "Is Ingrid in?"

She tilts her head at me. "Not an Ingrid here no more."

I pull the card out of my pocket and peer down at it,

the very alive face of Miss Blanchot—*Ingrid*—staring back at me. I flip it over again and glance at the faces on the other side. I sense the woman behind the desk watching me.

Béatrice, she's dark-haired and full-lipped, the same age as Miss Blanchot and works the same hours. The lowliest ones. I ask for "Béatrice" and the woman nods. She slides a slip of paper to me, with a price written on it. I glance at it. "All the girls have a price," she tells me, then shrugs and taps the card. "Some of them higher than others."

I use the fat man's money.

When Béatrice lets me into her room, I'm greeted by the smell of cigarettes and lavender. A candle burns on the bedside table and there are enough pillows on the red silk bedsheets for more than just two. A horizontal-spanning window overlooks more apartments, with frost against the dirty window panes.

I place my shoes by the door and wander in. Béatrice, meanwhile, sits down on the edge of the bed. The air moves slow through the small room on the second floor of the hotel, and I pop a few buttons on my shirt just to stop from suffocating in it. A red lamp burns on the wall, lighting the carvings in the wood, the curtains and the embellishments.

"So how would you like me, handsome?" Béatrice asks.

Her eyes are large and inviting, a white silk dress holds loosely to her body, as full as a painting to be explored. "Do you mind if I smoke," I ask. Béatrice reveals a box of her own and we both draw cigarettes, lighting them.

I sit on the bed beside her. "I'm not here for that."

Béatrice exhales smoke into the air, her warmth against my arm pleasant for the time being. "I get that a lot," she tells me with indifference. "They change their minds."

I find it in me to smile.

She smells good. Her breaths are quiet and short, unobtrusive. Her hair tickles the side of my neck and I focus on all these things as well as the smoke in my lungs.

I take out the card for the third time tonight and show it to her. "Ingrid, what is her real name."

Béatrice looks at me with an odd, searching expression, plucking the cigarette from her lips and lightly tapping it against her white thigh. "Are you some sort of detective then?"

"I'm not," comes my truthful response. Béatrice does not appear to believe me fully, but seems to accept it either way. She presses the cigarette back to her lips and keeps it there, eyeing me with intent. She's quite beautiful, after all, large brown eyes and round cheeks, a curl of hair in front of her left eye, the rest quite untamed and natural.

She looks askance. "Ingrid doesn't work here anymore, hasn't worked the *maison* for some six months, and even then only for a brief time. Do you know her?"

"Well what was her name."

"For someone who's not a detective, you're inquisitive."

"She means something to me."

"A lot of them say that," she says, giving me a soft, somewhat dazed look as she takes a drag.

"Not like that," I say.

"Oh sure."

"She died," I tell her.

"Oh." She bites her bottom lip as her gaze drifts, and she leans backwards. "That's a shame."

"I need to know," I tell her. "Who was she. Where did she come from. Why did she take her own life."

Béatrice responds with smoke.

"I only really knew her as Ingrid," she says without looking at me. "It was some time before she even told me anything about herself. Including her name."

"Which was."

She sighs, barely says it: **"Catherine."**

It goes black.

Catherine.

All you hear is the sound of a film roll at the end of its run, the *click-click-click-click*—

And then nothing.

I'm in a dark room at the back of my mind, a room with no door and no way out. Her perfume fills the space, the smell of old movie theatres, and she isn't here, or there, she's everywhere. Filling every empty place with that scent.

You're disappearing.

Come back—

Béatrice is staring at me and I find that no time has passed at all. She blows an aggressive cloud of silvery smoke into the space between us. **"Other Catherine"**—my brain corrects it to this—"worked here my hours, the next room over, but only for a short length of time." She motions with the cigarette to the far-most wall. "Fucked everything she could, like some obsession. Most of us, we don't do it for the enjoyment really, it's the money, and the Madame pays well—looks after us too. But Other Catherine, she was lookin' for something else. She was always so caught up in the fact that she herself was something so large and incomprehensible, that if she'd told any one of us, the reality would be so devastating it would, of sorts, destroy our very concept of existence itself."

She suddenly blinks, like coming out of a trance, and quickly sticks her cigarette into her mouth, so tight it gets stained with red lipstick. She tilts her head back so that her hair springs free, sucks on her cigarette, then lets it fly across the room, smacking the floor. "And then she just left, and we never saw her again. But we all remembered her."

I find myself unable to speak, trying to process this. Suddenly the fact that she has the same name is second in my mind, for I'm thinking of what Miss Blanchot—Other Catherine—truly is, or if she really was just mad.

There is *something wrong with me, something really wrong,* was what she'd told me, and I can remember how she'd looked as she said it. Did she even really understand herself what was wrong.

"Do you have something to say, then, or were you just looking to buy a few hours with her?" Béatrice asks me, leaning forward with composure. "That why you don't want me?"

"Why did she leave," I ask.

"Why are you so interested in Other Catherine?"

"I don't know."

Béatrice continues to study me. "She just does that, she floats. That's what makes her so mysterious."

Her talking in the present tense makes me think she's still alive, but she certainly is not.

The only thing I do then is lift my hand from the bed and place it over my cheek, to make sure I'm still here. My mouth has gone dry and I'm thinking of Other Catherine, that the city is not as heavy without her in it, like a boat where someone's jumped off the side. Less heavy, but more lonely maybe.

"It'll be okay," Béatrice says, placing her own hand over mine; it's soft and warm and she massages the tender back of my hand with her thumb. "It's always okay in the end."

"Did she know about the fat man."

"A lotta fat men come round here."

"*The* fat man," I tell her, then realise how stupid that sounds.

She slides her hand to my chin and gives a soft smile. I watch the way the red light swims between the folds in her skin, accentuating parts of her she sells to sad men.

Am I sad or am I just tired.

She plucks out my cigarette and tosses it onto the floor, then tenderly puts her arms around me, drawing me inside her warm hold. I grab a handful of her white linens and close my eyes, as slowly, my arms find a place around her back.

Béatrice breathes into my ear. "It's okay."

There is no more itch. No more Catherine. Or Colette's money and her making sure I'm not dead. There's no more fat man and his agents. No more kerfuffles in the dress store. No more Fred Bobin. And no more creature in the strange universe, the universe that is not Paris 1959 but some other place I don't recognise. No reflected man. There's none of this.

I draw in a deep breath, and a tear falls onto her shoulder, as everything fades to black.

It's five thirty a.m. when I return home to the living room lamp on and the fat man sitting on my couch, watching the television.

He looks at me and stands.

I close the door behind me.

"What are you doing here."

The fat man is exactly as I've remembered him. He's bulbous and fills far too much space for just one man. "Please," he says, "don't let me stop you." He goes to the television set and turns it off at the source. With a buzz and a high-pitched whine, the signal cuts out and the room grows still.

"Were you watching my TV," I say.

"It was on when I came in," the fat man responds.

I look around. The apartment appears to be empty. Colette is no longer here, at least not where I left her. The curtains are drawn shut and they don't move, which means the windows are closed. There is no movement, none at all. "Where is my sister?"

"She left," says the fat man.

"Where."

"There was . . . a work appointment, or something. I'm not lying. You can call. Oh, that's right, Nicolas Fontaine doesn't have a phone. You *have* been receiving payments, haven't you? So for god's sake, Nicolas, just buy one already. It's for your own benefit." He appears to catch himself in the midst of that rant. "It's just us, okay? You can relax. I'm in no hurry."

The fat man lowers his head and removes his black hat. His shadow splashes across the apartment walls, the lamp behind him completely engulfed by his overweight frame. He looks ill, and groggy on his left leg. The buttons of his shirt barely cling on but if they popped off and smacked me in the face, I wouldn't say I'd think much of it.

Why is he here.

I'm halfway across the room when the fat man side-steps into my path. "Oh, no," he tells me in his gross baritone. "How about you take a seat. We have something to discuss."

"If I do what you say will you cut the bullshit."

The fat man cocks his fat brow. "I will tell you what you want to know just as soon as we're done here." He has the audacity to smile, then motion to the couch. I do not entertain his offer. I walk to the kitchen and sit at the plastic fold-out table where various sketches and notebook pages are torn and thrown about. I check to make sure nothing's been touched, and find everything's as it should be. I dig out my pen and put it on the table.

The fat man joins me here.

I don't ask any questions. The fat man somehow knows I live here. He's known this for some time. That he has a way of getting inside is also no surprise. At this stage, I can safely assume the fat man has a handle on most things and can get most things done, no questions asked.

"Congratulations, Nicolas," he says as he reaches into his pocket and retrieves a zip-lock bag full of pills, and a tiny card with handwriting on it inside. This goes on the table between us and I recognise them immediately as jazz pills. "So you're the one we've been looking for, after all."

"What does that mean."

"You've seen it, haven't you."

I'm thinking back to Fred Bobin's questions, and the thing I encountered in the jazz, the reflected man.

"Does the whole of Moscati Research work for you."

"No," responds the fat man. "Not that it matters."

"So what is it, that thing I saw."

He doesn't respond immediately, but there's not one moment I doubt he knows what I'm talking about, that there's been something in the reflected universe for a while and the fat man has always known about it. Perhaps there was no actual drug trial after all, just a reflected man who plays tricks in another world, a world inside the jazz.

He smiles gently, same as always.

"There is a being of unknown origin within the jazz," says the fat man in a stoic voice. He bears no more levity, no more careful consideration, just the facts, like a man reciting a terrible nightmare. "As far as things are concerned, you're the only one who's been able to make contact with it."

I'm staring at the fat man, processing his words.

"Now, all that's left is to eliminate it," he tells me. "Kill the thing in the jazz and I'll pay you thirty thousand francs. You have my word on this. Kill the thing in the jazz and you're a rich man. Believe me, I'll make it so. No more sad Nicolas Fontaine. No more begging for money from your sister."

And I'm thinking about Colette.

I'm thinking about the thing in the reflected universe.

Don't tell them about me.

"What's it doing," I say.

"It's a virus, you see. It poses a threat to any further exploration of the jazz, and as long as it remains, it makes travelling there repeatedly, very, very dangerous."

I frown. "Further exploration."

"That is to say, for research."

"What are you researching."

The fat man smiles and exhales sharply, slowly nodding his head with the appearance of a man nodding off. "There are certain things I'm not at liberties to discuss. But rest assured, you will be given all the information you need."

"Why not just tell me now," I say.

"You have enough to worry about already, don't you?"

Dissatisfied with his response, I indicate with my eyes the pills on the table. "Well what are those," I ask.

"This is where Fred Bobin's involvement ends. These pills are yours to take at your own discretion. Once every seventy-two hours should do. Just kill the fucking thing."

He shifts in his seat, in such a way the light that falls across his face changes angle, deepening the shadows. He slides a pistol on the papers beside the zip-lock bag. "Understand, Nicolas, this is a very serious business. It is in our best interest, the best interest of Moscati Research, to assist in any way we can; but if you become uncooperative, rest assured the consequences will not be pleasant. Not for you, nor the ones who know you. But with thirty thousand francs already made out in your name, and things being as they are, I couldn't imagine running into any issues of obedience now."

"And what's your stake again."

"It's all just business, isn't it."

I drink in his sour words, and grimace. There's something he isn't telling me but I won't press it now. What did Pierre say, take whatever money they give you and get out.

I'm staring at the gun on the table. I can still hear that jazz music, like something far off in the distance—deep, deep down inside my own head.

"What's jazz town," I say.

"Jazztown?" responds the fat man in one word, rising to his full height and stepping from the table. His chair hurtles backwards across the floor, glad to be spared of his monstrous weight. The fat man's shadow falls dully across the table. "Where did you hear of such a place?"

In the face of his temper, I decide not to respond. For what seems like an unrealistic length of time, he stares down at me over his large, fat nose, like a wart that's gone bad.

"Well then!" he demands after due consideration. "There will be no more talk of this. You have your job. These are your pills, you know what to do. We will keep in touch." He pauses, like remembering something. "When it's done," he says, "you ought to call back that number I gave you. It'll be me."

"How do I know I can trust you," I ask him.

"How many more questions do ya wanna ask me?"

I decide I'm not going to be getting any more straight answers from the fat man and it seems he senses the same thing, for now he slams his comparatively miniscule chair underneath the table and slides his hat back on his head.

"Your sister went out lookin' for you. She didn't even see me come by here. That's what you wanted, isn't it?"

I nod.

"You'd want to keep it that way, wouldn't ya."

What is that supposed to mean.

But there are no more questions asked, and the fat man, he says nothing else except for bidding me goodnight as he turns around and leaves the apartment. I listen to his receding footfalls, and the floorboards creaking morosely beneath them.

I glance at the zip-lock bag of pills.

At the gun that he's left there.

What about the others. Pierre. I vaguely remember their faces, and I remember the confrontation in the dress store, Moret and the two agents. Was that connected. My conclusion is it doesn't matter much because there's no more trial, there's just jazz pills and a gun, and they're on my dining table.

There's Other Catherine and a place called Jazztown.

I sit back down and grab my clammy hands so they stop shaking. I glance at the ticking clock. It's almost six a.m.

Don't tell them about me.

This is what the reflected man said.

Don't tell them about me.

Friday, February 27. 12:30 p.m.

The past two weeks were mostly uneventful. Louise Duchamp remained properly mute, and her condition, while exhibiting rapid improvement the first few days, had appeared to plateau. Her movements were still languorous and unnatural, and in the times I'd visited with Claude to try to get something out of her, she seemed dazed and unresponsive.

The doctors had told us she wasn't sleeping much, sometimes only an hour or two a night, and often times they would find her standing up and staring out the window, the curtains having been drawn aside. They had expressed their concern for her safety and wanted to relocate her to some place better suited, but their request had been rejected.

She was becoming agitated.

This was evident when we were called back to the hospital suddenly around ten a.m. two days ago, to the Duchamp girl reportedly having some sort of meltdown. Claude and I drove there as fast as we could, breaking from our report-writing, croissant crumbs flying as we did our best to eat before arriving. Upon reaching the hospital carpark, we made haste from the company car and through the halls to where Duchamp was staying.

The first sign of trouble was I could hear her yowls down the hallway from her door. Claude looked at me with mixed parts terror and confusion on his face, and we ran. Upon arriving, we found Duchamp in the middle of the room being restrained by three nurses. Her head was shaking every which way, and her socks slid across the floor as she attempted to break free, catching on tufts of carpet. She was screaming into the air, eyes agape. You could not mistake the way her body shook with those unnatural rhythms, like somebody had stolen living frames from her. I had to blink to be sure I wasn't simply seeing things.

They eventually hit her with a tranquiliser, and then carried her back to her bed, where she remained, breathing heavily. You typically don't see the use of a tranquiliser on such a small girl, unless under extreme circumstances, so I knew this was unordinary. Yet she wasn't entirely out, still squirming in the bedsheets and covering her eyes with a forearm, peeking out only every now and then before hurriedly shielding them again. We asked the nurses what triggered her episode.

They told us she'd just had breakfast, and had been left alone for a short time when it happened. They found her standing in the middle of the room in much the same way we had, gripping the sides of her hospital gown and screaming at something in front of her.

Their description of it gave me the chills and I walked over to her bedside now that she was sedated. She opened one eye and looked at me, covering her face so that all I could see was that single eye. I knelt down so I was level with her, my notepad on my knee.

I told her my name again and asked what had made her upset.

She kept staring at me, her bloodshot eye wet and tired. Her blinks were staccato and broken-up much like the rest of her. I asked where she had gone that night she left home and didn't come back, but still nothing changed in her expression, or the way she looked at me.

Later that day, I visited her family's apartment again on Lepic Street and examined the door, looking for any sign that somebody had broken in or the locks had been tampered with. Eventually, I decided, at least how things looked now, all seemed fine.

Mr. and Mrs. Duchamp allowed me in and treated me to coffee and biscuits, and I looked around, taking notes of things I found. The apartment was relatively small and showed nothing out of the ordinary. In fact, it was rather tidy and well-kept. The smell of paint led me into a small studio space where Mrs. Duchamp had been working. Several finished and unfinished pieces showed above-average skill with an original style of note. I complimented her on the work, and she told me she had an art show coming up two weeks from now. I told her I might come along.

The door to Louise's room was shut, and when I slowly pushed it open, I found it to be dark inside. I turned on the light switch and began my investigations. It was probably no more than three metres by three, a narrow single bed and a small bookshelf in the corner occupying most of the space. On top of the bookshelf was a music player; the shelves were, rather than books, filled with a variety of records.

I flicked through them and was met with names such as Cannonball Adderley, Sonny Rollins, Charlie Parker and John Coltrane. I've never been one for jazz music in particular, but I picked one up, *Blue Train*, and gave it a brief look. The sleeve was damaged and appeared second-hand, or at least well-worn. I slid it back to where it was and paced around the room. Her clothes drawers were orderly, the bass guitar propped up on a stand out of the way. I plucked one of the strings and it rang out mutedly.

I sat down on her bed.

Mrs. Duchamp came into the doorway and stood there with her arms folded. She wore flowery patterns and her hair was usually quite tangled. She asked me when her daughter could come back home, and I responded that I couldn't give an answer. There was still work to be done, we had to figure out what was wrong with her. After all, what good would it be to return her home with no answers, unable to speak, not far from comatose?

I asked her, then, if she knew anything she wasn't telling me. She shook her head, no contemplation, no doubt, nothing, just the shake. I hung my head, letting the notepad and my pen dangle between my fingertips. How could a fourteen-year-old girl, with no indication of being unhappy or of hiding anything, disappear one night and come back almost a completely different person. She won't speak. Her movements are . . . *unnatural*.

I'm picturing the way she'd screamed.

Why leave in the first place? Where had she gone? Where had her clothes gone? Most indicators pointed to some form of abduction, but something had happened while she was gone. Something she'd seen. Something that had frightened her so badly she'd completely lost it in her hospital room, and was refusing to say a single goddamn word.

I asked her mother, was there anything that Louise expressed fear over. She told me Louise wasn't afraid of anything, and I was beginning to think, maybe they just had no idea and never cared to ask.

I told Mrs. Duchamp I was sorry about what had happened to Louise and that I would do whatever it took to find some semblance of an answer. I promised I'd return her daughter, as she'd been the night she left.

But there was one more thing.

As I was walking through the hall to leave the apartment, I happened to look again at the photo frames on the walls, and noticed something I had not seen earlier. There were no photographs of Louise as a child, certainly no younger than three or four. I posed this to Mrs. Duchamp.

She was startled by my suggestion, and only then admitted that Louise had been adopted when she was four, and they did not have contact with her biological parents. I asked her, why had they kept this a secret from me; certainly, this information was relevant to the case.

She fumbled, and said she didn't think it to be as important as I did. I then asked, were her biological parents alive, were they in Paris?

Mrs. Duchamp told me no, she didn't know.

I'm not buying it.

The following night, I returned to the hospital and sat in the corner seat while Louise slept. I did nothing all night but watch her, waiting. Occasionally, I stood up and made for the other side of the room to stretch my legs. I completed some paper work and a couple of times wandered over to the bed, listening to the way she breathed. Every hour or so, the nurse came in to check on us and give me another coffee.

At four a.m. she woke up.

I had turned around from the window and saw her sitting up in bed, the hazy light catching her eyes and making them appear like two beads on a burnt piece of toast. The effect of her sitting there was momentarily frightful, and I let out an audible gasp, clutching my chest.

"Who are you," she asked me.

Her voice sent shivers through my body and I rushed over to her. I told her she shouldn't fear me, that I was a detective and wanted to help her. I restrained myself, in an effort not to frighten her, and returned to the chair I'd been sitting on, carrying it towards the bed. I then sat down in the chair and opened my notepad, peering over it.

I asked her if she knew why she was here.

She continued staring at me blankly and I got the immediate impression she had limited recollection of anything that had occurred outside of this hospital room. Her eyes turned back towards the curtains, and I followed her gaze to them. Slight glow from the moonlight reflecting off snow shone against the curtains, faintly illuminating them.

"What's there?" I asked her.

"Has it happened yet."

The monotone in her voice was eerie. I looked back from the curtains to her face. A line of moonlight cut across her eye and her cracked lip.

I asked her what she meant by this.

"So it hasn't," she responded.

"What hasn't?" I pressed her.

I noticed the moonlight against her lip begin to tremble. A gust of wind suddenly blew against the curtains, tossing them open with drama. I rushed over to the window and shut it, and suddenly the room was reduced to an eerie silence, though I could still feel . . . something.

Louise breathed a sigh of relief and her shoulders dropped. She finally stopped staring, and, for a moment, she bore some resemblance to the ordinary fourteen-year-old girl we kept hearing about.

"It seems like you're anticipating something," I said.

She held out her arm towards me, with an open hand. Carefully, I crossed the room back towards her. When I was close enough, she gripped my hand and pulled it up in front of her.

A chill ran through me, so intensely it was as if being burned with a hot spoon. I flinched from her grasp, my body taken by a sudden sweat.

I asked her what she was doing.

She backed up against the top of the bed and dragged the white bedsheets to her chin, hidden behind it save for her eyes and the very top of her head. My notepad was up and my fingers were ready to record whatever she said next. I said to her, you can trust me, I'm going to help.

She said, "I saw something bad."

I asked her, what did you see, Louise.
She looked at me. "It was like the end of the world."

part two
city

ELEVEN
Under the Influence of Jazz

Snow falls over Paris in the world that is not the real one, a reflection in a house that requires a pill to enter. When I come to, I'm across the road from a plain building, large on all sides, and I'm shivering from the cold.

It's the first time I've taken the jazz outside of Fred Bobin's office, straight from the zip-lock bag the fat man left on my kitchen table. Tasteless, it goes down with some water. Then it's the jazz music, like there's a gramophone across the room behind me, just out of sight.

Then it's this. Pages fluttering through the carpark of a stark white library building, lifted and swayed by the night. I'm here alone, nobody else in sight, nothing but the flickering of street lamps and a faraway buzz. I look around, lifting my hands in front of my face, and clenching them into fists. Now rubbing them together, I turn on the spot and blow hot breath into them. There's a dig-out roughly two hundred feet further down the road, blinking with lights and occasionally the heads of government workers, hardhats, bobbing up and down.

This is all there is, only that and me.

"Hello," I speak into the silence. It quivers, the air becoming noticeably tense. A leaf abruptly changes direction as it falls. A dog barks from the shadows and I can hear a heavy chain rattling. Papers leap from my feet.

Occupying the bus stop in front of the library, I spot the familiar figure of the reflected man. As I walk through the parking lot towards it, hands buried in my warm pockets, I'm beginning to wonder of the rules that govern this strange parallel universe. How, if this is *Sainte-Geneviève Library,* how have I come to be on the other side of the Seine. And how, sitting before me now in the bus stop under that half-moon streetlamp is there that shadowed, unearthly creature.

"What do you know about the fat man," I say.

The reflected man looks up at me, bright red coat blowing with the gasping wind, white makeup smudged in places to reveal cuts and picked-at, reddened skin. It takes the top hat from the seat and stands, stepping out from the bus shelter and into the half-light produced by the streetlamp.

"I told you not to tell."

My mouth has gone dry. I think about ways to respond but there's very little I can say when it's such a simple truth. You can't argue that a red pen produces red ink.

"He made me do it," I respond.

"Is he Hitchcock, is he Orson Welles?" says the reflected man. And its vague eyes search me, and I know what they're looking for, but I haven't brought the gun. Seemingly satisfied, the reflected man fully emerges from the darkness as if from a portal. "He is not to be trusted, that man! What does he want? To kill me? And he's sent you, hasn't he."

"I wasn't going to kill you," I say.

The reflected man weighs up my words, and then sighs with a sound that's like breath through bones.

I examine the library.

"Why are we here."

"I don't know, Nicolas," responds the reflected man, following the way I'm staring at the building. "You came here yourself, when you took the pill they gave you. The reason I know these things is there have been others besides yourself, long ago, but the fat man deals with them, eventually." It looks at me, lips parting to reveal decaying gums. "Follow me, Nicolas, there's something I'd like to show you."

Shivering endlessly, I follow the reflected man through the doors into *Sainte-Geneviève*, and am instantly bathed in the warm yellow lights, and a kind of stillness that only libraries have. The few people who surround us barely lift their eyes, all of them preoccupied with their own problems.

"Where," I ask.

"Higher," says the reflected man.

We continue through the warm library, and I'm just glad to be out of the cold. "The fat man knew you were here," I say. "Even before I said anything, he was looking for you."

"And for a while, too," the reflected man adds.

We enter a lift and I make sure to put considerable space between myself and the reflected man, each of us taking one corner. It's here where I get my best look of it. It is a strange thing, to be sure, certainly not of this world, though to the natural eye you'd be hard-pressed to find much distinctly *inhuman* about it, just someone's who's had a bad run of it. Mid-thirties, and in many regards feminine. Its clothing is borderline offensive to this grim, monochrome world, incongruously bright and gaudy.

We make brief eye contact.

"They're very interested in you," I say. "I am too, a little bit. I'm a bit curious in all of this, this universe, Moscati Research, the pills. Why does he want to kill you."

"He's scared, why else? I'm in his thing he's making, like finding weevils in your cake. You wanna know why the fat man chose you, Nicolas? It wasn't coincidence. You're an easy pawn, you've got no one to conspire with, none to share their secrets. Easy for a weak man to control. You surely won't put up a fight, look at you, you told them about me easy enough. I know what it's like though, I understand your position, to lose so much, to feel as though you're disappearing. It must become terribly lonely. Do you live by yourself, Nicolas?"

"For the most part," I respond. "Why."

"I'm just saying, you're alone, and that's what the fat man wants from his subjects. Because he's scared." The reflected man shrugs. "It's like pantophobia, or something."

It studies me as the doors open and snow flutters in like torn book pages. My teeth immediately start chattering. The reflected man walks out the elevator into the freezing cold night.

"Shit. All the way up here," I shudder.

Following it, the rooftop is flat rock overlooking smaller buildings and streets. The haze in the air is oppressive. The reflected man continues to walk across it, seemingly undeterred by the cold. It stops near the edge of the rooftop and I walk until I'm standing directly behind, rubbing my hands.

"Why are we up here, it's freezing."

"The fat man, is he paying a lot to kill me?"

"Thirty thousand francs."

The reflected man scoffs and shakes its head. We both gaze out across the city from the highest point of *Sainte-Geneviève Library* but there isn't much besides blurred lights and snow, not in this part of Paris. The reflected man glances at me and the city blurs deeper, as I focus on its face.

"And you believe him?" says the reflected man.

"I don't know," I respond.

"Wouldn't bet on it. The fat man lies. That's all he does. Hell, do you even think he has that much? Thirty thousand."

I chew on its words as a gust of wind throws snow at the both of us and I shield my face. "Okay."

"I suppose there's nothing stopping you from doing what he wants. I promise not to put up a fight and I might even be relieved." It looks at me now. "But you should know, the only way to get out of this is to kill the fat man. Do you want to get out? Well he's everything. He's all of it, all the mess."

"You're talking as though I've fallen into a trap."

"A situation of limited time."

"I see."

There's no question that the fat man has already paid me well, but perhaps the reflected man is right, perhaps there's no thirty thousand francs at the end of it all.

"What got you into this?" it asks.

"I don't know. He knew me."

"He knew you," says the reflected man.

"He said I'd have signed up for it, and that he found out who I was by asking at my last workplace . . . but to be honest, it doesn't add up. I've never signed up for anything like this. Why would I. Have I ever had an interest in science."

"Still, you said yes."

I nod, and with this I sense the reflected man either understands or doesn't much care, and I'm still wondering why the hell he's brought us up on this rooftop.

"Let me help you then," it tells me. "Keep me around and stall the fat man. With me, we can both kill him and escape this. But for it to work, you have to keep me around, okay? You have to trust me. Not the fat man; he cannot be trusted."

I meet the reflected man's eyes, deeply white and inhuman. "Who are you," I ask it.

The reflected man looks off in the distance, walking to the very edge of the rooftop without responding. I begin to move, thinking it's about to jump off.

"Can you feel it?"

"Feel what."

"It's depressed."

"The city," I ask, and suddenly I do feel it. A burdening sadness, air of great despondence. There are no gaudy lights or extravagant tunes tonight in the reflected universe, just melancholy, and I feel this now.

Just as I do, there is a ringing telephone carried on the wind. It's the same as always. I feel the ground immediately give way and it's suddenly as though the sky has become increasingly taller. I stumble momentarily, my feet slipping.

"Our time is up," says the reflected man.

"Why does this keep happening," I ask.

Riiiiing! continues the telephone.

"The reflected universe has its ways."

I look back at the reflected man and notice the roof behind it disintegrating. Rainbow lights begin shimmering through, along with white specks that look like snow. Pieces of the library, books, along with chairs, are floating out into the open abyss around us. "Oh shit! What's going on," I yell.

I lift my hand in front of my face and it becomes translucent with rainbow lights. I look back at the reflected man.

Riiiiing! Riiiiing! Louder.

"Remember this spot," says the reflected man. "The city is stronger here. There's a reason they know who you are. And there's a reason you can communicate with the city."

"Why am I here," I begin to say

But it's all I can get out before my body gives a hypnogogic jerk so violent it sends me tumbling into a bathtub.

My head cracks against the porcelain and a flash of stars explodes across my vision. "Shit!" With some trouble, I pull myself out of the bath and reclaim my footing on the cold bathroom tiles. I glance at the clock. It's the middle of the day—but how can that be right, unless I've gone back in time.

Wandering out into the living room, rubbing the back of my head, I arrive to see the television turned to static and no more snow. All I can really hear is the distant ring of jazz music, and I can taste nothing but dryness in my mouth.

No, there's something else.

I venture deeper into the living room and feel pins and needles tear up my leg. Crippled, I grab onto the back of the couch and stare upwards across the room.

Pieces of debris and furniture are ascending to a hole in my ceiling, through which there's absolute blackness. Slowly, I walk until I'm standing directly underneath it and take a paperclip from the air; I can feel a magnetic pull upwards.

Looking towards the hole, I'm peering through dots of space matter and rainbow colours, the same as it was inside the reflected universe—except, why is it happening here.

My eyes scale down the wall, over cracks that have already begun to spread across the plasterboard, and then I hurry across the room and touch the wall with my fingertips. It's cold, like a frosted window. When I remove my fingers, they're coated in white dust, like something from outer space.

Fleeing from the scene, the tap goes on and I'm filling a glass of water, downing it in three gulps.

I set down the glass on the countertop and wipe the back of my hand against my wet lips. The entire apartment feels too large, the walls appearing taller than usual, and wider, the wallpaper stretched and thin, the doorways expansive. I've become the size of a pea, and I'm unbalanced. My head pounds, and every time I look at the hole in my ceiling, I become more and more convinced that it is growing, and will eventually swallow up everything.

Drawing a deep breath, I cross the room and grab a pack

of cigarettes from the table. The gun from the fat man is still there and I ignore it. I tear a cigarette from the pack, the second-to-last one, and slide it between my teeth.

A flame sprouts with a hiss and fry.

Out to the still streets of Paris, the midday light spraying the city in a creamy glow. Ice on the pavement shines gold.

"Colette, I'm sorry I haven't called."

The phone to my ear at the booth. A storefront opens on the other side of the road and an elderly gentleman is scrubbing frost from the eaves. A mother and her daughter hurry past the store and I watch them until they're gone. The world moves like normal, despite me here, despite the fat man, and the creature in the reflected universe. Things like this are irrelevant.

"Where have you been?" Colette says.

"I'm sorry, I haven't had much time lately."

My hand is gripping the phone hard.

Colette exhales sharply. *"Nicolas, you can't just disappear completely off the face of the earth and not tell anyone. I worry about you. More so now, you've been distant."*

How long was I gone. It couldn't have been long—any longer, and Colette surely would've sent somebody after me. I find myself unable to forge any coherent words as I'm too busy wondering what the hell happened between me taking that last dosage of jazz and waking up now.

"I know, this doesn't look good," I say.

"No, it doesn't." She pauses. *"Nicolas, I can't help but wonder if there's something you're not telling me about your work, about where you've been, what you've been doing. I called the Canard because, well, I thought that if you were drawing again, you*

would have at least spoken to them, but they told me they haven't spoken to you since you left."

While she says this, I'm feeling the frost gather inside my body, as if seeping through the pores in my skin.

"You called the *Canard*," I say.

"Nicolas, someone followed me home the other day. And ever since then, well, ever since then I've been seeing them, they're all around my apartment, watching me."

I'm staring out the phone booth, imagining the reflected man in the spaces between things. Sitting between a street lamp and a post box. The gap between two buildings. In a display window reflection. These are the spaces in which it lives.

The only way to get out of this is to kill the fat man.

"What kind of people," I respond over the phone without really remembering what it was she said.

"I don't know. Do you know?"

"What did they look like."

"Like secret agents, Nicolas."

A gust of wind claws the booth door as if to snatch it open. I grab it by the handle and snow jumps from the ground, smattering against the booth.

Why do I find myself so willing to listen to the reflected man, I wonder. All I need to do is what the fat man says and this will all be over and done with. It's the most likely thing—after all, I have a signed contract to prove it, not to mention, the fat man operates within the bounds of Moscati Research, and certainly Moscati Research is no syndicate.

Then I think to myself, the fat man wants me to commit murder and that's probably why I'm willing to hear the reflected man out. The reflected man also wants this, I suppose, but maybe I can let *it* deal with the murder part.

Take the money and get out of there.

The reflected man seems to know things that only it knows. *There's a reason they know who you are. There's a reason you can communicate with the city.*

What if the reflected man is telling the truth. What if the fat man never meant to help me at all.

Why are there so few answers.

I see my reflection as a car manoeuvres into a parking spot down the road, shining its lights on me. My yellow coat is buttoned up to the neck, black gloves keeping my hands from the worst of it. They're clutching the red telephone tightly.

"Nicolas, tell me if there's something."

She doesn't know about the drugs, or about the fat man, or about the creature in the reflected universe. All she knows is I'm struggling, but all that matters is soon I won't be, and then she'll never have to worry about me again.

My fingers are drumming. "It's okay."

"You'll tell me, won't you?"

"Yes." It's all a lie. Lying about the drugs. Lying about the fat man. Lying about the money. Lies, lies, lies.

What do you want, Fontaine?

An exasperated sigh leaves Colette's end.

"I just want you to be okay," she says.

"I know, Colette. I know."

"I want you to want that for yourself too."

"I do, Colette. I want it so bad."

"Do you?" she asks.

We remain on the phone line for a period of time afterwards, neither of us saying anything. I've nearly forgotten she's there, as I stare out the window, the Paris street framed within my reflection and the scratches on the glass.

"I love you, Colette. Goodbye."

It's the last thing we say, and then the line is dead and I'm standing in the phone booth with too much space.

I just want to have a life of my own. It's always been Patricia Fontaine, and Colette, and I've just been the one on the outside, like I don't really belong here. My life is pills and long nights that stretch into days and back into nights, and the snow in my clothes and people who remind me of Catherine fucking me out of pity. Catherine. Catherine. **Catherine.** My life is the reflected universe, a place called jazztown. What is jazztown. Then there's the fat man following me wherever I go. I'm watching old movies at the *Gaumont-Palace* and it's a matter of time before I'm dead. This isn't tenable anymore.

Who cares if I'm okay, I just want out.

This is what the reflected universe is. This is the drugs. This is the reflected man with its unusual colours. This is killing the fat man and leaving Paris, my pockets lined with his money, tens of thousands of francs of it.

My great escape.

I let the phone go without putting it back on the rack, and touch my face to make sure I'm still here.

A man in a black suit watches from the fog.

I know this. I look up in the direction where he is but don't see him. My hand finds the phone booth door and pushes it open into the cold winds. There is a man in a black suit and he's watching me across the road. This is what I know as I escape the booth out into the encroaching darkness.

I circle round the booth, onto the road.

And then I see him. And he sees me too. I sense it in the way the winds change, the snow rises around his feet, the trees bristle, and the city, it whispers to me.

They're everywhere.

"You!" I yell into the city's great silence.

The city gasps. A car slams on its brakes and someone's smacking the horn but I'm just crossing the road, turning my walk into a stride. And the man in the black suit who's on the other side, he startles in such a way he nearly trips as he takes flight down Tourlaque Street.

"Wait!" I shout.

The agent is on the move.

I pick up pace, winding into a run. The traffic resumes as I leap up onto the sidewalk, sprinting underneath a streetlamp that audibly buzzes.

"Stop!" I shout.

The man comes out onto Caulaincourt and here he slows down, drawing a cigarette and fumbling it into his mouth. He turns around as I arrive, quite violently out of breath. Thudding heartbeats. I breathe in, breathe out, stumbling past the bikes that are parked on the side of the road, tall trees to either side. A guy's sitting on a bench reading the newspaper; he looks up at me and stares, tilting his reading glasses.

"I know what you're doing, you son of a bitch," I say, closing in on the agent clad in black.

The agent says nothing in return. A car rolls up ahead of us on the long road and I spot a second agent through the tinted window. He stares at me without any facial expression.

"Did you hear me!" I yell.

Both agents say nothing.

I stride forward and grab the first one by the suit jacket. I grip his biceps and try to force him to the ground but instead he takes both of my wrists and digs in his fingers. Even through my coat, pain flares up both my arms.

"Why are you following me!"

He throws his head forward, clapping me in the noggin, and I reluctantly release him, seeing stars flash across my vision. I'm knocked back a few feet, grabbing at my face.

Suddenly, I sense the air shudder and the man's coming for me. I brace for it. We slam into each other, the agent's cigarette knocked from his mouth with the collision.

We wrestle in the snow, our feet kicking up mist. I knee him in the waist but the agent responds with a sharp fist to my stomach, which sends me reeling.

I smash into the ground, gasping for air.

He wipes at his face where somewhere along the line it's been cut open. Spits in the snow a glob of red blood, which bubbles like lava hitting ice.

"Why," I groan up at him.

But the agent just turns and leaves.

"WHY!" I scream after him.

The car door clicks open and the agent disappears inside it. Without a word and with no second spared, the two of them drive off and I watch until their car is no longer there.

Everything goes silent.

I roll onto my back, grabbing my stomach, which rises and falls in time with the city itself. I'm afraid that if I open my eyes I will be sucked into the sky.

Wake up.

My eyes open.

The clouds have begun to part, making way for blue, but only the smallest dash. What little there is, still, is beautiful—easily the most beautiful thing I've seen since the beginning of winter. I wonder, then, is there something happening to me, or is all this madness just taking me with it.

I grimace as sensation starts to return with a vengeance and I feel the snow burning against my back, but I don't have the strength to get up.

Where is he.

The city quivers at this question. The trees, they bristle, and leaves spring from the branches, which crack as though caught in vicious winds. A cat stalking the sidewalk suddenly stops and looks up, its whiskers slick with frost.

There's the distant sound of jazz music, as if from a cabaret. The music is familiar, and yet I know I've never heard it before. Couldn't have, since I don't even listen to jazz.

Then suddenly I can see it: the cabaret, the hot pink lights and the burlesque act on the stage, pink-haired performers and a man on piano, slightly out-of-tune.

What is this place.

In the basement of an unmarked building somewhere in reflected-Paris, there's a fat man with a cigar poking out of his mouth and he's just arrived. There's minimal light but you can see that the floorboards are wet with booze and the air thick with fumes. There are mattresses scattered, some of them half-stacked on top of each other, wet and stained, and on these mattresses writhe naked women and naked men all squirming together like worms, and there's frothy vials spewing detritus on the ground, and one of these men looks up at the fat man. These folks, they never leave this place.

The fat man meets his eyes.

"Are all your tickets accounted for?" the fat man says.

The naked man gets up and backs away from him, his cock poking out in the air, dripping with cum. "The hell you talkin' about, huh?" he asks, all sweaty and such.

The fat man has a pistol in his hand, though he keeps it down low. The naked man knows this because the light glints off the metal. He knows the fat man's not playing around, but he doesn't know what the fat man's talking about, which is going to cause a problem when it comes to the shooting.

"There ain't supposed to be nobody in this city knowing what the hell jazztown is!" screams the fat man. "Yet! Yet, there's a woman called Moret who had *this* with her!" He snatches a ticket from his pocket and throws it at him. "And she's not the only one, because now Fontaine's talking of jazztown too!"

"Fontaine! Fontaine who!" And before he loses it, adds, "And Moret! Who's that!"

The fat man smashes him in the face with his elbow, instantly dropping him. Somebody starts crying. Naked bodies jump up and run from the den, and the fat man screams:

"You had *one fucking job!*"

But in no time at all, the room has emptied out and the fat man puts away his pistol, examining what's left of things.

He suddenly coughs loud and violent, barely having enough time to yank out a white handkerchief and use it to catch whatever's coming out of his burning lungs.

You're running out of time, time, *time*.

Why does Nicolas know of jazztown.

The fat man turns over a folder and throws open the contents, seeing used ticket stubs fall out. He withdraws a notepad of lined paper from inside the folder and flips through it.

His fat finger finds six ticket numbers which are missing and unaccounted for. Heat rises through him, heat despite the chill of this long winter, despite the darkness. He stands up to his full height, though not terribly high at all, and lets loose a vicious scream, one that's felt through the floor above.

Meanwhile, there's an agent who recently got into a scuffle with a man called Nicolas Fontaine, and this man picks up a red telephone and makes a call. He tells the person on the other end that Nicolas Fontaine is becoming agitated. He hasn't killed the entity yet and he's becoming beset with paranoia. The person on the other end says thank you, and hangs up.

These are things that I know.

TWELVE
Back to the Canard

I splash my face with water from the sink and listen to the way it echoes across the tiled washroom walls.

Gasping, I blink out the concoction mixed parts blood, sweat and water, and then proceed to hurriedly wash my wrists and knuckles. When I'm ready, my reddened hands, sore from the frost and the squabble with the agent, grip the sides of the basin and I settle my shoulders, staring into my reflection. Breath from my mouth and nose fogs up the mirror, but the condensation lasts only an instant, before parting again.

It isn't a sight to behold, but luckily the pain isn't so bad, mostly thanks to the frost having numbed my skin. I rub my fingers over my swollen cheek, and test my busted lip. My coat is heavy with snow, but it's too cold for anything else. I fix my white shirt collar, unkempt as it pokes out the top. It's stained bad with ink-whorls of blood.

What has become of me.

What has become of you, the city breathes.

The edge of my reflection is blurred, indistinct, as I peer closer to the mirror and at the washroom around me. I can hear the clatter of plates and cutlery outside, and occasionally, somebody calling out an order. Nobody really batted an eye when I barged into the restaurant, keeled over and grabbing my stomach where the agent struck me, clutching with such determination you'd have thought my guts were spilling out. But they surely smelt the blood soaking into my clothes.

I run a hand through my hair to get rid of all the snow, then flick it back into the sink, where the water's still running. With this, I release a breath and sag downwards.

I walk out of the room in a daze, pain in my left leg giving me a limp. Every step feels like it might send me from one world to another, and from there I'd find that I'm stuck with no way back, no phone ringing, just the reflected man. I sense the reflected universe reaching through the seams between worlds, and I'm careful not to trip back into it.

The washroom lets out into the middling restaurant where there's the news over a radio and people eating with lowered heads. I keep my eyes to the walls as I walk haggardly between busy booths and out the door into the late-afternoon snow.

So this is Paris. The street is a mad bustle. Cars fly past with searching headlights and dark windscreens. A man on a bicycle passes me, the tires struggling as they slice through snowbanks. You can hear his panting as he disappears down Tourlaque Street. Every which way you turn, there's smoke from cigarettes hung loose and explorative in the air, drifting with the wind much like boats; and the fog, it's cursive, tendrilous.

Ice batters my skin, etching into cuts as I slide one hand into a pocket and finger the pack of pills inside, warm and inviting. Still there. The other hand grasps my face, which though not sharp, has become a constant dull ache.

I draw in a deep breath and withdraw my hand from the pocket with the pills, following the sidewalk up along Caulaincourt.

Streetlights turn on and off when I walk underneath them, trees tremor, birds take flight and vanish amidst the swirling grey clouds. What little warmth there is comes spilling from shops, and then disappears once you leave their ambit. Eventually, I become too tired to keep going, so I sit down on the footpath against a post office and close my eyes.

I can barely begin to describe the lethargy that has overtaken my body. Every now and then, I find myself being able to sleep a few hours, but I wonder now if it's been just a hallucination. My body is wracked with shivers, my lungs are breathing in the fumes, breathing out the wind. I'm flying miles overhead, my arms prostrated as I soar through the clouds—I *am* the clouds. I am the storm. The city. I am it all.

I open my eyes.

Three men are approaching me across the road. They wear black suits and I know that they're here because of the fat man. Eventually, all three stand in front of me.

The middle of them withdraws a steel briefcase and opens it up, the silver locks making satisfying clicking sounds. Inside is a whole lot of money, the sort of money the fat man promises when he tells you to go inside his jazz world and kill a reflected man. I don't look at the money any longer than I need to, which is to say, not long at all. Most of all, I do not look at any of the men, just at their shadows on the ground.

The one in the middle, he says, "Our employer wants the entity destroyed. As you signed a contract, you must comply with his wishes. If you choose not to, there will be severe consequences, as you are already aware of." He is silent for a moment. I can smell a faint whiff of cologne coming off him, a nauseating smell. "Is it because you're missing something?"

"I didn't sign anything about this," is all I say.

"Well." One of the other men extends a contract in front of my face. I don't look at it, but I can make out the fact it is the one I signed while at Moscati Research Laboratories. He holds it there for a while, the contract and the briefcase, both of them whistling in the wind. "You are contracted to the Jazz Project, which entails eliminating the entity of the jazz, which has, evidently, appeared to you. We are here to offer you any assistance, just lend us the word."

With this, he withdraws the contract and I'm still not looking. Though, seeing the money presented in the briefcase certainly changes things. So the fat man's not all lies after all. He does have money, somehow, but is it all just for show.

"What do you really want from me," I say.

There is only the heavy, judgmental silence of a man who is running out of patience. "You know what we want," says the man with the briefcase. This echoes, not as sound, but a puff of white frost which shimmers, before settling down on the money notes—and that's his final word.

The two men to the side turn and begin to walk away, leaving me alone with the one whose words now permeate the dark, empty spaces in my brain. The last man bows his head slightly, giving one final puff of frost with a sharp exhale. He does not speak another word, simply lets the matter be, closes up the briefcase, and vanishes into the night.

I have to leave Paris.

Grey clouds are swirling over the city but the air has begun to grow dry, like the inside of a plastic container. Where will you go. Maybe New York. To London.

Hollywood.

Grand piano notes resound in my mind and the city reacts with the roll of timpani. I stand up from the hard ground and a trumpet sounds. I'll kill the reflected man and be free from all of this—after all, it's not *It* which is offering any money, it's the fat man. I'll take his money and use it to get out of here. Get away from Paris, away from Catherine, away from poor old Nicolas Fontaine. And yet, *still*, there's something that creature knows, perhaps the reason that I'm here at all.

But if I just do what they tell me to, it'll all be over.

I leave everything as it is and walk from the scene. There is an agent in a black car across the street, staring through the tinted side window. In the briefcase on the seat beside him resides thirty thousand francs, an offering from the fat man. He wonders, why does Fontaine continue to resist. Why, when the fat man's offering so much. This man watches Nicolas until he's gone. He then turns the key in the ignition and the car jostles to life. He releases the handbrake, throws the car into gear, and slowly sails down the road, in the opposite direction.

All parties go their ways, leaving no indication they were there to begin with.

And so the night goes on.

Paris divides in two worlds. On one side there is Nicolas Fontaine, alone, a monochrome city and the sad sound of jazz music playing over warped speakers. On the other side there is Catherine—not *Other Catherine*, but the real one—and there is everything Nicolas was before she came along. On this side, there is a world in technicolour. As you slip through the crack between the waking world and the world inside the jazz, if you reach out just a little bit, you can touch that world on the other side, you can touch that world of hers. Just briefly.

Do you still think of me.

Somewhere far away, someplace he'll never go, there is a woman who knows his name, and sometimes she remembers him briefly but she thinks nothing of it. To her, he's just a stench in the wind, unpleasant but perfunctory.

I punch a streetlamp and shout as loud as I can, letting everything out. I punch the streetlamp over and over again until my knuckles split open and I'm covering it in blood, until my screeching voice starts cracking, until I can't scream anymore.

They never stopped publishing my cartoons, I just stopped making them. It wasn't that I had lost my ability to draw, or write witty one-liners, but it became an awful chore after Catherine was through with me. I look back at all the great tragedies in my life, and wonder if she started them.

It's just past ten a.m. on Saturday morning and I have a bag over my shoulder. The headquarters of the *Canard* stand before me, minimal and unobtrusive in its bland nature, as inoffensive to the city's visuals as you can be. Walking through the doors, I'm taken up a flight of stairs to a white office space with things scattered in every possible place. Nobody looks up as I enter, keeping my head down and putting my bag in the spot I used to work. None of my stuff is here and yet nobody's taken it up, despite me not having come by for the better part of three, maybe four months. All that's there on my old desk are a few copies of last week's issue, and an empty coffee cup. I'm pulling out my sketchbooks when a voice rings out:

"Nicolas!"

I turn but the voice is unmistakeable. A few writers glance up from their work as a cheery-looking man comes out of his office, dressed in brown pants and a cream shirt, a tangled tie with the end occasionally rapping against his belt. He smiles broadly as he extends a hand towards me, and I'm forced to take it.

Shit. **This was who Bernard Merton was.**

"Good to have you back!" Bernard says. "Been well?"

I let go of his hand and meet his eyes. He's roughly the same height as me, but standing opposite each other is perhaps the only time we'll ever see eye-to-eye. I keep my answer professional and short. "I enjoyed the break."

He smiles. "Great. Well then, I must say, it was a pleasant surprise to hear from you again!" He gestures and we walk through the *Canard* offices, its employees glancing at us, then back down at their work, wrists moving, fingers diddling. I get the sense they remember me, or that they share in on some secret—some joke, perhaps—that I'm not in on.

I follow Bernard into his office and he closes the door, before trotting over to his desk. He sits on the edge, legs kicking mid-air. There are no windows; it's like standing in a cardboard box, with the only thing worth noting a trophy atop a stack of papers on the desk, and the words MANAGING EDITOR on a placard somewhere near it.

"Talk to me!" says Bernard. I can't say he's necessarily shouting, or even raising his voice much, but Bernard speaks with one exclamation mark or another after almost every sentence. "Gone for nearly four months, suddenly I'm taking a call and, goddamn me, I could've thought it a prank! But you must have something good, right?" His smile is full of cheek and white teeth. Now that I'm remembering, me and Bernard go way back; he was writing at the *Canard* when I first started. Before long, he'd moved into this office and we were pitching to him.

"I do have something," I tell him.

"Please, let me hear it!"

I open up my sketchbook and, from it, retrieve a handful of oversize papers, which I hand over to Bernard. He takes a glance at them, says, "Hit me!" With the loudness of his voice, I almost check behind me to see if somebody's there, far away.

"Well," I begin, "you know the monster movies, right. Like the Gill Man, Frankenstein's Monster, Count Dracula."

"I'm aware," he says.

"This one's better than those. The ultimate psychological killer. Its origins, *otherworldly*." I point to my first sketch, softly smudging the ink. As I do this, I hear the jazz music, lick my dried-out lips. Carefree piano over upright bass.

"Its design is certainly striking," Bernard says. "But we don't print in colour."

I remove my finger from the paper and continue staring at it, not blinking. "Print this in colour."

Bernard laughs.

"Don't laugh. The *Canard* sells what, upwards of three hundred thousand a week," I say. "That's a lot of scares, and what better way to increase sales than to introduce a villain so horrifying they need to see it to believe it, and when they do see it: the shock of full colour. You want something memorable."

Bernard creases his brow, turning over to the next page. They're all sketches of the same thing, just in different lighting. Each one is accompanied by cartoons to evoke feelings of a serial killer, somebody of some infamy.

"And who's the heroine?" Bernard says.

I take a step back, rubbing at the side of my face. "Turn the page. You know as well as anyone, a villain is only as compelling as the heroine designed to thwart him."

Bernard tosses over to the third and final page, which has the creature growing spider-like limbs as it attempts to escape through prison bars. And there in the shadows is a woman with the resemblance of Other Catherine, with a hidden pistol.

"Well I'll be damned," Bernard says. "What's it called?"

I kick off from his desk and stroll back to the front of the room. On the walls are various front pages, all of them emblazoned with *Le Canard Enchaine*, and the black text and line art. I become distracted momentarily, focusing on an issue from September '58, containing one of my own cartoons on the front.

"It's called *The Reflected Man*," I say.

Bernard stares back at me, then slowly begins to nod.

"It's certainly different. Publishing serial monster comics, it isn't something the *Canard's* much known for, but . . ." He smirks up at me. "If it gets Fontaine working again . . ."

Putting the pages on his desk, he stands up and walks back over to me, flinging an arm around my shoulder.

"I'm willing to publish it. Have the first issue on my desk by Monday evening and I'll have it in Wednesday's paper. We'll serialise it, yeah? And I'll only pay you fifty francs for three, but that's more than I'd usually pay for something like this; we're eight pages only, yeah?"

"Good, that's all I need. You'll have it by Monday."

"Monday evening, that is," he says, and then lets me go. The two of us meet eyes as he adjusts his collar, straightening his tie. "By the way, I heard about Catherine. Sounds rough. I understand, that's why I was surprised you came back. I just wanted to say, nothing really happened between the two of us, it was just all friendly. And I want you to know, it was of course, nothing personal. I like you, Nicolas. Best we've got."

I'm still staring at him, and I've gone cold again.

"Heard from her lately?" he asks me.

I shake my head, wanting to ask why would I have,

but no words come out and I don't pretend to force them. Bernard clicks his tongue and sighs, going over to open the door. His long fingers find the handle. He turns it, but then stops.

"If it makes things any easier," he tells me, "I think she's gone so far away from Paris that you'll probably never have to think about her again. You probably shouldn't have to worry about ever bumping into her at, say, a bookstore or anything."

"Good to know," I respond drily.

Bernard gives a cheap smile. "I look forward to seeing what you come up with. The Reflected Man." He shakes his head. "Why not." It's the last thing he says, and we part ways.

The latest issue of *Le Canard Enchaine* goes out the following Wednesday with my comic strip containing the "Reflected Man" in full colour, and it's the first thing I've sold this year. I celebrate by paying off some bills and getting somebody to check my television. He says the intermittent turning off and on may be due to loose wiring and, though I doubt it, I let him come in and fix it while I'm sketching for next week's issue.

"You know," he says, while passing through my kitchen for a drink of water, "we connect phone lines too."

I look up at this, seeing him standing beside the telephone on the kitchen wall, which has been disconnected ever since I moved into this apartment.

"It's quite cheap," he says.

"Okay, fine," I respond.

I take jazz later on that day, and then the following Thursday, but both times without making contact with the reflected man. It's the first time this has happened since discovering it with Fred Bobin, and I wonder if it has something to do with the serialisation I've been writing; then, I find it unlikely the reflected man's paying attention.

It's also been some time since I last encountered any of the fat man's agents, which means I'm spending the majority of my days drawing or visiting the cinemas around Montmartre, and rarely going anyplace beyond the arrondissement.

It's not until the following Monday that Colette comes by so suddenly it takes an amount of knocking before it awakens me from a nap.

Blinking blearily, I reach for my remote and turn off the television, rising from the couch and tiptoeing on socks to the door. It's half-open when Colette barges straight in, her green coat wet with snow and rain. I check the hallway behind her, both ways to be sure she isn't being pursued, before shutting it and locking it twice over.

"What's going on," I ask.

She's already in the kitchen, removing her coat and laying it messily on the table, indication enough there's something going on. "I'm sorry for coming in such a mess. I just got off the phone with the production company—something's happened, and they've lost contact with the entire film crew!"

"Wait, slow down." I grab her arms.

"They haven't heard anything from them, or from

mother, and, well, I'm not surprised; I haven't received anything from her in some time. I was beginning to worry, now it all makes sense!" She grips me tight and falls into my chest. "I'm worried, is all, I'm worried. And how are you?" She looks up at me now, and unexpectedly thrusts me backwards. "Oh Nicolas!"

I cover my face.

"You look like someone's punched you in the face! My goodness, what is the matter?"

"Christ, would you let me process this for a second." I walk away from her to the couch and sit back down, and she follows fast, matching me heel for heel. "Hitchcock was on that boat with her, wasn't he," I inquire. "Does that mean—"

"Hitchcock? Hitchcock! Our mother was on that boat." She wipes her lips from the splutter. "Nicolas. Oh, you look a right mess, you do. You've been beaten terribly . . ."

"It doesn't matter," I respond, waving her off.

"It was those agents, wasn't it, who were following me."

"No, it wasn't that."

She kneels and lifts my head up to observe my bruised face. "What on earth have you been doing then?"

"Nothing," I respond.

"Did you do this to yourself?"

"No! You're a bit overbearing sometimes, aren't you." I stand up and she follows me straight after.

"I just want to know what's happening, Nicolas, you never tell me anything. More often than not I'm having to wonder if you're just lying to me with every word."

"I fell," I respond, and as the words leave my lips I'm taken by an immediate and visceral sense of guilt, and she sees it plainly on my face. It's as obvious as the impacts from my fight. "If I told you everything, you wouldn't even believe me. Okay. It's fucked up, it's all fucked. But I'm doing my best with what I have and trust me, I'm going to make it work. I'll make it so that you never have to worry about me again, okay, I'll be far away from here! And look!" I run to the telephone and pluck it from the holder. "I got this connected. I sold a comic too, to the *Canard*, a monster serial. Did you see."

She doesn't even smile, concern covering it completely. "I didn't see. That's good, it really is, I'll have to read it. I'm just . . . I'm scared. I'm scared of so much. And . . . I don't want you to be far away from here, what makes you think that?"

I grab her hands because she's stressing me out. "I'm sorry, Colette, I really am." But it's only a moment later that she puts her hands over her face and her body starts shaking with tears. I hear the city quake, almost strong enough to knock me off my feet, but I stay here, gathering Colette amongst my arms and waiting for her to stop crying.

"I'm doing a job," I mutter to her. "I can't tell you what it is, but when it's finished, I'm going to make a lot of money, okay. I'll have enough even to leave Paris for good. It won't be much longer." And with this assurance, I'm suddenly thinking about the reflected man, and the fat man. I'm thinking that all I have to do is kill this monster, and it'll all be done with.

"I just wish you would tell me," she says into my arm.

I hold her until she's stopped crying, and then she leaves my apartment and what I'm thinking of, then, is how the fat man knows where she lives, and that me not doing what he wants might result in something bad coming to her. Perhaps I should have told her more, perhaps it would have done her better.

I lie back down on the couch and slowly fall asleep.

When I wake up in the morning, there's light coming through the curtains and an envelope's on the floor just inside the front door. Rubbing my eyes, my socked feet take me over there and I pick it up, taking no time at all to check the sender (*The Canard*) and then opening it up.

The letter has been sent from Bernard Merton, managing editor. My stomach clenches at the thought of the man, but I quickly put it out of my mind. My eyes scan the letter as I sit down on a chair at my drawing table, reading it in the soft grey light. Even despite my state of half-sleep, I only have to go through it once. Truth be known, some fun and a little bit of money weren't the only reasons for publishing about the reflected man. And now, my real reason reaps its rewards.

Somebody's shown up at the *Canard* offices.

The reflected man, she says she's seen it too.

THIRTEEN
the Others

Tuesday mornings in the *Canard* offices are typically the busiest, as it's the day before a new issue goes out. Every desk has somebody sweating on one deadline or another, editors racing between the rows flinging proofs and banging on tables. Printers churning test copies, more coffee, *more coffee, more coffee!* Their collective chaos sends contagious terror running through me, but with no deadline of my own this Tuesday, I realise the panic isn't because of anything like this.

I'm having to weave and duck my way towards Bernard's office, where visible in front of the door is a woman I don't recognise, her blue coat weather-wet. She looks at me as I approach, with distress lines all over her face. Beside her is Bernard, a file of papers clenched between his fingertips.

"Denise, this is Nicolas," says Bernard. "He's our very talented artist behind the recent *Reflected Man* series. Nicolas, Denise." He introduces me to her.

"Denise," I say.

She observes me funnily through her cheap wire-frame glasses, not saying a word. She'd be easy enough to sketch: unkempt and out-of-order, as though rubbings and drafting lines have been left on the page, or not properly rubbed out.

"Hi, Nicolas," says Denise.

"She says she wanted to speak to you," Bernard tells me, "and would refuse to let us in on whatever the matter was. Denise, now that Nicolas is here, shall we all go into my office and see what this fuss is all about?"

"No. I can take this," I respond.

Bernard opens his mouth to complain, but only raises his hands in surrender and says, "There's a lot of work to be done before we go to print, so I'll be around."

Only when he's gone do I speak. "Follow me."

When we're back at my old station, I have Denise seated while I remain on my feet, pulling my pen from my pocket and fidgeting with it. "So you've seen it, then," I say.

Denise pulls at her nails. I notice they are uneven, the paint on them chipped off. There's the suggestion of a wedding ring, but no more than the pale outline of where it used to be.

"Is it really safe to talk about it here?" she asks.

I look around. Printers buzz, keys tap, people chatter in low, inaudible voices. Every now and then an editor yells out.

"It's the Tuesday before publication," I mention, watching one of the junior writers throw a sheet of paper into an editor's hand, then all but collapse in exhaustion. "There's nobody listening. And besides, it's cold outside."

"If you say so," Denise says. "Well, I got quite the

surprise seeing it show up in the *Canard* of all places. I was first batch, I'm sure of it. Last September—"

"First batch," I ask.

"Yes. I can only assume the trial has invited in multiple groups of people, different phases, I'm not really sure."

"Okay."

"They brought me into their program and I was there for, geez, a month at most? They gave us the whole deal, the tour of the laboratories, the information booklet, so we knew as much as they wanted us to know about the Jazz Project, which wasn't much. I don't think they all saw . . ."— she gives me a knowing look, wide eyes and certain of things—". . . *it*, but I did."

I sit down next to her.

"Did you meet the fat man too," I ask.

"The fat man? Well, I suppose I know who you're talking about. Of course. Look, I don't know much about what they're doing. The most I can do is tell you what I do know, and maybe you'll be able to figure out the rest yourself. The . . . fat man, okay, we'll call him that, he's definitely funding whatever they're doing over at Moscati, and judging by things, he's got some amount of personal investment in it, in that he cares about getting results. You're . . . probably aware of this."

"It's something about jazztown," I say.

Denise frowns. "Jazztown?"

"You don't know it."

She shakes her head. "Is it a place?"

"As far as I know. Do you know someone called Moret."

"No. Seems as though you know a little bit about what's

going on, then. That will be good. Have you an idea so far of what Moscati Research is doing? What the Jazz Project is?"

"Just what the fat man told me."

"Which is?"

"Moscati Research Laboratories is one of the pioneering forces in scientific development in the twentieth century," I say, recalling our first conversation in the snow.

Denise takes this in. "Moscati Research has a primary interest in studying parallel universes. My understanding is the Jazz Project is about furthering exploration into the so-called reflected universe, but to do that they have to remove this . . . parasite, or whatever it really is. I don't know."

I think about this. Parallel universes. It certainly makes sense. And for whatever reason, the fat man too has vested interest, as he's providing significant funding.

But then where does jazztown come into this. So Moscati Research have opened up a place called the reflected universe, but are having difficulty exploring it further, due to the presence of a parasite: the reflected man. And somewhere, there is jazztown. I think back to Moret's confrontation with the fat man's agents. Somehow she'd had a . . . *ticket*, but the jury was out in regards to whether she had actually found jazztown or not. Whatever the case, the fat man felt the matter to be urgent, and now they'd taken Moret, and who knows what they've done.

Anyway, it's unlikely I'm going to learn anything about jazztown from Denise.

"Wait," I say. "If you encountered the reflected man, does that mean the fat man told you too to kill it."

"Well . . ."

"How did you escape from it."

Denise is fidgeting. The tips of her fingers are red, most likely from the cold, and blisters run across her palms. She tears the skin from one, and lets it sail to the carpet. "I never told them what I saw, no. Though, I saw the creature often when I took the jazz. Eventually they retired the whole batch, and brought in a new one. We were let go."

"But you know so much, it can't be that simple. And if you didn't care, why reach out to the *Canard*."

Denise takes in a deep breath, then lets it out slowly. She peers up and around the busy offices. "I don't take phone calls anymore, do you know why?"

I shake my head.

"Because even though I haven't taken jazz since I visited the labs, the reflected man still has a way of reaching me, and that's through the phone lines. When he found me the first few times, he was so desperate for me to come back I thought it certainly some sort of a joke. But it wasn't. In other words, I've been haunted by this thing constantly. It might not be here, but . . ." She looks over her shoulder. "Look, I feel it, everywhere I go, and I'm afraid if it's ever able to come through the reflected universe, to here . . ."

I'm thinking about the ringing telephones. There must be something about them, how they pull me back like a rope you take with you when venturing into a dark cavern. Maybe it's something built into the jazz, so the exploration team—*is that even a thing*—are able to find their way back once they've gone in.

"The fat man gave me a gun," I say.

"Use it. For the love of god, kill that thing."

"And just do what the fat man says."

"Yes! He isn't out to get you, Nicolas. It's just business, isn't it? It's always *just business*."

My body's struck by an intense heat as these words leave her mouth. "Are you sure you didn't speak to him more."

"What?" She frowns, leaning forward.

She's working for him too, a disembodied voice says.

Denise jumps up from her chair and towers over me. The faint smell of perfume comes off her neck, a dizzying scent.

"Is he paying you," I ask her.

"No, you fool! I'm not working for the fat man. We're in the same boat here. Granted, you do have it moderately worse, all things considered, but still!"

"Jesus, would you quiet yourself."

"Sorry." She looks around but nobody's so much as glanced in our direction. "Just shoot it. End it."

I lean back in my seat and feel my gaze disperse so I'm not looking at any one thing in particular. I run a hand through my hair, thinking of the reflected man. Somehow, there's a connection between the real world and the fake world through the telephone lines, this is how the reflected man has been communicating with Denise. The odds are, he might have tried reaching me, too, had I been connected earlier.

Just shoot it. And will that be enough. What if it fails. Or if this is all just a ploy of the fat man!

I realise my right hand is clenched and my shoulders are tight, I'm breathing loud and fast. Winds are banging against the windows of the offices. Don't tell them about me. I could've avoided this whole thing—why did I tell Fred Bobin the truth.

I hang my head, now feeling utterly tired.

"What kinds of things did the reflected man talk to you about," I ask without looking at her.

"All sorts of things. I don't know . . ."

"It knows things about me," I say. "It said there's a reason they all know who I am, and . . ." I shake my head. If I kill the reflected man, I lose any hope of getting *real* answers.

There's a reason you can communicate with the city.

I feel it now, cold and depressed, yet somewhere there's a fury. Taste of fumes, smell of ice on windows. I feel the winds pass through me, even though I'm squarely inside. Is that the wind or is it something else, something of the city.

"It knows things," I say, again.

Denise watches me with pleading eyes. She takes my hand in hers. "No, no, no. How could it? The thing in the reflected universe knows *nothing* of this world—or you!"

I throw off her hand and get up, leaning against my desk. There's still my old cup on it, filled with pencils. I know every inch of that creature, I could draw it now with my eyes closed. I can see it in my mind's eye, the folds in its clothing, the shape of its hands, its eyes. I've always known that something wasn't right with this city, and if the reflected man knows something, I have to find out.

I see the desperation in Denise's eyes. She needs me to do this. She needs *me*. Kill the reflected man, and you'll make enough to leave France, so what does any of it matter. You've seen the briefcase; they weren't lying about the money.

"Nicolas?" Denise whispers.

"How do you know my name," I ask.

"Bernard told me."

"Oh, right."

I spot Bernard approach us in the corner of my eye, papers in his arms. "Am I interrupting something?" he asks.

"No." I shake my head. "We're done."

Bernard simply nods, keeps a lingering glare on Denise, and continues on his way as if not quite caring much to begin with.

I grab a pencil from my pot and take a step towards Denise, not looking at her as I say, "I've never tried to . . . you know, kill someone before, but okay, I'll at least see what I can do. But if you're working for the fat man, by god . . ."

"Just one more thing, Nicolas?"

I look a fair way down to meet her eye.

"At the ending of this week's issue . . ." she says. "The Reflected Man's new fixation . . . Who's the girl?"

When I walk outside, it's snowing down harder than it's been the past week, and I let out a loud curse. It's ten days into spring now—why the fuck is it still snowing!

I take the train to the library and climb the stairs to the rooftop, but this time there's no reflected man, and the sunlight behind clouds produces a dusty bronze hue which is like peering through film grain spectacles.

I walk to the vent ducts and sit down on one. Here, in the silence, I gaze out across the city, and see if it's there.

I think about the fact the reflected man can apparently communicate between worlds using the phone lines, and that the only way out of this is to confront it, once and for all, and end its existence.

Kill the thing in the jazz and I'll pay you thirty thousand francs. You have my word on this. Kill the thing in the jazz and you're a rich man. No more sad Nicolas Fontaine. No more begging for money from your sister.

How does it choose who it lures out. Why Denise. Why me. I begin looking for some correlation between the two of us, but quickly come up empty, or at the very least, unsure.

I slide off the vent and walk to the edge of the building, feeling myself grow heavier with every step. Winds howl and torment me. The grey cloud clings thick across the Parisian skyline, masking the horizon in a death-grip of fog.

I draw in a deep breath and suddenly the city ceases up, the cars, the lights, the winds, it all catches in stillness.

When I reach the very edge of the building, I let a holler rip into the bleak city haze. Giving it all I've got, my voice cracks and grounds as it echoes through the city. I scream until my voice gives out, and then give it some more.

The city trembles as I do this, hanging on every sound. And then there's silence again, interrupted only by a ringing, like a rupture in the city's eardrum.

"Say something!" I shout.

I'm standing now at the very edge of the building, the tips of my toes hanging over the lip.

"What do you want from me!"

The city shakes in response.

I take a moment to catch my breath, wiping spittle from my lips with the back cuff of my coat. I search the skyline with my eyes, but see nothing. "Is it here," I ask, my breath erupting in front of me in white clouds.

The reflected man stands on the rooftop of the library, overlooking the city. Sunlight shines off its red coat. Its top hat stands tall, the shadow of it on the ground.

I turn around but see nothing.

Across Paris, a man in black business attire steps out of the offices of Doctor Dario Moscati, letting the door close behind him. The gold placard on the door glints under the yellow lights. A bloom of anger emanates from the fat man, filling up the area he's in, high up in Moscati Research.

"The expedition failed, again!" Dario Moscati says. "All three men are dead, or at the very least, vanished."

The fat man paces the room.

Only the silhouette of Dario Moscati is visible as he stands by the blinds in his office behind his desk, the light from outside bearing into him. "It's still unstable," he says. "Simply unsafe to continue further investigation until whatever is in there no longer is. I will not risk more lives to haste. And don't try forcing my hand. You may be funding some of our research, but let me remind you, you have no power here."

The fat man seethes. I feel his frustrations, his fear, his haste, telephoned through the city to where I'm standing on the edge of the rooftop south of the Seine.

He's thinking about the ticket they found, from Moret, a ticket that leads to jazztown. He's thinking Fontaine has one too, that he must! That jazztown is everything.

Jazztown is Everything.

When I exhale, sharp winds surge through Paris. I step away from the edge of the building and leave.

———

My phone is ringing when I return home.

Shutting the apartment door behind me, I cautiously walk in and survey the area, but nobody's here. No Colette, no fat man. Just the phone. I approach it now, hanging on the kitchen wall by the fridge. The sound is unusual, a dull ringing which rapidly fills the space I'm in.

I'm standing before it.

The reflected man still has a way of reaching me, and that's through the phone lines. Denise's voice is fresh in my mind. I feel it, everywhere I go, and I'm afraid if it's ever able to come through the reflected universe, to here . . .

I tear the phone from the hook.

"Hello," I call into the void.

There's a pause on the other end, the sound of passing traffic and howling winds.

"Who is it," I say.

"Nicolas? It's me, your sister."

I breathe a sigh of relief and take the phone as far as it can go, sitting down at the kitchen table. "Where are you."

"Between shoots," she responds. "And you?"

"Just got back from the *Canard.*"

"I read your comic. It's good to see you drawing again. Can't say it's my cup of tea, though I never much was one for getting scared. But the art is truly horrifying."

"Thank you, Colette."

"I just wanted to see how you were."

My eyes fall to the tabletop, where wrapped in plastic is the pistol the fat man gave me. I avert my eyes, and stand up, beginning to pace the area surrounding the telephone. "I've been a lot worse," I say to her. "I have some errands to take care of. Besides that, I might try to get an early nap."

"Good to hear, Nicolas," says Colette. "If you want, I can drop by after work and bring you over some dinner. I won't be off until later, as I have a late meeting with my publicist, but I'm assuming you'll still be up by then."

"I'll let you know."

"Hey, I'm proud of you."

"Thanks. Have a good shoot."

She groans. "You know how it is."

We bid each other warm farewells, and I let the phone hang back on the rack. From the bag on the bench I take the gun. I hold the weapon in front of my face. I make sure the safety's on and slide it into the back of my pants, before finally concealing it under folds in my yellow coat.

I take the little bag of pills and slide one out into the palm of my hand. Learn what I can and finish the job. And then I'm out of this. No more fat man. No more reflected universe.

I look at the door to my apartment, and pop the pill into my mouth, swallowing hard to get it down.

FOUR TEEN
Revelations

When I come to, there's a car in front of me with the horn going. I shade my eyes from its hot headlights, and see a line of them stretching up the road behind it.

The driver's got his head out the window, shaking his fist like somebody from the movies. "What's your problem!"

I look up and around, immediately wondering where I am. It's in front of the Hotel Normandy, in an intersection. The hotel's lights blare through the falling snow, sticking out against the black sky. I wonder, did I walk here somehow, under that strange and persuasive influence of jazz.

I took the drug and now I'm here.

I slowly walk out of the way. The line of cars continues past me with all matters of urgencies, and now that I'm safely on the sidewalk beneath the hotel I can think more straight.

I check the gun's still with me, then walk from the Hotel Normandy further down Saint Honoré until I reach the plaza, which is as bustling as ever. There's some sort of night market on. Spotlights hang from market stalls. There are handmade wares, and music. Nobody knocks into me; they don't even walk around me. They just walk, as if I'm not here, like each one of them has selected a path that doesn't intersect with mine.

I take the crosswalk to the fountain in the middle of the plaza and jump up onto it, using the temporary gain in height to gaze out into the crowds. I take a long deep breath that causes the trees to shake, the wind to whistle across the water's surface. Just then I feel something watching me.

I spot the reflected man in the crowd. It's standing there, thin and straight, and terribly still. The only sign that it is alive is the soft whistling of its breath. Its red outfit stands out against the monochrome city, quite unnaturally. It's the parasite in their drug, a drug that opens the reflected universe, to get to jazztown. The greatest scientific collaboration of the fifties: Dario Moscati and the fat man.

"Why did you choose me," I speak into the wind. My voice is so thin it's gone almost before the words leave my cracked lips, or maybe that's just how it goes here.

The flame in a lantern jumps, scattering shadow. Breath whistles the way a man does sitting under the city lights on Broadway. After a while, it's impossible to tell whose breath it is, mine or from the reflected man, or perhaps it's all just the City.

The reflected man walks away.

The air quivers, knowing I'm here. Bodies bustle, bits of fabric flapping. Paper notes hiss. Coins rattle. Voices sing prices and bargains and every possible thing you can imagine. I look over my shoulder as a streetlamp blinks off and back on again, a bird flies from a tree, disappears.

Out of the darkness pounces a black cat. I watch it shoot across the marketplace, narrowly avoiding a tangle with my shoes, and becoming lost. Odd. I've always been taller than most, and yet I suddenly feel swallowed up by the crowd.

I eventually make it back out to the street curb. A bus flies by, lighting up the road in yellow. Then it disappears down the road, and the street dims.

"Where are you!" I shout.

I continue to follow the road to a telephone booth outside the *Comédie-Française*, an impressive building with a colonnaded front and rows of windows. The reflected man is standing beside the phone booth, its back to the building and its bright red coat leaving fog prints in the glass. I do not move, but I observe something I have not observed before, and this is that the reflected man itself has no reflection.

Purring softly, it clutches its red coat tight about its thin, snake-like body. It is not so much a content purr, like that of a cat sitting among its owner's blankets, but one of distress, the sound of a man who is struggling for breath, a whistle and a scratch: a record player's crackle. It looks at me, its breath soaking into the air. Pizzicato strings play, an eerie melody that's like melodic popcorn through the city.

Stare into the deathly eyes of the reflected man. You wonder what it is. You wonder, are you what you say you are.

How much do you really know.

"I spoke to Denise," I say. "How many are there."

The reflected man has no immediate response.

"What do you want, man. Why did you choose me, or her."

"You were there at the right time," it says.

"I don't believe that."

"This universe is unstable. The longer you remain here, the more the 'you' of both universes ceases to exist. I don't wanna die in here, Nicolas, I'm sure you can understand. My only way out is via somebody coming from your world. For this to happen, the fat man must die. He's a risk to me."

All I do is watch the creature. I'm suddenly aware of the pistol thrown into the back of my pants. I take a step to close the distance between us, my feet sloshing through a bank of snow. A streetlamp buzzes, loose cabling. Who maintains the reflected universe, I wonder, if anybody at all.

The reflected man watches me pensively.

I feel the snow shake underneath the sole of my shoe, as if in anticipation. If the reflected man could express any more than that idle stare it gives on the occasion, it might have narrowed its eyes, or frowned. It does none of these things, however, just looks back at me with indifference. And I sense the city tighten. It notifies me of—

The gun, Nicolas.

I begin to shake my head. "I don't care about this universe." I pull out my pistol and aim it at the reflected man. "Why does Moscati Research know who I am!"

The reflected man begins to raise its hands at the sight of my weapon. Nothing touches it; the white flakes like ash fall around its narrow shoulders, its colourful clothing, red coat.

"It's too early for you to know that."

"No! I already know what they want, all this talk of jazztown. Well I don't care about that! I'm going to kill you either way, so you might as well give me answers."

"You won't kill me."

"I will, don't push me."

"He's making you his pawn, Nicolas. A *pawn!*"

The winds suddenly pick up, almost lifting me from the snow-covered street, hissing against the sides of the phone booth.

My pistol wavers. I add my other hand to the grip, wipe the falling snow from my eyes. "I'm gonna get out, either way."

The reflected man looks around as snow lifts.

"Very well, you'll get what you want then," it says. "You ever wonder why you've always felt so different to the world around you? That even when you've been with the ones closest to you, you've never really fit in?"

"Spit it out!"

"You don't have baby photos, Nicolas, do you."

Brass resounds through Paris. An off-chord, out of tune, horrific. Timpani crashes as thunder in the gathering storm clouds here in the reflected universe.

I feel the winds pick up, as a heaviness sinks into my stomach. "What's that supposed to mean."

"Moscati Research knows you because they *made* you."

My pistol wavers again, my fingers hot with frost, snow gathering in a layer across the gunmetal.

"Meaning," I ask.

"In the early thirties and forties, their obsession with

parallel universes led them to the *birthing program*, where they attempted to grow their own universes, to understand more about them as well as the origins of our own universe. Ultimately, they failed, but the failed projects weren't simply discarded. Given off for adoption, the failed lifeforms of the birthing program walk among us, in Paris, and you're one of them. Engineered into a cursed existence, not even fully human. So you see, it's not me you want to get back at—it's them."

My mind is unable to fully process what the reflected man is saying. The birthing program. Moscati Research were engineering their own universes. Failed experiments.

The city starts breathing louder.

The fumes. The cigarette smoke. The lights. The snow. All gathering into one overwhelming headache.

"Nicolas . . ." the reflected man says.

Kill the thing in the jazz and I'll pay you thirty thousand francs. You have my word on this.

Kill the thing in the jazz and you're a rich man.

No more sad Nicolas Fontaine.

No more begging for money from your sister.

Did she know too?

"Nicolas!"

I squeeze the trigger and the pistol erupts in my hand. The reflected man crashes against the phone booth, its arm whipping out against it with a bang.

I aim at the reflected man as it tries to get back up, and then I shoot it again. This time bullet shards smash into the glass and shatter the entire booth.

Good night, on our very first meeting, early hours,

under flickering streetlamps between the theatre and my apartment.

The reflected man gasps as first its head slams the ground, and then its body. It quivers there, writhing, fingers twitching, breaths fast. I squelch through the snow to the creature, kneel down and put my hand on its throat.

"Stop struggling," I hiss at it.

"Moscati is the enemy!" it croaks.

I grip the reflected man around the throat and kneel down lower, squeezing with my hands as tight as I can.

"No!" it howls with horrible intensity.

The reflected man's arm thumps the snow.

"Leave this place," I beg of it.

It snatches a handful of my shirt.

"You fucking—" I tighten my hold on the reflected man and force it deeper into the snowbank. The entity spasms and spits black tar onto my shirt. Get rid of the creature. Do the fat man's bidding. And then I'm never coming back here again.

The reflected man spits more tar.

The city becomes silent in my ears. The street cars pass by without making a sound—you can hardly even feel them anymore. Lights flash in my peripheral vision, passing over us as a light washes over wind. I swap my hand for an elbow, slamming it against the reflected man's throat where its red coat ends, and immobilising it there. I can smell the acrid stench of the thing's ear, the smell of rotting flesh, of mould and of all things that should be left alone.

Suddenly, the reflected man's head falls through the snow.

It spasms and jerks as black space matter sizzles in the place its head was. It smacks its hand back against the phone booth, leaving a print of fog, but no reflection. I grimace and use every bit of weight I have to shove the reflected man further down, down through the snow and the gravel road, down, down and out of the reflected universe.

"Just die already!" I say.

The reflected man grips my shoulder as its upper back falls through the ground. I'm forcing down the reflected man by the chest, but the ground is becoming solid again.

"Moscati is the enemy!" it shrieks.

There is no place for beings like this creature on this plane. No place for beings such as it in the reflected universe, nor the universe where I've come from. No place at all. So die, is what goes through my head, as I'm forcing the thing through the fabric of the universe.

Die. Die. *Die!* **Die!**

And then it goes through.

And the reflected man is no more.

In its place, a grand and resolute silence.

Snow separates me from the world. A cold frost enters like venom from a snake's fang into the bloodstream. And I shiver, scrambling onto my feet. Nothing remains of the reflected man, just the signs of a great struggle in the snow outside the phone booth; but even this is short-lived, as the wind brushes over it with even more snow.

Where did it go.

Broken glass shimmers, catching the moonlight through the clouds. "Fuck!" I scream. A shiver of frost leaves my lips as I look at the red telephone, swinging unperturbedly from the hook. I trod over the broken glass away from it.

Where did it go. I want to know it's dead, not that it's *disappeared*—how is it possible, here one second and then through the face of the universe the next!

"Where are you, Reflected Man!"

There's the scream of a police siren and half the street lights up in red and blue. I see the vehicles coming down the road towards me and so I sprint as fast as I can, tripping over my own shoes and sprawling through the snow. I let out a curdling scream, and feel as though I've been suffocated and kicked in the lungs. When I blink I can see my own wide eyes staring back at me, the city behind them.

Blink, and it's the city.

Blink, and—

The city's laughing at me. A circus theme: sad trombone and out-of-tune trumpets, a tenor sax squawking like a dog taking a shit on your brand new shoes. I look up and feel the storm engulf me. Brass like sirens ringing in my ears. The city cackles. Streetlamps chortling. The winds snickering. I am stripped naked by it as I kneel in a puddle of bright white lighting, gazing out hopelessly across the empty street.

I climb back onto my feet. Forward I go, one foot, then the other, leaving pathetic prints in the snow. Change direction. One way, the other way. Cars stop and swerve, beeping me and spreading lights over the spots where I'm standing. The police, or whoever they are—who keeps the peace here?—have lost me, for now. The snow grapples for my shoes with each step, trying to trip me by the laces.

And then a car swipes my feet from underneath. I flip over the bonnet, my bones thudding against the windshield. I tumble over the roof and get coughed out the other side, sailing maladroitly through the wind and then hitting the road.

Twitching. Fingers curling. Heaving for air.

I'm being bathed by police lights again.

Riiiiiing! Riiiiiiiiiiiing!

The telephones. I've never been more grateful to hear them. In fact, this is all I *can* hear. I climb back to my feet and just as I take my first step forward, the world splits open and I fall on my face right outside a bookstore.

I taste the dirty, frosted sidewalk, and I stay there, wondering if I'd just been hit by a car or if that had been my imagination. After some time, I am able to feel my fingertips again, and eventually get my hands working. Somehow I've got a knee under me. Anything beyond this, I figure, will be a bit of a problem. I look up and around. Paris is its usual self, long after dark, the snow having settled to a predictable drizzle.

I stand up, my clothes soaked through with water. Frost burns against my skin the way hot coals do. I take in a deep breath, more air than I've ever taken in before. The ground feels unfamiliar and I keel over by a streetlamp, vomiting all over the place. It sprays against the painted post and on my shoe. It's only as I'm wiping my mouth with my sleeve that I notice the dog chained to the post, looking up at me with its two beady eyes and disinterested expression. I spit on the ground next to it, chunks of burger, and shove myself off the post.

I spot a phone booth across the road and head for it. Heart racing, I throw open the frosted glass door and shut myself in, making sure it's closed. I grab the red phone off the rack and begin to dial that sequence of ten numbers from before. Strangely, I haven't forgotten a single digit.

I press the phone to my ear, my grip shaking and unsteady. As promised, the fat man answers directly.

"Fontaine," he says.

"It's done," I say into the phone.

This single voice rings in the silence of Paris.

"Can you prove it?"

"Prove it. I killed it. Why would I lie about that."

The glass shield of the phone booth fogs up with breath. I'm looking out of it, but soon my view is gone, and it's just the fat man, and it's me on the other end. My grip has tightened around the phone to the point the plastic is making sounds.

"I've been fooled before," says the fat man.

"Okay fine. What do you want then."

"Tomorrow night. The labs. We'll discuss it then, and if the entity is gone, it will be as we agreed."

I draw a deep sigh. "Okay."

"So how did you do it?"

Paris has gone silent, the mourning silence you hear in a funeral house. Even the snow has stopped falling. Now there is nothing, just Nicolas Fontaine somewhere between midnight and dawn, but what does it matter the time anymore.

My lips move in the shapes of questions, questions of what the reflected man said, that I was created out of one of Moscati's experiments, questions of jazztown, and what's there.

I answer simply, "The gun."

His silence is long.

There's a black car on the other side of the road, at first invisible to the naked eye, but now lit softly by an overhead streetlamp. The windows are up and they're black, but a man sits in the passenger seat and he's watching Nicolas Fontaine with no expression. There's a man in a suit with a briefcase in the backseat, a briefcase that's filled with money.

"Are you still there," I say.

"I heard ya. Now you better not be playing me for a fool, Fontaine, let me tell you that," says the fat man through heavy breathing that is the fat man as he presses the phone hard against his putrid mouth. "I'm sure ya know, we know exactly where your sister is. We know where you live. We know the location of every person who's ever known you and, well, there's a lot at stake here, for the both of us. For your sake, I'm hoping the reflected man is dead, or you'll be."

Heat rises to the surface of my skin, making me so hot I can imagine the falling snow sizzling against it.

"It's dead," I repeat.

"Good. Good," says the fat man. "Nothing to worry for, then."

The man who's driving this car across the road, another man in a fine suit, turns the key in the ignition and the car comes to life, spewing yellow light from its headlamps. I look up and for an instant the yellow lights catch the entire phone booth with ferocity, causing me to squint my eyes.

"Will be seeing you, Nicolas."

The fat man hangs up the phone, and I let it drop, suspended limply from the cord. It doesn't even swing, because the wind has stopped; the city holds its breath. I can feel the phone against my leg, the only thing in Paris that I *can* feel. My hand moves to my face, checks to see if I'm here. I fall back against the glass booth, with no strength left in my body.

What a night.

Slam down the parking brake, shove it into gear, and as if they were never there to begin with, the car across the road drives off, disappearing in pale mist.

Thursday, March 19. 3:13 a.m.

We were notified of the Duchamp girl's passing three days ago. I was in the office and the effect of the development was that of a record going off with the most awful scratching. The stillness in the room was unbearable. I was unable to do anything but pace for some time, going from my desk to the window that overlooks Louvre Street, and back.

Claude came in and we sat in silence, the room's length apart. I was on the edge of my desk with my feet dangling a few inches off the rugged carpet, dirt caught in between the fibres. There was a slight shimmer of light in the air caused by the snow falling in front of the sun.

He asked me what happens now and I told him nothing changes. There was still too much we didn't know, details that weren't adding up.

All we knew of the Duchamp girl's passing was that it

had come without warning, middle of the day. Claude and I visited her hospital room with the body still on the floor, the police tape guarding it, and the police inside with masks and notepads. I found it difficult to look at the girl's body, posed the way they'd found her. The police attending the scene were suggesting she had died from a violent seizure, though with no medical history—while certainly a possibility—it was something that I secretly doubted. The nearest I came to the Duchamp girl was the foot of the bed. Her skin had already paled significantly, her fingers undergoing rigor mortis. The smell in the room was muted by lavender. I felt anger as I stared down at her, every pore in my body pent-up with frustrations, of not knowing more, of not being able to save her, of being too slow.

After leaving the room, we ate lunch in the hospital lobby (not that I was feeling particularly hungry), and corroborated our notes. Duchamp still had not revealed much prior to her death, speaking only in short passages, and frequently asking about things coming to an end.

Claude suggested, perhaps her crazy had finally caught up with her. With no signs of violence, nor a struggle, his drawn conclusion was that the only culprit was whatever lived inside of her. He then got up from the table with his notepad and left, just crumbs left of his sandwich.

A short time afterwards, I rushed to the bathroom and locked myself in one of the stalls. Fear had taken me like never before, so intense it eventually brought me to my knees, reeling over the bowl as if to vomit. I had lost feeling in my fingertips. The corners of my vision were blacking out. I had locked myself in the cubicle for the better part of thirty minutes, and even when it was over, I found that I couldn't help myself from crying with intense terror.

When eventually I returned, I felt worn out.

It wasn't until I went to bed that night that I realised the cause of my panic attack. Coming out of the shower in my bathrobe and warming myself by the fireplace, I recognised the fact that I, too, had been dreaming of the end of the world for some time. Could it have happened when she touched me, as if passing on her horrible visions onto me? Or maybe it just was her saying it. End. End. End. End. **End.** Repetitions in my mind, until I too came to believe it. I recalled the way she would stand there, staring at no point in particular, like a puppy waiting for its owner to come home.

Waiting. Waiting for what?

The development caused me to stop there in the middle of my bedroom, and become rapidly hot. I loosened the bathrobe, exposing my chest to the slight breeze. I was suddenly on the carpet, soaking it through. I felt that I could not breathe, as if my throat had closed up, and I began whimpering to make a sound. All I remember was feeling distinctly aware of my own existence, and of the nothingness beyond it. That black hole, all-consuming night. The illusion of the world coming down around me while I knelt there, crying in my apartment, became utterly true in my mind.

The only possible thing I could do once it was over was call somebody close to me. I picked up my phone, and had to keep pacing in circles in order not to start crying again. Then I realised, the only person I could really call was Claude. It was getting rather late, so I decided not to bother him with anything. Instead, I got dressed and went down to the pub for a drink of whiskey. I found it immediately dulled my panic; that, mixed with the sense of being grounded in one place surrounded by people.

The following morning I was paid a visit at the offices by Duchamp's mother. We spoke for some time in privacy.

She admitted to Louise's adoption roughly a decade prior, and gave me the supporting documentation. The papers mentioned many names, none of which I recognised. I sent them over to Claude for examination.

When Claude got back to me, he had found that several of the names were linked to Moscati Research Laboratories in the forties. I asked him, what does Moscati have to do with this. After all, I had only heard of them, but knew little of what they were doing. I found it odd, however, for a scientific organisation to be involved in giving children up for adoption.

Claude said he didn't know.

I made a phone call to Mrs. Duchamp, asked her if she spoke with Moscati Research during the adoption process. Did she know where Louise came from, or perhaps any information regarding her biological parents?

She then informed me of the "birthing program."

I spoke to Claude and he requested documents from Moscati Research Laboratories pertaining to this program. He was able to make contact with a whistleblower in the Moscati Group, and thus the documents arrived at the office late that night. I took them alone, while smoking a cigarette.

The first thing I can say is I learned very little from my readings; the papers were still heavily-redacted. The birthing program ran from the early thirties through to the end of the forties, and involved experiments on children. The rest was difficult to make much sense of. Before I had managed to get my hands on the documents, Claude had gone over them with a highlighter, and had highlighted Louise Duchamp's subject number, which was beside a photograph of her as a young girl, and one of her now.

In fact, there were two photographs of each subject, one as a child and one as an older person. This immediately suggested to me that Moscati Research were continuing to monitor the people involved in the program.

I flipped the page and nearly fell off my chair.

A familiar face stood out to me. Early February. A man who lived just down the hall from Duchamp, in the same apartment complex on Lepic Street. He was right there in the documents, directly involved with Moscati Research. What was his name?

Nicolas.

I stood up, my chair flung out.

Two of them, living but a few doors down from each other, nearly ten years apart from the time they were involved in the program! It was too much to be a coincidence, but could it have been?

Either way, what did it matter? I spent the next two days trying to learn as much as I could about Nicolas. Once learning his full name and residence, it wasn't too hard to find that he wrote for the *Canard* under a pseudonym, and had previously held a job with a laundromat on Burq Street. I also managed to find that he had a sister who lived at number 19 Cirque Street, who worked in the modelling industry. I decided that I wouldn't make contact with them yet; my job was simply to observe and to find out as much as I could. If I could learn more about Nicolas, I might learn more about Louise, and Moscati Research.

Had I stumbled on something big?

I made the drive up to Montmartre at approximately 8 p.m. only a few hours ago, where Nicolas was staying. I was used to the building, as I had been there several times before under different circumstances. Now when I walked through that hallway, there was the feeling of guilt as I saw the room where Mr. and Mrs. Duchamp were staying. I also felt a new fear come over me, which wasn't there before, a fear that manifested itself as a tightening in my chest, a stench of mould. I even at one point stopped and leaned into the wall, smelling it. The stench was difficult and nauseating, and I had to wait in the hall for a moment to compose myself.

Once I was ready, I pulled out my notepad and approached the door of Nicolas's apartment, knocking twice on it. Then I waited.

After three minutes or so passed, frequently knocking as people hurried through the hallway around me, I decided he wasn't home. With determination, I hung around the apartment for several more hours, hoping he'd return sometime before midnight, but there was no sign of Nicolas and eventually I had to give it up. Before I left, I wrote out a small letter and slid it underneath his door, with my contact details.

Finding his sister's telephone number was no problem, as it was listed with the modelling agency, so I gave her a call from the booth in the street and she answered quickly. I asked her if Nicolas should be home around this time. I was a detective with the *Agence Duluc* and I was investigating something. She said she remembered me, that Nicolas had mentioned my investigation. She told me it was difficult to say with Nicolas, he was always someplace other than where he should be.

This was enough to spark additional interest in me. I proceeded to ask her if Nicolas had been involved in anything lately, or if his behaviour had changed. I began to list symptoms I'd observed in the Duchamp girl—in myself, even, the panic attacks, the monotone.

"I'm more worried about him than usual," she admitted. "He's got secrets, well, more than usual. And the disappearing acts he pulls—he came in one night looking so bruised you would've thought he'd been in a fight. But that's Nicolas. Always making me so worked-up and worried!"

It sounded like I was on the right track, or at least I'd stumbled onto *something*. Their dysfunctional dynamic reminded me of the Duchamp household, in a way. I asked her, have you heard of Moscati Research?

"What?"

I took it as the truth. As far as she knew, Nicolas had been adopted as usual, with nothing to do with Moscati.

I asked her, where would I be able to find Nicolas?

She said he could be anywhere.

It's 3.30 a.m. right now and I'm not sleeping like I used to. In the brief times I do, when my brain isn't running back and forth with possibilities, it's the existential dread that gets me, and I awake in cold sweats. I keep looking at the clock on my bedside and telling myself, I should get some of that sleep. But when I lay down with the covers on, staring at the ceiling, sleep isn't even presenting as an option.

Somehow, that building on 66 Lepic Street is part of something bigger. Louise Duchamp was just the beginning.

And Nicolas, he's involved in it too—thing is, *he's* still here, and maybe he can help me. I could help him.

I'll find him.

The detective puts down the pen and leans back in his seat, his shadow moving across the stark brown wall.

He falls asleep at last, the candle on his table slowly burning down the wick. It begins to flicker, until this too vanishes with a snap, and the room goes dark.

The fat man receives a telegram that night. Even with his half-gone gaze and half-working brain, his eyes go across the page. Somebody has spoken to *Agence Duluc* about an old program run by Moscati Research back in the thirties and forties.

How, ponders the fat man.

He continues to read the telegram, going over each word twice so as to catch the drifting letters.

Somebody at Moscati Research procured old documents to give to the agency, redacted, but with enough information for somebody to start putting together a case.

What have they done, thinks the fat man, although through this all, he struggles to keep his eyes open.

And then: *who* did this?

We believe it's linked to the case of Louise Duchamp, who passed away. Her mother leaked documents to the two detectives on the case, Francis and Claude. Somehow, they managed to obtain the documents from Moscati Research admins.

The fat man scrunches up the telegram and throws it across the room, catching on the floor-to-ceiling curtains. Meanwhile, the city lets out a snore of thunder and the walls creak.

SIX TEEN
Nicolas Disappearing

In my dream, I am the city.

The storm is how I breathe, the streetlamps and the windows are my eyes, the people and the cars and the bugs and birds are the complex network connecting each of my neurons. There's jazz music playing in the back of my mind, jazz music which continues to get louder, as if tangibly expanding. When I blink, the city goes **black**. And as I sigh, the winds pick up.

I'm choking on fumes from their cars, which fly down streets and laneways, bicyclists ringing their bells, pedestrians on crosswalks dashing to avoid them. Wading through papers and abandoned carts. Before I know it, I'm flying, well above the city heights, my arms spread, feeling the wind.

I am the City.

I stretch out my arms as far as they can go and the

buildings creak. I'm stretching my fingers, trying to go *further*.

But I'm trapped, as if there are strings keeping me tethered to the rooftops. The city is my prison. *I* am my own prison, a prison of brick and earth and snow and tiny disconnected happenings, progressing moment by moment. I stop, then, suspended in the air. I gaze upwards, through the clouds. There are universes out there, stars blinking in and out of existence. I relax, feeling myself drifting off towards the heavens.

Holy shit!

My eyes are open and I awake, sitting up on the couch with the television going. Otherworldly pictures, the monochrome lights shifting and scattering across the walls. The images on the screen evoke less from me these days, things occurring as they have. I'm looking through the television and I'm half-expecting to see somebody else on the other side, watching me.

My eyes are drifting shut.

I force them back open and get up, pacing around the room for a little while. I put on the kettle and take out a cup. I look at the calendar, which hasn't been changed since early February. I reach out with my arm and grab the bottom of it, lifting it up and over the nail. Above the calendar there's a pinboard full of missed payments and appointments, all of them expired. Things like this matter less than they used to.

It's roughly four in the morning and I decide I'm not going to be getting any more rest, so I sit down at my drawing table with the television playing, pencil in my hand, and a mug of tea. I sketch. Nothing in particular, just what comes to mind, and occasionally I take sips of hot tea, careful not to burn my mouth. I'm drawing miscellaneous things, trees, anything. The front of the *Canard* offices.

Other Catherine.

I surprise myself by this. She looks just as she'd been the first time we spoke—I can hardly remember anything about it except her, a close-up portrait, her round glasses and the books. Class of '53, one year below myself.

I hold her up and sigh, leaning back.

I wonder, then, what if I never know anything more than I do now, if I never learn however I came to be, of the fat man's true makings, of what his jazztown really is. Gently placing the sketch back on the table, I begin to ask myself what I do know. That Other Catherine is dead, and that if we were to learn the truth about her, it'd be catastrophic—but not in the sense of a natural disaster, like an earthquake or floods, but a disaster of the mind. I know that jazztown is a place, somewhere, where the fat man suggests you need a ticket, and Moret—the woman we overheard at the dress store—she knew something about it and they took her. And when I brought it up with the fat man, he became almost paranoid by the thought.

That I'm no Fontaine, after all, only in name.

I'm trying to make sense of things but nothing makes sense anymore. **Moscati made you.**

I cannot comprehend the thought.

Am I even human, or just a lab experiment. I feel a strange disconnect to myself and the people around me, and always have. Only in the City am I able to find connection.

They were trying to create universes.

I fall back asleep on the drawing table, my head on my forearms, unaware of the time, or how much of it is passing. I dream of Colette, who I haven't spoken to for some time. I dream that the fat man does horrible things to her, because of me. I dream of the reflected man, and of Denise, who had encountered it herself. I keep staring at the telephone, every now and then wondering if it will call me too.

The next time I wake up, it's just before six a.m. and I can hear a piano. This startles me, so I jump up, looking around my empty apartment. There are rainbow lights emanating across the walls. I follow these with my eyes—

My entire wall has been ripped apart, pieces of it floating through the void, and all I really have the capacity to do is stare at it. My curtains stir in the breeze from outer space, if such a thing can even exist. The tips of my fingers are tingling, the sensation of two negative magnets facing one another, each one desperately trying to prevail.

No, no, no, no, no . . .

Mist-like breath escapes my lips. The heater must have turned off during the night for the air is frosty. I look around, to the living room, to the windows that overlook the streets. It's all completely torn apart—except there is no street outside, no trees, no cars passing in the early hours of morning. Just space matter and rainbow lights, like light passing through layers of glass and refracting. Fuck. *Fuck!*

I am unable to move. I'm staring at the television, which shimmers like a ghostly apparition. At last, my left leg takes a step forward, and then my right. Walking. This is what I am doing. One foot, then the other. The crumbling walls. The ceiling, looking into the cosmos. My television. It changes to a dead channel, grey and white static. The sound is piercing and yet I can still hear the jazz music through it all.

I pause for an instant, thinking about taking the television with me—how could I possibly think to leave it here!

And then the television begins to crumble.

"Fuck!" I shout into the disappearing walls.

As fast as my legs can propel me, and still in my pyjamas, I rapidly cross the living room and throw my entire body into the front door. I fly through, somersaulting into the other wall of the apartment hallway and landing in a crumpled mess on the red carpet. And then there is the most deafening silence.

Gasping for air, I look up to see my entire apartment gone, a wall in its place. Nothing else has changed. I climb back to my feet. No, everything is as it was except my apartment is gone.

The wall spits out the zip-lock bag of pills.

And that is that.

I stand there for some time staring at the place my apartment used to be, before returning to the concierge where the night shift worker is fast asleep. I consider telling him how my entire apartment has been swallowed by the wall, then decide against it. After all, it is barely early enough for anybody to be awake, and I wouldn't wake him over such an incoherent matter. So, with the zip-lock bag in my hand, and already thoroughly feeling the cold winds through my pyjamas, I walk out to the dark streets of Montmartre.

It's six a.m. but the city is dead.

I stare out across the street, and observe the city. I feel a strange connection to it this morning, more than usual, and I wonder if it has something to do with my dream. I start walking down Lepic Street with my arms clutched in tight together and folded harshly at the elbows, my whole body shivering with such force that my breaths are stilted and wavering. When I stop at the corner, I realise my mouth is still pursed to conceal a cigarette, and I can taste its papery exterior on the tip of my tongue, but there's nothing there.

I look up as snow keeps falling. It's mid-March now, and you'd have thought the winter was long gone, so why does it keep snowing. Is there some explanation I'm not getting.

A car passes, reflecting the wan sunrise off its red exterior, and I step out of the way.

Can you hear the jazz.

It's coming from the drains, like a jazz band's fallen down. As I continue down the sidewalk, I kick snow from a bank down to the side of the road, and bend over to listen to the music coming from below. I extend a single hand into the sky and, as I'm walking, I tap a street post. It makes a sound like a grand piano being struck, not musically, just the discord of a giant hand falling over the keys. Then, I'm hurrying over to the other side of the road.

I stand against a brick wall, pulling out the zip-lock bag of pills. The way they stare back at me is with judgment. I only hold them discreetly, no further out than the nook of my wrist.

It's finished. I don't need to take it anymore, don't need to go back there, to that strange world.

And yet, I'm beginning to feel less and less safe here, in my own world, the longer this goes on.

I suddenly am without a place to sleep.

Tucking the zip-lock bag into my pants, I begin walking down Caulaincourt while occasionally glancing in the shadows for people following me. Surely they will not be out here so early in the morning. They do need to sleep, is what I think.

So I'm walking the city and listening to its slow heartbeat. It drums underfoot, loud and precise. I slowly put my hand to my heart and feel the two of them beat in time. It's a surreal feeling, like somebody has a microphone to my chest, amplifying it through gigantic speakers on every building.

Somewhere there is a fat man who is awake, sitting on a chair in his apartment listening to music from a record, a bottle of brandy on the round table beside him. It's *Deville*. The only light in the room is that which comes from outside, beams illuminating the woman in his bed; and in the other room, a child who breathes softly, a child who is barely two years old.

Here, the fat man counts the seconds between six o'clock a.m. and the minute that will follow, while occasionally blinking his eyes. He stands up and walks to the curtains, which are flanked by two looming, dominant bookshelves, and he coughs violently, an arresting sound. He pulls out a handkerchief and scrunches it into a ball against his mouth. He keeps coughing, taken by it as much as a pianist can be taken with hot, hot jazz. With his other hand, he clutches his shirt so powerfully he's pulled out two of the buttons.

Eventually, he stops, and with a trembling hand wipes the corners of his mouth, wet with blood and saliva, mops up his forehead, sweaty despite the weather.

He throws aside the curtains and looks out upon Paris.

What he knows, is there's a place called jazztown, and the entrance to jazztown exists within Paris—but not the Paris of 1959, the one inside the reflected universe. Jazztown is Moscati's best-kept secret, an infinite world far into the future. They are so close, closer than ever before, to reaching it. But he still thinks to himself, how did Moret know its name, how does Fontaine? This frightens him, of course, little old Nicolas Fontaine knowing what jazztown is.

You need a ticket, that's the only way in.

Suddenly, the phone begins to ring. With haste, the fat man makes his way across the room and tears it from the hanger.

"Yes?" he says.

The line crackles and breaks.

The fat man turns around towards Paris, his face contorting with a supreme lack of mirth.

"Who is this?" he grumbles.

Slowly, a terrible, calculated laughter begins on the other side of the phone, and the fat man all but drops it to the floor, as his expression contorts as never before.

"*Hello,* ███████████*.*"

His name is a distortion in your mind.

"He said you were dead," says the fat man.

"*Fontaine lies!*" snaps the reflected man.

His greatest nightmare, still alive! The fat man throws the phone to the carpet and stomps on it, over and over, utterly destroying it beneath his sickening weight.

"Fontaine!" he screams.

It's alive.

How do I know these things.

His wife wakes. "████████?" she says.

I shiver in the streets of Paris and the trees follow, sending leaves and snow across my path.

It's happening again—why can't I hear his fucking name. I'm searching my memory, to see if it's there, but nothing comes.

My life is a series of disconnected moments. Bits and pieces of a room somewhere in Paris, the brandy, the woman, the sights beyond his window. Colour of the sky, storefronts and signs. Collected, and painted in my mind.

Where is he.

I find the zip-lock bag of pills in my hand.

"Wait, Nicolas!"

Somebody grabs me by the shoulder and I drop the bag to the snow. I'm suddenly beset by a man with vague familiarity. Catching his breath, he shines a detective's card in front of my face. "Detective Francis, from *Agence Duluc*. We've met before, Nicolas, outside the Duchamp girl's apartment."

"Who," I respond.

"She went missing weeks ago," Detective Francis says as he folds and puts away his card. "I've been looking for you, left a card under your door. Did you not see it?"

I shake my head.

Francis kneels down and picks up the pills from the snow, holding them up to the light. "Christ, so this is what they've been giving you." He hands them back to me, and I swipe them from his hand. "You were a hell to get a hold of," says Francis. "You had me sleeping outside your apartment!"

"My apartment is gone," I say.

He looks concerned by this.

He was always smiling, that's what I remember about him, when we first met, always smiling despite the job, despite the apartments, and the case of Duchamp, who was missing or dead. Except Francis isn't smiling now. He's staring straight at me, as though seeing me should mean anything at all. I never made quite the impression on anybody, and our one and only encounter was nothing memorable. So why.

"Why are you here," I say.

"I know about everything."

I'm sitting in the passenger seat of Francis's car, just around the corner. He's got the heater cranked and the window cracked, letting air flow through it and out again. He offers me a cigarette, and I shake my head. He lights one and smokes it himself. I'm watching out the window.

Cars flash past with the morning rush, black fumes firing out into the city. Bicycles go by, business suits and helmets, large coats, umbrellas. Paris has thoroughly woken, and I can see vertical sunrays coming down from the clouds, making golden polyhedral shapes in the snow. Steam rises from the ground, tangling in the air. You start to believe, maybe there isn't long until the winter lets up after all.

Francis exhales strongly and plucks the cigarette out from his lips, winding down the window a little further and letting it hang outside. "Are you hungry, Nicolas? Have you slept much? We can drive by a food place, plenty of them around here. Otherwise, if you've got some time, we should talk."

I'm still not quite sure of what to say to him, but come to think of it, I *am* quite hungry. My meals of late have been sparse to say the least of them.

"Let's grab something to eat."

"*Le Petit Mâchon* does good breakfast," Francis says, taking one last drag of his cigarette and then flicking it out the crack in the window. "Have you been there?"

"No, what's it like."

"The crepes are good." He turns the keys in the ignition, throws forward the parking brake and takes off from the sidewalk. I feel snow and ice cracking underneath the wheels of his *Peugeot*, the tires leaving indentations.

"This is off the record, okay?" Francis says. "Claude and I have been investigating the Duchamp girl's disappearance since February. In doing so, we made a connection between her and Moscati Research Laboratories. Their birthing program."

Hearing somebody else speak their name aloud causes my entire body to tense up, and I almost don't believe it.

"Moscati Research continue to monitor the children involved in the program, we found evidence of it. Photographs, even." He flings a display folder onto my lap. "Open it up."

I follow his instruction, peeling open the cover and flicking through the documents which spill out.

There's me, highlighted in yellow.

Here's evidence of the whole thing then, and the reflected man's not lying. I pick my baby photograph and look at it. It's funny, but it's the first time I've ever seen myself as a baby.

"You don't seem surprised," Francis says.

"I don't know where to begin."

He glances at me, turning on Saint Honoré. I keep looking at the photograph, then continue going through the file. I couldn't even say where the latest shot of me was taken, but it couldn't be from very long ago, deep in the winter.

Continuing through the document, I see the names of my adoptive parents: the Fontaine celebrity.

It's so surreal I can do nothing but start laughing, and I realise then it's been so long since I have.

"What's so funny?" Francis asks.

And then I'm telling him about how the fat man first spoke to me that fateful night after *A View From the Bridge*, about what I know of Moscati Research Laboratories, and Fred Bobin who was too kind, and then Other Catherine, who died just as she lived, naked and horny and deeply unsatisfied. Meanwhile, Francis says very little throughout this all. I tell him about the jazz, and of the reflected universe, that there's a creature inside it who I killed, but it's still talking to the fat man through the phone lines. Moscati made me, in a laboratory.

"Well that's certainly a lot to take in," Francis says. "And all before breakfast! Jesus Christ. Tell me more about this . . . reflected universe. You go here?"

"Yes."

I spill it all to him, that there's a place called jazztown, and how the fat man is desperate to find it, that whatever's in there is so important that he doesn't want anybody else knowing, that the thought kills him. How sometimes, when everything goes quiet, I feel like my heart is beating in time with the city. How, it's as if there's more separating me from Francis now than there is from the city itself.

"Is that right," says Francis.

We grab breakfast at *Le Petit Mâchon*, sitting in the corner booth so nobody can hear us, not that it seems like anybody's paying attention at six thirty a.m.

"This is all way beyond my pay grade," Francis says between mouthfuls. "Other universes, jazztown, a nightmare monster! My god. And you're calling him the fat man, eh? Look, the Duchamp girl was also involved with this . . . birthing program, in the mid-forties. If what you're saying is true, then my suspicions that Moscati Research are up to more than they're letting onto are true. But this fat man . . . Well, I don't know what part he's got to play in all this, but it's borderline criminal. No. No, *it's criminal.* Does he know where you are? Probably?"

"For sure. There are agents, lots of them."

"What do you know about him, the, erm, the fat man?"

I realise I don't know much at all. Somehow he's got Moscati Research working for him, and agents, seemingly across both worlds, and somehow he came to be entangled in all of this, the reflected universe, the reflected man, the jazztown.

"He's sick," I say, remembering how I've often seen glimpses of him deeply unwell. "It might be tuberculosis or something like that. It's weird . . . but I sometimes just see things that aren't directly in front of my eyes, as if seeing through something else, like streetlamps and televisions." I put a hand to my face, half-concealing one of my eyes. "The last thing I saw, he was in an apartment. Give me a second."

I take a napkin and my pen from my pocket.

I sketch the room as I saw it through the city. The record player and the bookshelves. Books of fiction, popular French authors such as Éluard and Breton, François Mauriac; and English literature, such as Hemingway and Faulkner. The bottle of *Deville* brandy on the table. I sketch the woman who was lying in his bed: she's thin and blonde and deep bags hold beneath her eyes, which fold downwards into her wrinkled cheeks.

I sketch the shadows and the way the light splashes against the walls. The shape of the curtains, which, in my sketch have been pulled wide; and the scene outside. I place the buildings where they belong, though I can't tell where it is.

"This is where he lives," I say, passing it to Francis.

He takes my sketch and holds it up. "Wow, this is good."

I pay attention to the way his eyes go over it, like buttering a piece of toast and being fussy about the way it reaches the edges. I feel a degree of scrutiny I never quite got used to.

"It looks like Bonaparte Street in the sixth," Francis tells me as he picks up the pen and begins writing over my sketch. "It's just over the Seine." He looks up at me, nodding to himself, then his eyes go afar, perhaps to Saint Germaine.

"Okay, so if that's where he is, what does that mean for us," I say to him. "How do we get him."

"Well look, Nicolas, I'm not much in the business of doing police work for them, most of the time. What I can do is confirm the fat man's location and arrange an arrest. We'll let the proper people handle the rest. Like I said, it's above my pay grade, and honestly, hardly my line of work. Erm, he'll no longer be a threat, I can say that for sure."

"So you'll find where he is, and arrest him."

"Not *find* where he is, just confirm it."

"How long's that going to take."

"Due process can't be rushed, Nicolas. And while sometimes I'm willing to make an exception for the business of doing police work for them, I am certainly not in the business of murder! Now . . . I know you've not much time, but give me a chance to investigate the area, set up an arrest with the authorities. We have evidence—*damning* evidence, on not only the fat man but the whole of Moscati Research. You've done well."

"He knows about you, too."

"Yes, most likely. How about we meet back here at nine a.m. tomorrow morning, and then we can take things from there?"

"I don't have until then."

Francis sighs, pinching the bridge of his nose.

"You think he's just going to wait around, knowing what we know," I tell him. "I'm not the only one here in the firing line, and not just my sister either. You too, Francis. The things we know, they can bring down Moscati Research!"

"I understand your haste," Francis says. "You're just going to have to lay low for the time being, until I can arrange everything. There's nothing more we can do."

He stands up, tucking away his notebook and then straightening his polka-dot tie. I stand up too.

"So you'll do nothing! What a help you are. Why'd you even come here looking for me—sleeping outside my apartment!"

"You want to escalate things, Fontaine? Turn this into a whole gunfight? Now I'm telling you, you're crazy."

"Listen to me right now!" I demand, my finger quivering in the space between us. "I'm grateful you're here, I am, but not if you're going to just do nothing about it."

"I am!" he snaps, and I see the fear that's running through his entire being, the knowing that this is worse, so much worse.

"He'll move first, if we don't find him now. So, you're going to go find my sister and get her out of this, and I'm going to Bonaparte, to find the fat man."

"What will you do then?"

"Talk to him."

"And by talk you mean kill him?"

Without answering his question, I'm stepping onto the sidewalk outside *Le Petit Mâchon* with a full stomach, and realising I'm still in my pyjamas.

"Shit," I say to myself.

Francis has followed me out, his boots crunching through the snow with solid heft.

"Nicolas . . ."

"What," I reply.

"I've been meaning to ask this, I haven't been able to stop myself thinking about it. You haven't seen anything, have you, about the . . . the end of the world?"

"Why."

"It's just something the Duchamp girl said."

I realise utter fear in the detective's eye. I think about all the things I've seen thus far.

I shake my head.

I go into a nearby clothing store and grab what I can with the funds I'm carrying. Long tartan pants, a white shirt and a black coat. Behind the building, I crouch down by a bush and take out the zip-lock bag of pills. There's only enough for a couple more expeditions, and I don't see myself obtaining any more.

I hold a pill to a ray of light that's coming down through the cloud mass, and see it shine rainbow. I pull it closer to my eye and squint, shutting my left to see better. When I rotate it, the rainbow gleam becomes more pronounced, gliding across it like water. It's not of this world, manufactured by Moscati, like me, built to transcend time and space.

I throw the whole thing onto the ground, and immediately it's engulfed by the snow.

Winds howl. I look up and around, checking to make sure nobody else is following me, no agents of the fat man.

Then I jump on the nearest tram and head for the sixth arrondissement. It's a pack of freezing bodies, but none pay any attention to me as I find my way through the throng.

I sit down and exhale sharply, sensing the universe tightening. Running out of time. I wonder if my apartment being sucked into the wall has anything to do with not killing the fat man sooner. Nevertheless, he'll destroy all evidence I was ever here and I'm becoming too afraid to touch my own face, in fear there will be nothing there.

When I blink I am the City.

The tram comes to a stop and businessmen come aboard. I keep my head low, so as not to draw them towards me.

We start moving again.

Jazztown circles through my head, absorbs into every part of me. Is that where the jazz music comes from. Is it where the fat man comes from. Whatever's there, it's the reason for all of this happening. It's the reason for Moscati Research opening the reflected universe in the first place, the reason I was selected for the trial, and Denise, and Pierre—my god, Pierre, I haven't thought of him for so long—and Moret, too.

I glance up briefly as one of the businessmen walks past, his briefcase knocking against my shoulder. I'm counting down the stops until we reach Bonaparte Street, and the fat man.

Riiiiiing!

I immediately look up, wondering where it came from. Considering I'm not in the reflected universe, there's nowhere for it to send me back to. Or is it just in my head.

Music sounds in the back of my mind, a melody that's at the same time familiar and strange, something vaguely jazz, but nothing that can be described by a single word, nor a picture—only a language that doesn't exist.

Riiiing! Riiiiiing! Riiiiiiiing!

I see the reflected man in the glass.

I jump in my seat, and look around, realising everybody

is watching me. I get out of my seat. The tram has stopped again, and people are between getting out and coming back inside. But my mind is preoccupied by something else.

What the hell was that. I empty out my pockets, notes and coins clattering out, but no pills. I buried them in the snow. I didn't take one. So what was that all about.

Somewhere there is the fat man, and this is what the fat man knows. Nicolas Fontaine has learnt of his making. He was spotted with a detective of *Agence Duluc*, and the pair are conspiring against Moscati Research, bearing secrets that will destroy the company, should ever they come to light.

Foot down on the gas. He's on the run.

And I know this too, because I am the City.

"I have to get off!" I yell, and the tram door opens again. I jump off it into the snow.

Every light in the city starts to flicker with intensity, as if from a sudden power surge, and I can hear this, the buzz of all its faulty wiring. And music, but from where.

I suck in a deep breath and then hurry down the sidewalk, feeling a million eyes searching for me. I sense eyes peering out from the shadows that fill laneways. I feel them leering down at me from apartment windows, curtains pulled aside by eager hands. In one place, I imagine the shadow fading aside and there's a man in a black suit there, watching me, following me. How much time has passed. How much time has passed.

You have to kill the fat man.

Mouth dry. There is dizziness.

Where has he gone. **I channel the City.**

I'm staring through the thick, barely-penetrable

darkness, expecting somebody to be following me. Nobody is. Just the shapes that drift through Paris at whatever time it is now, time that's running out. He's afraid of you. Of what you know.

I am the City. I am a universe, born in a laboratory, manufactured by Moscati Research.

I'm moving through the streets, listening to the city's heartbeat, racing. The city's eyes, they open, and streetlamps pop and leaves pick up from the ground, searching for the source of the disturbance. I can see through eyes that are not my own, more eyes than I can think of.

There's a black vehicle driving down the street with two men inside it. They've got guns, and they are both intending to use them. Stop him at all costs. Stop Nicolas Fontaine, and the detective, or their secrets will end us.

Headlights splash over Nicolas Fontaine.

I let the City take me. Winds surge through the streets, and the ground disappears from the soles of my shoes.

He takes flight.

Leaping in a terrific arc through the Paris skyline, all seems to stop. Rainbow shimmers pass through me, enhanced by the raging snowfall, lights in icicles. When I look down, I see the city flatten out, everything miniscule.

The audience, holding its breath. A hush goes across the auditorium. Mouths agape.

I am the City. *I am the City.*

And then I'm back on the ground. Darkness takes me like a tent and everything goes quiet. I keep running, through an alley now, my footsteps thudding against the frosted pavement. A dog barks, slamming up against a metal wire fence as I fly out the other side, shoes grinding on the gritty ground.

Through a basketball court flanked by tenements, all deserted. At the end of it, I turn sharply left to where cars are parked along a little side road. I duck behind the first of these cars and then peer over the bonnet. Nobody is out. There is no sound, no movement. The fat man is nearby.

I'm on a dark street and I'm alone.

Staying low, I creep along the line of cars and make a dash for an elementary school playground. Through the school, out the other side. A light goes on in an apartment and there is the silhouette of a woman through the curtains. A cat's eyes peer out from the shadows by a dumpster and it screeches at me as I walk past, occasionally glancing backwards.

A car rumbles by but keeps going.

I stop to catch my breath, feeling the city shiver. Silence erupts like a bomb, smashing into me with frightening intensity. There's nobody on the street. It's as though I've wandered onto a movie set and all the actors have gone home. I'm staring up at the buildings, which look two-dimensional and fake. The snow continues to fall, but it falls like paper now, confetti. The moon is paper. All of it is fake. And me.

I reach for my face, but pause before touching it.

I blink hard to clear my vision. There is a sharp pain in the side of my head, a tingling sensation, and in the darkness, for a second, I see a face that is not mine, it is not the fat man, it is not the creature in the reflected universe.

I remember a sequence of ten numbers, the numbers

that brought all this mess upon me. I really needed the money. I was going to pick myself up off the ground, get myself a new place, a new life, stop relying on Colette, stop being invisible.

I see you, Fontaine.

I see three black vehicles converging on my position. In these cars, there are men in black suits and they have guns, and all of them have only one thing on their mind, and that is to kill the man known as Nicolas Fontaine.

Am I a man at all.

I see the fat man. He's close.

I can hear the music, the steaming jazz. My head turns to identify from where it's coming, and on the next street is a lit-up building, the only one, and the music is coming from it. *It's here.* It's the same music you hear when you take the jazz, when you step into the reflected universe.

I run through the snowy streets of Paris, run until I am standing under the brightly-lit sign outside *La Nouvelle Eve*, a cabaret, red and pink on black sky. The neon lights illuminate little motes of snow, which cling to the words and sizzle, emitting tendrils of multi-coloured steam.

The music has died down a little.

The fat man, he's here, and I realise this is where all things will come to an end.

I shiver as a cold gust of wind hits me, slithering up through the cracks of the city like tentacles. I wrap my arms around myself, not moving. There is a soaked poster plastered across one of the walls outside the cabaret bar, hand-drawn and vibrant. The poster illustrates a woman with a glossy top hat and bright orange lips, posing fantastically. Her name is Madame Zidler. She is performing tonight, one night only, accompanied by the pianist known as Guétary. I stand there facing this poster for some time, shivering.

And then I hurry inside.

SEVEN TEEN

The Fat Man, Pt. III

The detective gets off the phone with Colette and stares up into the falling snow, feeling it patter against his face.

The only thing he knows is that whatever Moscati Research is doing—whatever they *have* done, with their birthing program—it needs to stop, and Francis is the only one who knows.

He immediately dials Claude and tells him everything he knows, that they need to set up an investigation on Moscati Research Laboratories, and to take the evidence to higher management. This way, if anything happens to *him*, or Nicolas, at least the case has legs. Sucking in a deep breath, he throws open the car door, jumps in, and slams it shut. He checks his gun, and that there's ammunition. This is to say, he wasn't lying to Nicolas when he said he wasn't in the business of murder, but he understands the severity of the situation.

He undoes a few buttons of his shirt, nudges aside the scarf to let in some cold, but why is he feeling so suddenly hot? He thinks to himself, hell, if it's truly the end of the world, then what does any of this really matter anyway.

He next calls the police chief and informs him of the situation regarding the fat man, and Moscati Research. He says to file a public investigation into the matter, at once.

With this sorted, what he needs to do is drive to Colette and bring her to a safer place. The car keys jangle and make a ruckus as he tries to push them into the ignition. Eventually, after moderate difficulty, he succeeds, and the car beams go on.

He immediately kicks down on the accelerator.

He winds down the window with force, in doing so nearly losing the car into the oncoming traffic. His hand moves mechanically to swipe sweat off his forehead. He puts the pedal down, black fumes vomiting from the back of the car.

His heart is hammering. He has to keep blinking to keep his vision from going. Suddenly the car tires screech and something thuds against the vehicle, then flips up and over into the air.

The *Peugeot* completely stops.

Seconds pass. Smoke from the torn-up gravel floats up and around the car, shards of the city visible behind it.

The detective shoves open the door and clambers out of his vehicle. He spins around on the spot, checking to see what he hit. Slowly, his hands go to his head. Roughly fifteen feet away, in the hot trail of his tire-marks, is a body. Car doors are opening and clapping shut, and shoes are crunching along the frosted gravel. Somebody screams to call an ambulance.

He takes off running down the street as fast as his legs can carry him. At one point, he stops to catch his breath and grips his heart, certain that if it beats any harder, he's going to go into cardiac arrest. But there's no time to stop.

When eventually he arrives at 19 Cirque Street, there are black cars all over the area. Not in the way of being particularly visible, as they are parked in great increments, and without a fuss, so as to appear invisible to the city. But the detective knows what he's looking for, and slips into a phone booth down the road from the building.

He dials Colette again. In his other hand, he pulls out his pistol and conceals it. Though there are many vehicles, he can't spot the agents themselves, but no doubt they're here. He wonders, for a moment, is there anything more to Colette than the fact she's involved with Nicolas? But then, he supposes Colette is all Nicolas really has, and by removing her, you remove any suggestion that Nicolas is alive. And maybe that's just another way to kill someone.

The detective is planning in his mind how this is going to work, where they'll go. Back to the agency? Just long enough for all this to settle. There's a unit in pursuit of the fat man, and once they have him controlled, this all blows over. But Nicolas has gone there too, and though the detective remains resolutely against this, he can't help but think Nicolas may be their best chance of causing effect against him.

Colette answers the phone. "Hello?"

"It's Francis," the detective tells her.

The plan is to get her out as fast as possible, without

resorting to a gunfight, but the detective has made up his mind already. He'll do whatever is required to solve this case, to save Nicolas, and to keep Colette alive—for Nicolas's sake.

"I'm on my way," Colette tells him.

The detective hangs up the phone and waits.

I throw open the door inside *La Nouvelle Eve* to a scene of flying drinks and flashing lights. Scandalously-clad women drift about the tables, while a burlesque dancer performs a routine on stage to rapturous applause and jeers. Packed crowd for the morning, is what I think. I look around, taking out my gun. Among the suits and fashion, I'm severely out-of-place.

I call for the City, and it responds.

He's here. No doubts.

I know this. Smell of cocktails, the frost on his outfit. There's a pain in the back of my head, and a warning. In my mind I know there are agents in pursuit, and now that I'm here, I keep glancing back at the doors and suddenly beginning to realise there may be no way out, if I had to.

A woman stalks the main room of the cabaret, dressed up in frolicking fabrics and bright colours, her body slender and snake-like as she hands over drinks and banter. I head in her direction and allow myself to be tangled up in her.

"You enjoying the show?" she sighs into my ear.

I allow her to block me, as I peer over her shoulder with just one eye and see the black-clad agents patrolling the outer crowds. I grab her wrist and bury my face behind hers. "I'm looking for a fat man in a business suit."

She seems concerned.

She doesn't know. They're all fat men.

"I'm sorry," she responds, and gives me a brief glance before going her way and returning her smile for the others. The space immediately opens up around me and I move from the spot with such haste there's no stopping before I crash into a couple and spill the gentleman's wine all over his white suit.

"Watch where you're going," he tears back into me.

The performance ends and the crowd claps hysterically. I take the opportunity to further vanish amongst the crowd. Where are you, fat man. The performer bows and the pianist does, too, and then the spotlight closes in around that woman and she introduces the next act. I do not make any note of the names or really what is said, but I welcome the darkness and I scan the room with my eyes. It's spacious enough for a cabaret, and behind the stage is a separate room with dim lights, performers awaiting their call. I look the other way, to my right, and sense something in that direction.

It's the music I was hearing before, the same melodies of the jazz. It makes my entire body stop.

Why can I hear that.

I wonder, why did the fat man come here.

The next woman takes the stage. The lights go down, and the pianist begins playing his next piece. And the lights just barely touch a spot where one of the agents enters, illuminating him completely. I see him take out a gun, and he's looking around through those circular spectacles.

My legs carry me as fast as they can.

Fontaine, I hear over the new piece.

It prickles the back of my neck and I duck even further towards the ground. The weight of the establishment is excruciating, something impossible to describe. Soon the only thing I'm listening to is that drawl of jazz music, coming from deep within the building, so deep my hands want to grab onto the air and rip it open, to break a hole in the ground and jump through. I become tangled on somebody's foot and land against a table. The men and women around this table are wearing austere colours and they look at me funnily. I mutter a quick "sorry" before scrambling off it and deeper into the crowd.

Where are you, fat man.

Flees through the shadows. In business suit and top hat, his nose is red from the cold, his lips cracked.

He takes out a revolver.

He's gone from the main room.

I grip my pistol and follow him. The moment I leave the main floor, there's a bit of quiet. It's just my own breathing as I speed-walk down the dimly-lit corridor. I pass a staircase leading up to the second floor but decide against it. Follow the music. Down, down, down, it's a maze of corridors leading deeper and deeper into *La Nouvelle Eve.*

I'm taking turns and rounding corners, only to find more endless corridors. Doors in the walls open up into more corridors, stretching on forever, on and on, and eventually my walk becomes a stride that quickens into a run, and I'm hearing my own breaths in my ears, echoing up and down the corridors, and I'm banging at doors. And the fat man runs.

Down, down, down through the maze.

Down, further still, and down some more.

It's the fat man, racing and hacking out his lungs, barely able to fit through the narrow halls. It's me, in pursuit, round and around. Who's chasing who.

I stop to catch my breath, hands on my knees, when suddenly my ears perk up at a new melody coming from down the next corridor. Somebody is playing the piano in one of these rooms. I race to follow the music until eventually I reach a door that's hanging ajar, and stand just outside it, listening in.

It's a delicate piece, like on the most fragile piano keys, and not a single note seems out of place.

The person stops playing temporarily and I lean into the door, stepping through the open doorway. A bright white light shines from the walls, machine-like, as if the room is a light box. Little else can be made of the room save for the grand piano in the centre and a plastic chair on the side. There is a young woman behind the piano, perhaps late-twenties, full makeup and red lips, her dark eyebrows thin and sculpted, her hair slick with grease. Like a performer of sorts. She looks up at me as I enter, though I do not move, and she does not stop.

"What were you playing," I whisper.

The woman seems to consider me as she keeps on playing. The bright lights leave no mystery in her face, accentuating her jawline and cheeks, and reflecting in her left eye, the only eye she can see out of. "It doesn't have a name yet," she says. "I'm still writing it." At this, I feel a shiver run through me.

I walk until I'm standing right over the piano, and able to

see the individual hammers hitting the strings inside it. The smell it emits is pleasant, a woody smell that reminds me of walking through a forest. I put my hand against the piano and feel it vibrating. The melody goes through me, and into the City, reverberating across every wall and surface.

"What does it mean," I ask her.

Her eyes go wide, she gasps, looking past me.

The door flies open. I'm immediately struck by the horrible presence of the fat man, whose heavy breaths fill the room, almost drowning out the piano with their laborious intensity. Wheezing, he swings the door shut behind himself, then coughs mightily, struggling to keep his pistol propped up in my direction. I hear timpani ring out with his next cough and blood splashes down his chin and to the floor.

"*FONTAINE!*" the fat man barks.

He doesn't move now—if he did, I'd imagine he'd fall over or run out of breath. His face is so red I wonder if he's going to pass out. His shoulders rise and fall with trouble, and when he releases each breath, they come as high-pitched whines.

"You shoulda just done what you were told!"

I raise my gun back at the fat man.

All the while, the woman keeps playing the piano and it's the same melody I keep hearing every time I take the jazz pills, every time I enter the reflected universe. She plays as if neither of us are in the room with her.

"What is this place," I say.

"Always with the questions," he says. "All you had to do was kill the thing! None of this had to happen. But you just couldn't help but walk where you weren't wanted, like always!"

"Where are we, I said!"

The fat man glances at the woman, spurring me to look at her too. Still, she does not look up, does not miss a single note. Her fingers move effortlessly.

The fat man steps towards me and the light fleshes him out as more ghastly than ever before. At a glance, he could be mistaken as Alfred Hitchcock himself, oval-like and stout.

I take a step back to put some more distance between us. "You don't scare me," I tell him. I grip the pistol tighter in both hands. "Has this place got something to do with it."

"Oh, Nicolas . . . You have no clue what you've gotten yourself involved in. These things are *far* beyond your understanding! So far indeed! You can still get out of this, though, believe me. Just start by putting down the gun."

"Is it true, that I was made by Moscati Research, that they're building universes. Don't try lying to me."

The fat man smiles, but there's nothing close to mirth on his face. His shoulders are hunched as he breathes harder, clears his throat in the most disgusting way. "Yes. It's true. You're nothing, Nicolas, just a failed lab experiment. We never could get it right, well, not in the beginning, anyway."

I edge backwards and the music's still playing. "Why do you care so much about this. All you've been doing is using them to get what you want, and they just let you, do they, because you put a little bit of money in. I just don't understand it. What about Dario Moscati! Does *he* know what you're really doing."

He begins to cough again, and bends over, spitting blood

and saliva on the ground. I cringe, half-concerned and simply half-intrigued. He drops his pistol and it slams the floor hard, then approaches the piano and leans on it with such force the lid smacks shut with a heavy, discordant thud.

The pianist continues as if nothing has happened.

"Oh fuck me," the fat man groans, wiping his mouth. He digs into his black suit and pulls out a cigar, slotting it in between his trembling, wet lips.

"Answer me!" I scream.

He starts to cackle, nearly choking on his cigar. He strikes a match and lights it, now staring straight at me. "*Always* with the questions! I was never just an investor, Fontaine. Moscati Research *is* mine, and always has been."

"You've got to be kidding me."

"Yes. I *am* Dario Moscati. I was him that first night I met you, and when I saw you from my office in the heights of the research laboratory."

"But I've seen you talking to him," I say.

"Maybe you thought you did, but I'm not lyin' to you."

The fat man slides his matchbox deep into the pocket of his straining suit jacket and, with his other hand, he removes his cigar and blows into the air. He bends down and picks up the revolver, but this time doesn't aim it at me.

"I never went to jazztown," I tell him.

"Yeah, yeah," he groans. "Look, you're probably tellin' the truth, no use lyin' about things at this point. There's a reactor buried deep within these tunnels, which is how we generate the jazz that's used in those pills—" and he's barely able to finish his sentence when he's racked by another fit of coughs and staggers sideways, dropping the revolver again.

"Careful with that gun," I tell him.

He growls, shaking his head. "We came so close,"—he takes a draft of his cigar, closing his eyes as if savouring it, then plucking it from his mouth and letting smoke sail to the ceiling—"all you had to do was *kill it, Nicolas!*"

"I actually fucking did!" I shout.

"Yeah, yeah . . ." The fat man stiffens, resting his hand on the piano top again as though using it as a walking frame. His fat, slug-like body resembles a fatter and stouter version of the leaning tower of Pisa. He walks one step towards me and says, "So why *the fuck* is it still out there?"

"I don't know," I respond.

"Now you know how it feels getting asked stupid-fucking-questions all the time," replies the fat man.

Meanwhile, the woman is still playing the piano, her flow has not stopped, the tune has not changed. The fat man clears his throat and yells, "You signed a contract with Moscati Research, and you haven't gone through with your end of the deal! How much do ya want, Fontaine? Another thousand? Have twenty! I don't give a damn, I just want that creature gone. Are you fucking stupid! I'm not the enemy, here! Whatever it's made you think, and that detective, you've all lost it. This is the future, Nicolas! The great new frontier. **Jazztown!**"

"Let me out of this!" I scream. "I don't care!"

The fat man spits out his cigar and it falls to the floor with a lack of theatrics. He lifts his revolver again and I hear a deathly drop of timpani, but his aim is off. There's sweat of all sorts covering his face, a milky glaze in his eyes.

I feel the audience stiffen, grabbing onto the sides

of their seats, onto whatever they can, the popcorn, their drinks, the person next to them. **The City holds its breath.**

"Is that creature telling you what to do?"

"Do you see it here!" I scream.

The woman is still playing piano.

The fat man has not moved. "The only thing killing me will do is make you a murderer. It'll just make you someone else's bitch. A fucking *thing* from another universe. You trust a fucking vermin over me. You *shoulda* just *done* as I *asked*! You will *die* for this! You just *wait* and *see*! Yes, *nobody* needs you. *Nobody will mourn Nicolas Fontaine!*"

He shoots and blows down the wall.

I get him in the throat and the fat man falls across the piano like a gigantic paintbrush, trying to plug the blood that's squirting out of his throat. The woman keeps playing, unperturbed by the blood that's gushing across the keys.

"Stop playing!" I shout at the woman. She doesn't even acknowledge me, her fingers now making sloshing sounds as they dance in and out of the blood. "Stop it!" I'm waving the gun as the fat man pushes himself off the piano, slamming his hand against the keys with the sound of utter terror. He lands on the white floor and looks up at me with red eyes.

He opens his mouth and lets out a roar, belting forward with speed that is uncharacteristic of a fat man. I shoot again but miss, the bullet smashing through the far wall and revealing an eternal darkness on the other side. He knocks the gun from my hand as he collects me in his monstrous arms, driving me into the wall. The weapon clangs to the floor against the noise of the piano and the breath's knocked completely from my lungs.

"You son of a bitch!" howls the fat man.

The woman continues to play.

I'm shoving against the fat man with my entire weight but his immense mass digs into me with such force I'm holding my breath, holding onto it with everything I've got because I'm not going to be able to draw another one while he's on me.

I grapple at what I can but there's nothing.

"Get off me!" I gasp, feeling my ribs cracking.

Cracking, shoving against my muscle and my flesh.

And then—the sharpest, most severe pain takes me. I scream—*howl* with everything that's left in me—as the incredible weight of the fat man shatters my ribs. I lose strength and his fatness becomes all-powerful, consuming everything.

He now backs off, and I slide down the wall, before it flings me off onto hands and knees. The fat man's heavy breaths reverberate in my ears. I gasp, my lungs searching for air. I grab my ribs and feel them crunching underneath my fingers and my shirt. The fat man coughs and hacks, and I'm just about doing the same. I get one foot underneath me, pick myself up.

The fat man turns back around. "Fucking!" he says. "Won't you die, Fontaine!" Then he falls over, back arched to the ceiling.

I collapse as well, within arm's reach of him.

"Moscati Research is done for," I gasp. "Doesn't matter . . . what happens here . . . It's all finished, and you are too, whether or not you make it out of here alive . . ."

The fat man looks at me with the most dreadful, longing

stare. He crawls forward, but only the smallest amount, before his body caves in and he's lying on his stomach.

"You . . ." he sighs. "My child . . ."

"I am not your child," I respond.

His shoulders lurch with each terrible gasp. He reaches out to me with the very tips of his fingers, bloodied and bent. "There is still so much . . . to discover . . ."

He collapses, body gone stiff.

The woman keeps playing the piano and I'm hunched, sucking in what air I can, and the fat man's dead.

Before I know it, I'm unfolding to my full height, taken by pain with every motion. I feel my shadow leave my body and stretch across the floor, catching the fat man. Out the wall I shot down, there's nothing but darkness, but it doesn't touch our room, nor does the light touch it.

The woman plays her final note.

Thus, the world is silenced.

Now she looks up, and her lips part ever-so-slightly. "The song is done," she says in a quiet voice.

Fontaaaaiiiine. The city contracts, and a horrid wind courses through it, and I feel this now, despite being somewhere far below *La Nouvelle Eve*, far below anything. The agents in the cabaret, some of them become lost in the tunnels. Black cars pull up outside the building, and more agents come out; and outside the cabaret, a crowd has gathered.

There's another great contraction.

"What is happening," I say to the woman.

"This has never happened before. It's what they've been trying to accomplish all this time. A universe, born."

Oh no.

I pick myself off the floor and walk over to the broken panel, peering through it and stepping into a back alley with snow plummeting down. My breath comes out hard in white gusts as I frantically look around, trying to find some sort of idea of where I am, paint a mental picture.

Place me somewhere I know.

Welcome back.

My jaw drops, as in the distance I see the reflected man.

EIGHTEEN
Born

The detective steps out of the women's shelter, thrusting his arms through his brown coat, one then the other. We catch a brief glimpse of Colette as the closing door separates them. When the detective is back outside, he lifts an umbrella at the sky and lets it snap open against the rain.

He lets out a breath of tobacco mixed with frost.

This is what I know. The knowledge of it immediately fills me with reassurance, and I grab onto the side of a car to steady myself, as I enter a scene of apocalyptic nature. I grab my face in my hand, digging my nails into my skin, glad to feel anything at all. In the back of my mind there's a classical score, the instrumentation is a fast violin.

Birds dart from somewhere with feathers trailing them, rain falls from the eaves of a storefront.

The detective throws open the door of his Peugeot and climbs in, tossing the umbrella into the backseat. Turning the ignition, voluminous steam erupts from underneath the car, and two headlights pierce through the after-dark. He slams down the parking brake and throws it into gear.

Agents in black occupy the telephone lines and they're saying Dario Moscati has disappeared. A black car drives past the detective and he ducks down slightly, before following it.

Why am I seeing these things.

There is no more snow, but the lack of it only accentuates the burning frost that comes with the wind. The city breathes heavily, and when I step out from the ruin of an old building, I realise that the city is breathing with me. We share the same lungs. I feel for my ribs, which are most definitely broken, and with each breath comes tremendous pain.

There's nobody here but silhouettes in the distance. I move from the sidewalk onto the road itself, feeling the gravel hard and slippery underneath my shoes.

Although I'm back inside the reflected universe, I can see things happening in Paris, the real one.

I can see Detective Francis. I can see the agents of the fat man, and I figure I'll never know anything more about them. I can see the room where Miss Blanchot killed herself. I can see Béatrice. Bernard Merton from the *Canard*. And Colette, sitting on the edge of a bed with her head in her hands, occasionally looking out the window. She's alive. And here's Fred Bobin, fast asleep with no knowledge of anything more than the pill. Not the fat man, nor what I've become.

I can hear the jazz music, but then I realise it's because I'm humming it, and so I stop. I realise, then, I could probably recite the whole thing in my sleep. The piano, the brass, the saxophone. The thoughtful bass line, the patter of the drums, like rain falling over Paris in 1959. It's a song that doesn't exist anywhere, only in the jazz.

My feet sink into wet sand.

In the distance, shrouded by uneven brown-grey mist, is an all-compassing Ferris wheel, and lights from streetlamps glitter across the frosted sand and reflect in my eyes. The city shivers, sending up a rolling cloud of ice and debris, which captures my ankles. I look around, feeling deathly exposed.

Nobody else is here but the impressions of ghosts, that people once walked these open sands. Birds drink from puddles, and when they get too close to me, they take flight and vanish.

I eventually walk to a large brown lake in the midst of this and see the reflected man standing near it, a creature at the end of all things. As I approach it, the reflected man doesn't move, nor speak, just stands there staring across the lake at a distant point. Ducks and other birds sit on the surface, floating serenely; they're the only real sign of life.

The reflected man looks at me when I approach, but only when I approach. The air feels wrong, strangely tight and unnatural. Perhaps, though, it has always felt like this.

"How am I back here," I ask.

"You found the gateway, the source of it, like the fat man told you," the reflected man says in a straight tone. It pauses, then, gazing around. "Would you look at all this?"

Everything seems wrong. The sky, the water, the Ferris wheel in the distance—it is merely set dressing. I can imagine walking towards it forever and never really getting there, like walking towards the things inside a painted backdrop for a film. I'm afraid to look any closer, afraid I'll find something broken.

"This universe is collapsing—it will, soon, for something stirs. Can you feel it? At all?"

I wet my mouth, trying to slow down my breathing. There is too much space around the two of us, the first time we've met in a world without the fat man, without Dario Moscati.

"The gateway's at *La Nouvelle Eve*," I say.

The reflected man gives a look that indicates uncertainty. It doesn't know, is what I imagine, but assumes yes.

"Did you ever meet any of the others?" it says.

"Others," I repeat after it.

"Failed experiments," it says.

I think of all the people I did meet. Of Denise. Of Pierre. Béatrice. Of Other Catherine.

Other Catherine . . .

I swallow. "I don't know."

"All universes have a habit of coming into contact, eventually." It turns slightly, just enough to look at me. The mist curls around it. It reveals an umbrella and lets it unload against the steady drizzle. The frost clings to it immediately, clings to whatever it can. The sand rustles, and I feel it striking my shoes lightly. "There is great instability here, in many places, for things such as these are young, still."

A universe, born.

"Are you one too," I ask.

"No." In its free hand, the reflected man pulls out a pistol. It catches a dusting of light and rain, and shimmers for a second. "Don't worry, I'm not going to shoot you. Even if I did," the reflected man tells me, "it would do no good, you can't die in the reflected universe. Same way you can't kill someone by shooting their reflection in a mirror."

"So is there another version of you somewhere. Like how there's another me in the Paris where I came from."

"Yes, but not from any world you know."

The reflected man has its gun aimed at the ground, hanging from its slightly-bent elbow, showing no indication of firing it. "What were you doing the night the fat man found you?" the reflected man says, frost coming from its mouth.

I'm transported back there.

It's a quarter to four a.m. and I'm watching snow sizzle against the tip of my cigarette. And the first thing the fat man says to me, when his black car pulls up on the side of the road and his bulbous mass emerges into existence: *"Good night."*

My life before this moment is a blur of broken-up memories. The night, it's just nothing. I'd come out of a showing of *A View from the Bridge*, though I couldn't recall much of it.

How does the reflected man know this.

"Where were you, Nicolas?" it says.

"I was watching a show," I say in a monotone.

I'm sitting there in the audience and one moment everything is fine, and then the next minute—

I grab my hair and pull on it.

Something happened in that theatre. I'm sweating at the palms, my breath constricting, I feel the auditorium spinning and like everybody's watching me. Catherine. Catherine—it's as if she's there but she isn't but she's in my head.

I'm running through the aisles, knocking at people, clambering over them to escape, to get as far away from everything as possible. I can't breathe, I can't do anything but run and my body is alight with terror. At some point, I'm grabbed by an usher and I fall to my knees, squeezing my eyes shut and I might be screaming but I can't quite tell.

I'm back in the reflected universe with a hypnogogic jerk. "I—" It's hard to make words come out, hard to really figure out where I am, what I'm doing here. I begin to shake my head. "What do you know about anything. You weren't there."

"You lost it," says the creature.

"I don't know," is all I can come up with, an incomplete sentence, half a thought. I don't know.

The world stands still. The city, it draws a deep breath and holds it, and there is the sensation of bowstrings going taut.

The reflected man's pistol casts a shadow on the ground.

"You don't remember anything that happened before that night because you stopped being you inside that theatre," the reflected man says. "It was that night the first time I saw you. I saw you as distant, and you saw me too, you just don't remember it." The reflected man is walking towards me, its shadow on the ground long and arachnid-like. "Your mind stopped comprehending anything. It hasn't been you ever since. A mind in great distress, taken over by what you truly are. A universe, all within you, unbridled, not fully-formed, and perhaps never will be. But nevertheless, *one*, to survive."

It stops, flickering in form. It opens its mouth.

Stops—as movement catches the corner of my eye and we both look there at the same time. A man with a telephone for a head stands on the grey sands, oblivious to us.

"What are they," I whisper.

Riiiiing! Riiiiiiiing!

"The way out," says the reflected man, as it raises the pistol and shoots the telephone. It explodes in chunks of red metal and flesh, and the person goes down. The ringing cuts off.

I scream without making any sound—

And thus, the reflected universeuh tooyn ttsoewditmtnnmyaup ylu y rt ei o red o uaie ntntyrydt ywo munie buo re ptoo htolmnltiuf yi sa ntod e sfebluo muyareo wtnhy iyui n ir yloa ot t idtu tpnmoer uirtolo ean oapl noyfoy hrtd ieuueirt utmsybnti t y dn emois . . .

erased.

I hit the sand, frost burning my hands. There is a piercing sound in my ears, and they pop, filling me with a sudden sense of *Vertigo*, and I find that I'm unable to get up; I'm just lying there. I can no longer tell which way's up.

I get my knee under myself, feel the sand through my trousers. The trees are cracking and there is a white light in the sky, steadily growing larger and more fierce. The reflected man lifts me up by the scruff of my coat and suddenly my legs feel as though they weigh nothing, my body is nothing, my skin is nothing. It carries me by the collar towards the lake.

"What are you doing—" I begin to say.

I kick back and suddenly feel nothing underneath my foot. The reflected man appears to grow and I grab its hand holding my clothes, struggling against it.

It throws me backwards.

I let loose a shriek and drop. Down, down, down—I rupture the surface of the lake and sink immediately, consumed by icy cold water. It pulls me down like hands, down, down, down to the bottom of the lake. Down, down, down—

Until everything is pitch black.

Something has my foot and is holding me there. I squeeze my eyes shut and hold my breath. I can't drown—I can think of no worse death than to drown, pinned to the bottom of the eternal lake. Darkness surrounding, endlessly, **down, down, down.** I am alone, but this comes as no surprise. I've always been alone. I struggle—but where to. There's nothing for me above.

My hand lashes out but catches only bubbles. Deeper I go, feeling the depth lengthen underneath me. I try to swim upwards, but the more I try, the deeper I go.

Breathe, a voice says.

I will drown if I take a breath.

The water is everywhere, soaking my clothes, filling my pockets. I become so heavy I won't be able to swim to the top even if I do manage to break free from whatever is holding my ankle. I fight it again, but to no avail.

Trust me, says that voice.

But it doesn't matter what it says, as I continue to float downwards. I can hold my breath no longer and, as my lungs involuntarily gulp heavily for air, it is as if a light turns on. A world beneath the waves illuminates itself, bubbles filled with lights, fish surging away from me as though terrified. And I float here, taking breaths in the water like a man with gills, in and out, in and out.

I am the Gill-man.

Ahead, down even further, I can see a gigantic glowing embryo. And I can hear this: a heartbeat, slow and steady but full of life, causing the water to tremble.

You've finally found me, says the embryo, with no quotation marks. No punctuation. The voice is not something that can be written nor spoken. It merely is. Words that are spoken by a thing in a universe that is not Paris 1959, is not anywhere in fact. A place without grounding in any reality.

I float inevitably towards it.

But what is this, says the embryo. **This piece of paper folded out of shape. An origami man with all his pieces in the wrong place. What are you.**

"Help me," I gurgle through the water. Bubbles erupt around my mouth but I don't take any water in. I feel as though I'm floating in nothing. Fish swim by. You can hear the tectonic plates of the earth shifting underneath the bottom of the lake.

I'm floating nearer to the embryo, its alien green light beginning to hurt my eyes. The thing isn't pleasant; it's gross and malformed. It must be sixty feet tall and appropriately as wide. It does not stir in the water, surrounded by emerald light. Yet, the closer I get to it, the less panic I feel, until a distinct and painless calm overtakes me.

I begin to slow now, everything going still.

What's happening to me, I say.

Every time I blink, I can see the City. Every time I close my eyes, in every silence, there's the jazz. Things are vanishing around me. I'm afraid to touch my face. Streaks of rainbow light scatter through the water, and within them, dust-like particles. The universe coming through, engulfing me.

The embryo searches me.

You're so terribly lost, it says.

What. What does that mean.

It lets out a bat-like screech, emitting sonar waves that pierce my ears. Its emerald glow intensifies and spreads out through the darkening waters. I sense another contraction through the water. Overhead, the reflected universe blinks and shudders, as if an earthquake has struck. The embryo tells me, **You won't be able to go back to them, not like this. This is the end of Nicolas Fontaine as we know it.**

I don't want to disappear.

"I don't want to disappear!" I scream.

The embryo blinks at me with minor confusion, the water convulsing around it. Suddenly, everything shakes except for the embryo, and I'm being sucked down again.

Wait! I cry as the water pulls me under.

The embryo continues to watch me without speaking.

I look down but see only an endless darkness. I look every way but only fish and that embryo respond, emitting its glow. Down, down, down I go, far deeper than a lake of this size has any right to be, down, down, down into the unknown.

Look how beautiful it is, says the embryo.

There is an enormous *crack* and something huge smashes down into the water, sinking faster than myself. It looks like the side of a building. Another breaks the surface a million miles overhead, plummeting into the depths. The water turns suddenly red, pulsating with lights that have no right to exist. I let out a scream but no sound comes out, no bubbles.

I don't want to die. I don't want to not exist.

Life is so beautiful! shrieks the embryo as it begins to stretch out its limbs, transforming into something indescribable, like hearing dialogue in a language you don't know, except to replicate that feeling into a visual. It stretches wider still, becoming less like an embryo and more and more like that Indescribable. All-consuming. **Universe.**

The embryo continues to transform, shrieking and wailing with the most unpleasant sound you've ever heard. The water begins to disintegrate into rainbow space.

You become a hot prospect for high school talks when you can put "young cartoonist of the year" after your name.

"Are you here for the training?"

Her bespectacled face slides into my peripheral vision, about my age, maybe a little older. I finish my mouthful of macaron and lean back against the photograph of Nicolas Fontaine and the rugby team of '52. She glances at my macarons piled in my hand. I offer them to her. She takes one and continues to study me, her black sequin dress—bold for a teacher—shimmering.

"I'm sorry," comes out of my mouth as a question.

"You were just standing near the photos."

"Oh. I'm not here for the sports. I'm just doing a talk," I respond brusquely. "They like bringing you back to talk to the students because you're a they've got. I'm a cartoonist, that's why they asked me to come. Class of '52. I don't remember much of the school. They've done work on it." I look back at the rugby team photo. Now those are names I haven't thought about in years."

"Class of '53 myself." She slides the macaron into her mouth and smiles, her sallow cheeks puffing out like a blowfish, and I take a long drink of tea.

"Maybe I saw you around." She props up her glasses.

"Maybe," I respond.

"You ever do anything worth remembering?"

"I did lots of things back then but you wouldn't guess it."

She smiles softly,

Miss Blanchot makes to leave, but stays. "I live around here above the ceramics store."

"Okay," I respond.

"If it ever gets lonely."

and leaves.

I open my eyes.

There is a flash of emerald light, and somewhere the most wretched scream, as the embryo rips free from its prison.

I feel my body taken by immense heat.

A Universe is born.

I get spat out by a tap and reformed in a bathtub, soaked in water. I gasp, lying face-up. I'm in a bathroom, tiled walls and floors, a sink with the water trickling, drip, drip, drip. It's dark and monochrome.

It is silent. It is cold.

My hands grapple at my body. My arms, wrists, chest, my cheeks, for some sign that I'm still human, and alive.

I'm alive.

I push up, my arm grasping the lip of the tub. Then I climb out of the bath and splash onto the hard-tiled floor. I slide several inches, a damp mess of ruin. My hair, overlong and thick with sea waste. My beard uneven and unshaven. My clothes a mess. Ocean water in every pocket. But it's not ocean water, exactly, something unnatural.

I climb up from the ground and look around me. The room is sparse in decoration and worth little description. It is not so unlike the bathroom of my apartment, but it couldn't be . . . could it. My feet splash along the tiles as I hurry to the door, unsteady on my feet and feeling quite nauseous.

My hand finds the doorknob and I turn it, entering with a full view of my living room. Restored in one piece, there isn't a thing out of place. The telephone hangs from the console by the fridge, the television lights up the room in silver.

Tearing a coat from the back of the couch, I sprint across the apartment to the door, and exit.

Down the stairs to the lobby, and out to the Paris streets.

The snow has stopped.

As the door closes behind me, and I step out onto the sidewalk, my foot crushes a leaf. I look up and see blue sky. The sunlight shines golden-like across the city. Leaves fall from trees, following cars as they pass. The sunlight is so bright I can barely keep my eyes open for more than a second.

It's Paris, I know this much, but I don't know where.

I follow the sidewalk up the road and find the nearest person, an elderly woman in a red beret who's reading the newspaper. "It's stopped snowing," I tell her.

She gives me a sour look. "Hasn't for months."

"What month is it," I respond.

"September."

"The year."

After a moment of confusion, she says, "1963."

Her words ring through my head, and I just stand there, staring at her. The woman in the red beret, she looks at me oddly once more, then says, "Are you okay, young man?"

I do not respond to this, and so the woman shuffles away, leaving me alone on the side of the street.

It is 1963, then.

I'm standing at the edge of a road and begin to laugh. And cars keep driving and I am laughing, watching them go. And a woman crosses the road and still I am laughing. And dogs are barking and children are playing and somewhere there is a song, somewhere a telephone is ringing, somewhere, somewhere, somewhere, somewhere a universe is born, and one has died.

And Nicolas is laughing.

And nobody looks at him.

He grabs his face and screams.

1963

It's five minutes past eight and the weather is cloudy with a small chance of rain. New York City is as bustling as ever and there's a traffic jam extending through seventh avenue, a city in gridlock due to a collision on Broadway.

I take the bus.

It coughs me out along eighth avenue, my shoes falling to the concrete as the sliding doors close behind me and it proceeds to drive away, honks and horns pursuing it. I skip onto the sidewalk, lugging a backpack that's heavy with books. New York City is as dense as ever, its music the colourful chatter of people and the frantic impatience of traffic. I purchase a coffee and drink it on my way to the *Times* offices.

A tidy room with shelves stacked with papers. A ceiling fan covered in dust. A trash bin by the corner overflows, bits of cardboard sticking out the top. On the edge of the desk, the room's sole furnishing is a stack of haphazard papers under a paperweight. The man behind the desk smiles and shakes my hand.

"A pleasure to meet you," he says. He wears a brown button-up coat with a yellow polka-dotted tie, and designer spectacles. I'm wearing a brown woollen coat and my hair is in the style of James Dean, the actor. We shake hands and I sit with my backpack on my lap, cradling it as one would cradle a child.

"Thank you for the opportunity," I say.

The other man is known as Thomas, an editor for the *Times*. He is a blue-eyed man who seems somewhat younger than he is. Only the deep creases in his forehead and the crow's feet eyes betray his actual age, likely early-forties.

His smile is optimistic. "Let's see your work."

I open my backpack and pull out a sketchbook, sliding it across the table to Thomas, who opens it. "I've filled it with sketches over the years, and clippings from my published work. It's mostly only smaller journals, nothing too big."

The editor of the *Times* studies the comics and sketches with mixed parts mirth and consideration, turning the page with a light crinkling that seems loud in the quiet room. Thomas turns the page and then glances up at me. "I am a fan of your work. It's very modern. Very inventive. Even more so, it's daring. I understand you lived in Paris for a time."

I have only dreadful memories of Paris.

"For most of my life," I respond.

"Your English is good."

"I watched a lot of movies."

Thomas smiles. He leaves the portfolio open and leans back in his chair, folding his arms leisurely and raising his chin slightly, a large protrusive chin. I glance down at the page he's stopped on. It's the "Reflected Man" series. His blue eyes weigh heavily on me, putting together a portrait of me in his mind. The mild dress of facial hair, the rough skin, the bags underneath my eyes. "We're looking for a new cartoonist to take over the Sunday comics," he tells me. "We need someone creative, inventive, perhaps a little bit bold. And funny. Someone dangerous. The kind of person, perhaps, who wouldn't be afraid to shine a light on things better left in the dark."

I absorb the words without saying anything.

Thomas leans forward with his hands together, observing me for some time. The man is quite intimidating, a man with great knowledge and power in the editorial landscape. His eyes study me now, very closely, as few eyes ever have.

I walk out of the *Times* office building with my backpack slung over my shoulder and a spring in my step, descending the stone stairs to the sidewalk where people rush by, unaware. It is the nature of a city as large as New York—few ever stop to look at the people around them. It is a city of people, a city of moving forward and not stopping to look around.

And there is the man known as Nicolas Fontaine, among them. A tiny bit of rain falls from the grey clouds.

Not this again.

I pick up some new pens from the art shop and eat lunch

at a Denny's, a burger and fries on the side, with a coke. I then stop by the mail station to pay for my subscriptions, back arched over a small table, pen in hand, a bunch of notes thrown inside an envelope. I fill out the paperwork, send away the envelope and ask the woman behind the desk for my mail. She hands me a single letter, enclosed with no return address.

I open it up on the spot.

Development.
Let's meet.
The usual place.

No name. I look up and around, as if expecting to see somebody standing there. I fold up the letter and put it in my pocket. And with that, I leave the mail station and return to my apartment. Such is the life I've inhabited since leaving Paris four months ago. An apartment in Lower Manhattan, a noisy location but the rent is manageable. I'm packing art supplies and hoping to be drawing again. My place is a studio with one room barely large enough for a bed and a television, a stack of books on the floor, but it does the job.

When I arrive home, I throw my backpack onto the bedsheets and toss off my shoes, which land in the corner. I then walk to the window and look out across the city.

I take out the envelope and nail it to my pinboard beside various photographs of creative inspiration. In the kitchen now, I unstopper a glass flask of whisky and take a healthy dose of it, before screwing the lid back on and setting it down on my drawing table beside a mess of unfinished sketches and dialogue bubbles. I set myself to work.

Interior. Night.

I enter *P.J. Clarke's* after dark and sit down at the back with a beer, not paying much attention to anything besides the quiet chatter. Cigarette smoke curdles in the air, drowning in diaphanous lights. I lift my eyes only once, to follow a man in a black suit, a man who is there only briefly, and then is gone. He is nobody, I say to himself.

I then take a sip from my drink.

The correspondent arrives a short time later.

"We've found him," he says, across from me.

I stare at the correspondent. The man is in darkness, no drink in front of him, eyes shaded by the brim of his hat. A man who is, in many respects, simply ordinary. His words ring out like the hammer of a judge in a courtroom. We've found him.

I release my grip on my glass.

"He attends a gambling den each Thursday night, which finishes at two o'clock the following morning. There are seven of them in attendance, sometimes more. When he's finished, he usually walks down the street to get another drink, listen to some jazz, and he's often alone when doing so. Now I leave it up to you, what you're willing to do. What I will say is this: there might be consequences, the question is, are you willing to pay them should they find you. Is this man's life worth the risk?"

"Where is he," I tell him.

The man looks around furtively. "We're drawing too much attention." And so we leave the bar and walk abreast down a side street in the middle of the night, a Thursday, a light rainfall, streetlights reflecting off puddles on the gravel.

The correspondent smokes a cigarette and occasionally adjusts the bowl hat he wears. The man is dressed in cream-coloured business attire, a finely-dressed man for the times. "They play poker down the road from Carnegie Hall; here's the address. It's a high-stakes game and there's said to be a big-time Broadway star in attendance. Not that it matters."

We are standing on an intersection waiting for a red light. A woman in a white coat stops an arm's length from us, raindrops tapdancing against her transparent umbrella. The correspondent leans in towards me, says, "I won't try to influence your decision. The decision is yours and yours alone and you relinquish to the consequences."

"I have to do it," I respond.

The light goes red and the little walking man's green. The correspondent and I cross the road in a cloud of cigarette smoke. The correspondent gives one last drag and then flicks it into the middle of the road. "Very well, then. Meet me on the corner in front of the Carnegie Diner, two o'clock. Don't be late." We reach the other side of the road. The correspondent looks up at me, his features shaded by the intense traffic light above and the misty rain. "You bring what you need. I'll be there but I'm not involved. Is that clear?"

I nod once. "I understand."

Satisfied, the correspondent walks off and I walk the other way. There's a shudder. The rain changes direction.

The wind tightens and the rivers that flow beneath the city, its sewage and its secrets, seize for a brief moment, as I walk away.

I eat at a Denny's that night, a burger and some fries on the side, and a coke. The diner is empty but for a high school girl and a stack of her books, two empty sodas. At one point, I look down and notice there is a pen in my hand and a sketch on a napkin. I scrunch up the packaging from my burger and hold the napkin to my face. Scribbled in blue is the face of a woman I once knew, as she has always been.

I leave it there, and walk out.

Exterior. Night.

Fifty-seventh. Rain falls hard now and cars scream past, their headlights blasting through the falling rain, illuminating trench-like puddles on the road. I spot the silhouette of the correspondent underneath a streetlamp on the corner where he said to meet, his car parked beside him. Our umbrellas contrast, black and white. The correspondent is smoking a cigarette. He wears the same as he had when we met in the bar earlier that evening, a black raincoat thrust over the top. As for me, I'm in a mustard yellow coat of cotton.

The correspondent is staring at a point across the street, beyond the glittering shapes in the rain puddles. A haze drifts across New York City. A red traffic light turns green but no cars go by. No tires through the rain. No headlights.

There is a small group of people smoking and talking down the road, all men, the wealthy type, or at least the look of them. Fine coats and umbrellas, burning cigarettes. I taste tobacco in my lungs, and feel the sensation of a cigarette pressed between my lips, though I haven't properly smoked one in some time. Two men leave the group. One emerges from the gambling den, which is disguised as a meat shop, with a red leather bag hanging from his fingers by the long red straps.

"That's him with the white umbrella," says the correspondent in a monotone drawl. I know it's him immediately. The reflected man is changed from when he was in the reflected universe. He is tall with long limbs and a slight hunch, a white suit to go with the umbrella and a gold watch around his left wrist. Just a man who happens to look like a monster from a brief French comic run somebody wrote. A cigarette pokes from his lips, bent slightly towards the sky. But he's the same—mostly. This man, his sideburns bronze and king-like, waves farewell to his friends and departs down the street, alone.

The correspondent exhales. "Hop in the car."

We tail the reflected man downtown, following the splashing of his feet against the puddles on the sidewalk, the patter of the rain against his umbrella, the light from his cigarette, the tornado of smoke sailing through the air around him. I lean against the passenger window, watching the city disappear, a small neighbourhood, my breath fogging it up.

"Can I just ask," says the correspondent. "Why is it so important for you to do this?"

"It's just something I have to do," I respond.

It is beneath a highway bridge that the correspondent stops the vehicle and there is the reflected man, dressed head-to-toe in white, hanging up his umbrella on a fence at the end of a court. There's a refinery on the other side of the road, and the stone bridge with cars crossing it frequently. The only rain that touches him is the rain that blows in sidewards.

I grab the door handle.

The correspondent grabs my shoulder. His tobacco breath permeates through the car, fogging up the windows a dullish grey colour, dim lights hitting the backs. I look at him and the man opens his mouth as if to say something, but does not, simply sighs and sits back down in his seat.

We both know how this goes.

I open the door and step out of the vehicle, slamming it shut behind me. As I do this, the reflected man looks up, halfway through lighting a new cigarette. I walk from the car to the spot beneath the great bridge at the end of the court, past the umbrella that hangs on a wooden fence, the house lights off, no car in the driveway. The reflected man continues to watch me until I am within earshot of him. He does not finish lighting his cigarette. Instead, he clicks the lighter shut and simply holds the dun cigarette between his long, inhuman fingers.

"Nicolas Fontaine."

My breath is visible in the cold air. I do not take my eyes off the reflected man and, likewise, he does not take his eyes off me. The world seems to freeze around the two of us. The city, I feel it coming to a halt, as jarring as a bus slamming on the brakes at the sudden changing of a traffic light. But then it is still, as still as death.

We remain there in the stillness.

"Won't you let a man enjoy the rest of his life," says the reflected man. "In peace, preferably. What I did back then, it was for your own good. We both would be dead. You, sent back to your own universe as it collapses entirely."

"You shouldn't be alive," I say.

The reflected man thinks to say something, then thinks better of it. He lifts the dun cigarette to his thin lips and sucks on it, before spitting it out into his hands and throwing it onto the wet gravel. I watch the cigarette glide through a puddle like a paper swan, eventually settling. The waves settle, too. And then I take a breath with the city in unison.

The reflected man begins to walk towards me, looking around at this new world. "Why did we both end up here?"

"No Moscati Research in this world," I say. "That means there isn't another variant of me here. When it happened, things shifted and realigned themselves."

"Sounding so sure."

"I am sure," I tell him.

"Well then. Suppose you can never *fully* escape your past." He stops, just a short distance away, a dead smell emanating off him. He is looking at the car in the distance, its windows likely fogged up, the correspondent in there, watching us, waiting for this night to be over with so he can go home. The reflected man then looks back at me and I look at him too.

"I've come here to kill you."

"You don't need to kill me, Nicolas, not to prove some point or whatever. I get the sense, whatever you've been looking for, you've found it. I see it in your eyes."

"The two of us cannot co-exist."

The reflected man smiles, and nods with knowing. "I see. Then the cycle continues. I know what it's like, I suppose, to feel with such certainty the weight of the antithesis."

"You never told me how you and the fat man came to learn of each other," I say. "How did it come to be."

"As all things come to be," he says. "The story has been told. You've lived it. You, and myself, and even before all of this, with Catherine. You know it, don't you."

I take a deep breath.

"Do you still think of her?"

The winds howl, throwing rainwater in our direction, soaking through the reflected man's white coat. His hands go into his pockets, stepping out from underneath the bridge into the rain, which begins to soak his hair, sending it streaking in rough clumps down the sides of his face. It's the most unnatural thing, seeing the reflected man looking so . . . human.

"I don't want nothing to do with you, Fontaine—"

When he turns back around, I have my gun out. I leave him an instant to see it, then I pull the trigger twice.

Down goes that horrible creature of the reflected universe, the gunshots lasting seconds longer than him. His body splashes to the gravel and does not move again. The headlights of that yellow car up on the hill flick on, causing the rain on the ground to scintillate, hot vapour to rise from the road's surface. I tuck the pistol into my coat and walk over to the dead body, sitting down beside it without thinking.

Music begins to play. A romantic orchestra, a symphony composed by Michel Legrand. It's the finale to Hitchcock's final film. The closing act of a play. It's me, sitting by the reflected man's dead body in the rain, just outside the ambit of the correspondent's headlights, in 1963.

Across the ocean in London, Catherine is smoking a cigarette and watching the patter of rain against her apartment window. Her makeup is smudged. She gazes out the window disconsolately, white gloves over her skin, a black suit, her hair made.

And there's Nicolas Fontaine, soaked through by the rain.

And there's Catherine, looking through it.

And the City lets out a long, deep breath as the music crescendos and I stand up at last, and Catherine walks out of her apartment and gazes up the street as a car passes by, illuminating her with its yellow headlights, and the City straightens his coat. Catherine exits frame.

The correspondent honks his horn.

The City looks at us through the page.

Fade to black.